SETTLING His HASH

WILLIAM W. JOHNSTONE

AND J. A. JOHNSTONE

SETTLING His HASH

PINNACLE BOOKS
Kensington Publishing Corp.
www.kensingtonbooks.com

PINNACLE BOOKS are published by

Kensington Publishing Corp.
119 West 40th Street
New York, NY 10018

Copyright © 2022 by J.A. Johnstone

PUBLISHER'S NOTE
Following the death of William W. Johnstone, the Johnstone family is working with a carefully selected writer to organize and complete Mr. Johnstone's outlines and many unfinished manuscripts to create additional novels in all of his series like The Last Gunfighter, Mountain Man, and Eagles, among others. This novel was inspired by Mr. Johnstone's superb storytelling.

PINNACLE BOOKS, the Pinnacle logo, and the WWJ steer head logo are Reg. U.S. Pat. & TM Off.

ISBN: 978-0-7860-4892-2

First Kensington Hardcover Edition: September 2022
First Kensington Mass Market Edition: December 2022

ISBN: 978-0-7860-4893-9 (ebook)

10 9 8 7 6 5 4 3 2 1

Printed in the United States of America

Chapter 1

Dewey "Mac" Mackenzie couldn't make up his mind whether to feel bitterly amused or just plain bitter. Either way, it came down to years of chasing a goal, practically an obsession, and then, when having finally attained it . . . having it turn out to be a big disappointment.

California.

That had been the goal. The dream. The place where Mac had figured he'd put all his past troubles behind him, lay them to rest, and start building a new life and a solid future. As it turned out, a big part of his past trouble, in the form of a polecat named Pierre Leclerc—the schemer responsible for stealing Mac's fiancée, framing him for a murder, and causing him to flee Louisiana—had been taken care of in a Montana mining settlement called Rattlesnake Creek. Leclerc had ended up dead, but not before his conniving ways and his own responsibility for the murder Mac had gotten framed for were exposed in front of witnesses.

Mac could have returned to Louisiana at that point, with those witnesses willing to testify on his behalf in order for him to try to reclaim all he'd been cheated out of. Instead, he'd decided there was nothing in Louisiana worth going back for, other than having his name cleared. The testimony of others could accomplish that with or without him. So he'd entrusted the necessary folks to handle that task while he proceeded with his dream of making it to California.

Once there, however, it wasn't long before the dream began to fray and then gradually unravel.

He entered at the state's northern end, after crossing through Idaho and a corner of Oregon. He found the people friendly enough, but the weather was dismally rainy and damp all the time. Along the coast, after the initial awe of seeing the mighty, endlessly rolling Pacific, he found himself feeling ill at ease and out of place. This was especially true during the time he spent on the docks of San Francisco.

When he worked his way south, conditions swung to the other extreme, and everything became miserably hot and dry. Again, the people were friendly—especially the dusky, beautiful señoritas—but none of it added up to a place that made him want to stick and put down roots.

The very thing that first caused him to think of California as a destination for escaping the troubles that had chased him out of Louisiana and put him on the drift to begin with turned out to be another dashed hope.

While Leclerc had been dealt with, and his poisonous lies were being revealed and crushed back where they had originated, the numerous circulars the damnably determined Frenchman was responsible for spreading far and wide, offering a generous dead or alive bounty on Mac, remained scattered across the western frontier, including California. Though a general recall had been issued, the word was slow reaching every distant corner. Which meant there were still those who, upon recognizing Mac, saw him as the chance for a big money return on the investment of a bullet. As he made his way down the length of the Golden State, Mac more than once was forced to dodge close calls on account of this.

And then one day in the sleepy little town of Rio Cisco, just off the north end of the Temescal Mountains, it all came to a head. Mac had arrived there riding guard on a string of freight wagons delivering goods from Los Angeles. He had understood from the start it was only a one-way job, meaning he'd be welcome to return with the off-loaded wagons if he wanted, but the freight boss, Kruger, could promise no further need of his services right away.

This was an arrangement that suited Mac okay since he had no desire to go back to Los Angeles, anyway. He reckoned Rio Cisco would do well enough as a point from which to take aim at some new pursuit. Which wasn't to say, however, he was in any particular hurry to head out. Especially not with a pocketful of wages and no clear notion what it was he intended to do next. So, to help ponder out an answer, Mac set his sights on a nameless yet inviting-looking little cantina he'd spotted on one corner of the town square.

At the hitch rail out front, he tied his horse, a deep-chested paint he'd come to call Pard in recognition of the animal having carried him and been his loyal companion all the way down the length of California, not to mention over several states and many miles prior, and went inside. The interior was smoky and dim and, thanks to its thick adobe walls, several degrees cooler than the baking air outside. The tangy aroma of fried meats and spices filled his nostrils.

Mac walked to a plank bar spread across the back of the room. He moved with the measured stride of someone always alert, always aware of his surroundings. A young man of average height with a solidly muscled frame, he retained a boyish handsomeness in spite of exposure to long hours of sun and wind, which had weathered and hardened his face some. His attire was the kind of standard range garb he had got used to wearing on the various cattle drives he'd worked as he made his way up through Texas, Colorado, and eventually to Montana.

At the bar, he laid his Winchester Yellowboy flat across the plank in front of him, lowered his elbows just behind it. The repeating rifle had been supplied to him when he signed on to guard the recently completed freight haul. He liked the feel and balance of it so well that he'd negotiated keeping it as part of his payoff from Kruger. He was aware that carrying it with him now might seem like a showy display, but the truth was that he simply hadn't yet had the chance to pick up a saddle scabbard for it. He planned to do so before leaving town.

Although he would balk at considering himself a "gun man" of any significance, there was no getting around the fact Mac had succeeded in surviving a number of confrontations over recent years only by relying on firearms.

His standard weapon was a Smith & Wesson Model 3 revolver that had even more miles on it than him and Pard. It was the only thing his father had ever left him, and he wore it tucked in the belt of his pants, never feeling comfortable with a gun belt and holster strapped around his waist. This was something of an unconventional choice, but it had served him well enough.

Mac wasn't quite sure what had brought about the yearning to hang on to the Yellowboy, too, other than knowing whatever lay ahead was bound to take him on the drift once again, likely into wild country. So maybe some gut instinct had kicked in to suggest it was time to give the Model 3 a little backup.

"What can I serve you, señor?" asked the plump middle-aged Mexican woman on the other side of the bar. She had a perfectly round face, a genuinely pleasant smile, and lovely almond eyes.

"A cold beer, for starters," Mac told her. Then, because he hadn't eaten lunch yet, he added, "And what kind of food do you have to go with that pleasant aroma I smell?"

The woman's smile widened. "Enchiladas and refried beans. And you will find it tastes as good as it smells."

"Then bring on a plate of it to go with the beer."

When the woman asked if he would rather sit at a table, Mac told her no, his spot at the bar would do fine.

After his beer came and he'd drained half the mug of cool, crisp brew in one thirsty gulp, he turned partway around and made a more leisurely survey of his surroundings. As he'd noted upon first entering, the place wasn't doing much business during this lull time of the afternoon. At a table over in one corner, two old men sat playing dominoes and sharing a bottle of wine. At the far end of the bar, a pasty-faced, weary-looking man in a frayed, dusty business suit—a none too successful drummer of some sort, Mac guessed—was silently, methodically working his way through his own plate of tortillas. That was it; otherwise, except for Mac and the woman behind the bar, the joint was empty.

Yes indeed, Mac mused, all the makings for a good spot to have a meal, have a couple more beers, and map out some kind of plan for what course he'd set from here.

Come to think of it, maybe he should change his mind and take a seat at one of the cantina tables, where he could sit more comfortably while he rolled things around inside his head.

He was still considering this when the front door opened and three men walked in.

Chapter 2

After glancing around, Mac quickly saw that he knew the trio entering amidst a wash of hot outside air. Lester Riley and the Buchwald brothers, Clyde and Clem, three of the teamsters he'd rolled into town with. Their eyes fell on him right away, and they moved toward him. Mac was ready with a grin and a greeting.

"Hey, fellas. Doggone, you made quick work of getting those wagons unloaded."

"Not quite. Not all the way," responded Riley, sauntering a half step ahead of the brothers. "Too blasted hot out there to be in a big hurry with anything."

"You can say that again," agreed Clyde, the older of the Buchwalds. "The beaners hereabouts got the right idea with that siesta thing they make a habit of."

His brother, Clem, bobbed his head. "That's right. Takin' it slow and easy when the afternoon heat lays on you the heaviest, that's the only way."

"In that case," said Mac, "let me help you take it easy by offering to buy the first round. I can testify they serve some real good beer here."

"Long as it's cold. That's the main thing," Clem said.

The men bellied up to the bar on either side of Mac, Riley to his right, the Buchwalds to his left. As they were settling into place, the Mexican woman reappeared with Mac's plate of food. When she set it in front of him, he said, "Gracias, señora. Now how about lining up some beers for my amigos and another for me, por favor?"

The woman smiled and went to fill some glasses.

Clyde Buchwald cast a sidelong scowl in Mac's direction. He was a tall, lanky number with a V-shaped face, perpetually squinted eyes, and a pencil mustache above a thin-lipped slash of a mouth. "You toss that Mex lingo around pretty handy, don't you?"

Mac shrugged. "You just heard the extent of it. Please, thank you, and I know the difference between *señora* and *señorita*. That's got me far enough to have some luck, on a few occasions, at saying please to a pretty señorita and then having cause to say thank you afterwards."

Clyde grunted. "I can't argue the beaners turn out some mighty pretty gals. But that don't mean I'm gonna change the way I talk to get next to any of 'em. This is America, by God, and I speak only American."

"Siesta," Mac said.

Clyde looked puzzled. "What?"

"A minute ago you said you liked the idea of a siesta in the afternoon heat," Mac pointed out. "That was you speaking Mexican. By the way, that makes one more word I know, too. *Siesta*."

On the other side of Clyde, his brother couldn't hold back a sort of honking chuckle. "You walked right into that one, brother. Dogged if you didn't!"

Younger than Clyde by a couple of years, Clem had the same lanky frame, squinty eyes, and narrow face, though his was a bit more rectangular and minus any attempt at a mustache. His most notable feature was a long nose with a bladelike bridge and a bulbous tip that flared out suddenly like a bubble. This apparently accounted for the faint honking tone discernible in many of the words and other sounds that came out of him.

Spurred by his brother's remark, Clyde aimed a fresh scowl at Mac. "Seems to me you go out of your way to be annoying sometimes, Mackenzie."

Before Mac could reply, Riley spoke up. "Hey, take it easy, Clyde. The kid was just needling you a little. And like Clem said, you walked right into it."

Riley was a beefy, florid-faced man some years older than Mac and the Buchwalds. His voice had a booming quality and he tended to sound like he was issuing commands, even in casual conversation. And when he spoke, he displayed a set of oversized teeth that made Mac think of rows of tightly spaced tombstones.

The bartender cut the tension by returning with glasses of foamy brew, which she lined up in front of the men. "Can I get you gentlemen anything else?"

Glad for the interruption, Mac said, "Maybe these gents will want some vittles, too." Then, glancing to either side, he asked, "How about it? You fellas can't have had lunch yet, right? Might as well slap on the feed bag while you're taking your break. Ain't had a chance to try my own order yet, but by the look and smell of it, I'm betting it's gonna be right tasty."

Riley paused with his glass raised partway to his mouth. Frowning, he said, "Tempting as that sounds, reckon we'd best hold off for now. The thing is, see, old man Kruger don't exactly know we took a notion to step out of the heat for a spell. He's still clearing invoices with the town merchants. He finishes that and finds out we ain't done unloading those wagons yet, he's liable to get his nose bent out of joint."

"Guess that makes me the lucky one for not being on the clock no more," said Mac. "Although that also means I got no job no more, so in the long run it sorta evens out."

"Yeah, about that," grunted Clyde, lowering his glass after downing a big gulp of its contents. "We just heard how you called it quits with Kruger. Was you gonna haul off and ride away without even sayin' good-bye to the rest of us after bein' part of our crew these past days?"

Mac shook his head. "No, that wasn't what I had in mind at all, Clyde. I knew you boys would be in town for the rest of today and tonight before rolling out tomorrow to return to Los Angeles. I figured I'd run into you again before then and have the chance to say good-bye. As for me, I ain't in no particular hurry to be riding off. Don't even know for sure which way I'll be heading when I do."

"Any direction but Louisiana, right?" said Clem from the other side of his brother.

His tone was totally casual, but Mac had no trouble immediately recognizing what was behind it. Nor did he have any trouble recognizing the warning tingle that suddenly trickled down his spine like a cold droplet falling from the tip of an icicle.

Straining to keep his own tone casual, Mac glanced over and said, "Louisiana, Clem? Why would you think that might even be an option?"

All at once Clem appeared very uncomfortable. Not just due to Mac's question and probing look, but also because of the glare Clyde had turned his head to aim at him. What was more, Mac had a hunch, Riley was likely joining in, as well.

Clem licked his lips and said stammeringly, "Well, I, uh . . . what I meant was . . . Well, you bein' from Louisiana and, uh, havin' stayed away all this time already . . . I guess I figured you must have some reason for not *wantin'* to go back."

"Who said I was from Louisiana to begin with, Clem?" Mac prodded.

Clem blinked. "Well . . . ain't you? I . . . I heard it somewhere. I guess it must've—"

"Knock it off!" Mac cut him short, his words ringing sharply. He'd been through this too many times in too many places. He was damned sick of it and in no mood to allow this faltering new attempt to play out any farther. Raking his eyes first over both of the Buchwald brothers and then snapping his face around to brand Riley with a blazing look, Mac snarled, "If this is about that damned reward poster, then spit it out and let's get to the bottom of it! I'll tell you right now you're in for a big disappointment, and if you try to crowd me over it, you'll be biting off more trouble than you can chew."

Riley's lips peeled back, and he flashed those big square teeth in a wide sneer. "That's awful big talk from somebody who's looking at three to one odds."

"I'm telling you straight, and to hell with the odds," Mac countered. "The first thing you need to know is that the skunk who issued that reward is dead, so there's no longer any money behind it. The rest is that the charges he based it on have been proven false."

"Says you," Clyde said.

"I can give you the names of several different legal authorities who'll be willing to confirm by telegram that what I'm saying is the truth."

Now it was Clem's turn to show a sneer. "That's real convenient, seein' how there ain't no telegraph office in this town nor any other for at least twenty miles."

"That's your tough luck," Mac responded.

Clyde shook his head. "No. I say it's the other way around. If you ain't got no way to back up your claim, then that's your hard luck. And if you think we're just going to take your word on how things are, it's you who's in for a big disappointment."

"There's a simple solution," Riley spoke up. "You stick with us when we head out tomorrow, like we been figuring all along, ever since Clyde here recognized you from that reward poster. We were going to wait and turn you in when we got back to Los Angeles. But now, based on what you're telling us, we'd be willing to stop at the first telegraph we come to and give you the chance to make good on your claim. If you're right, no hard feelings . . . If you're lying, then we haul you in like we counted on and make ourselves a tidy sum of money."

Mac cocked an eyebrow. "And until it gets sorted out, I'm supposed to cooperate and basically be your prisoner. Is that the idea?"

"That's one way of lookin' at it," said Clyde. "Another idea to keep in mind is that the reward poster says, *Dead or alive*. If you decide to try to buck against Riley's offer, I'm willin' to gamble on you bein' a liar and go for the payout by haulin' in your carcass, if that's the way we have to do it."

"In that case," Mac said, his voice tight, "I guess I don't have much choice."

Riley gave a curt nod. "That's playing it smart."

The problem was what Riley and the Buchwalds figured to be the smart play for Mac was a lot different than what he saw as the only real choice he had. Deciding there was no sense wasting any more time over it, Mac seized the Yellowboy laid out before him in both hands, lifted it just a few inches off the bar top, and then thrust it hard to his right, driving the butt end straight into Riley's rib cage. Over the crack of bones and the rush of breath pounded out of him, the florid-faced man expelled a roar of pain as he bent sharply to one side and went staggering away, until he crashed into a nearby table and its surrounding chairs.

Still gripping the Yellowboy in both hands, Mac twisted at the waist and whirled hard and fast to his left, bringing the rifle butt around with him in a flat arc and this time smashing it into the surprised expression on Clyde's face. The older Buchwald's head snapped back, blood and bits of broken teeth flying from his mouth. He staggered backward a step and a half before toppling flat onto the floor.

By the time Clyde landed, Mac had readjusted his grip on the Yellowboy and was now holding it aimed level and steady on Clem, the only still standing member of the threatening trio. Clem's face also showed surprise at the sudden turn of events, but he'd managed to work some anger into it, as well. His clawed right hand was reaching for the six-shooter holstered on his hip. But the reach halted as soon as Clem's eyes locked on the rifle muzzle staring back at him.

"I took it easy on the other two," Mac told him through gritted teeth. "But don't make the mistake of thinking I'll hesitate to use the business end of this Winchester if you try to push your luck."

Clem lifted his right hand away from the gun and, along with his left, raised it to shoulder level and held both of them palms out. "No need for that. I believe you," he said. "I'll give you no call to pull that trigger on me. I'm done with this whole business."

Chapter 3

Old man Kruger had worked himself into such a frenzy that his face looked red and bloated, like a boiled tomato ready to burst out of its skin.

"You can't leave me in a lurch like this! You busted up two of my best men so bad they can't handle their teams. I got to get those wagons back to Los Angeles right away in order to satisfy the hauling jobs I already have lined up!"

Mac put as much sympathy as he could muster into his tone as he said, "Sorry for the hard place you find yourself in, Mr. Kruger, but I fulfilled any obligation I have to you. And thanks to your three idiot teamsters, I've worn out my welcome around here and need to be moving on before the local lawman returns from his fishing trip."

"Yes, by all means that's what I'm talking about, too," Kruger said eagerly. "Moving on, heading out once again with us—this time driving one of the wagons. I'll pay you double my regular teamster wages, and I'll vouch for you to clear up any issue with the town marshal. I know him from my previous trips here."

Mac shook his head. "Thanks, but no thanks. I got no intention of going back with you, especially if you figure on taking those three along."

"There's no kind of doctor in this town. I've got to get Lester and Clyde someplace where their injuries can be properly treated." Kruger's sweat-beaded brow puckered with anguish. "They're my employees. I owe them at least that much."

"That's real decent of you, Mr. Kruger. In your place, I guess it's the responsible thing," Mac allowed. "But me, I don't give much of a damn about proper treatment for those jackasses. They were ready and willing to put a bullet in me over a lousy piece of paper with a pack of lies printed on it. They're lucky I didn't do more than just bust 'em up."

This conversation was taking place on the edge of the street outside Rio Cisco's largest general store, where Mac had just finished stocking up on some trail supplies before heading out of town. Pard stood waiting patiently at the hitch rail. Kruger had caught up with them here, hurrying up as Mac was getting ready to plant one foot in a stirrup and swing into the saddle.

"But if that reward poster Clyde got hold of is false—and you say you can prove it is, as soon as we get somewhere with a telegraph office—then the whole matter will be put to rest. Right?"

Mac twisted his mouth ruefully. "The whole mess should have already been put to rest. But it keeps cropping up. One of these times there's the risk it might be in the hands of some out-of-touch, trigger-happy fool who takes the notion it'd be easier to shoot first and worry about confirming things later. This latest go-round with

Riley and the Buchwalds has about got me convinced that my best bet is to plain steer clear of people."

"There are people everywhere, Mackenzie."

"Maybe so. But there are places where they're a lot sparser than others. And Los Angeles sure ain't one of 'em."

Mac toed a stirrup and pulled himself up onto Pard's hurricane deck. After gripping the reins and backing the big paint a couple steps away from the rail, he gazed down at the freight boss.

"Good luck to you, Mr. Kruger. With the money you're offering, you won't have no trouble finding drivers to get you back in time for those other hauls you got scheduled. As for the hombres I put out of commission, make sure they understand this. If they're still not convinced I ain't worth any reward money or if they take a notion to come looking for revenge . . . I catch sight of any one of their ugly mugs again, I won't hesitate to greet it with lead."

If Kruger made any reply, Mac didn't hear it. He wheeled Pard around, gave a light slap of his heels, and put dusty, sunbaked Rio Cisco behind them without a backward glance.

A rose-hued sundown found Mac camped in a grassy meadow off the eastern foothills of the Temescals. He sat cross-legged before a small fire, leaned back against his saddle, with a supper of beans, bacon, and biscuits resting comfortably in his belly and a cup of coffee balanced in one hand. A small cluster of cottonwoods rose up behind him, and a narrow, fast-moving stream ran off to one side. Pard was picketed over near the stream, giving him access to plenty of good graze and water.

"Just so you know," Mac was explaining to the horse,

"this ain't exactly the pampered level of comfort I had pictured for the two of us tonight. I figured to treat you to a livery stall with a big scoop of grain, some good hay, and a bed of fresh straw. Me, I had in mind a hot bath and a barber shave, a steak dinner with all the trimmings, and then a fresh, soft bed of my own . . . well, maybe shared with the right kind of company, if any such happened to be available."

Pard made no comment, just kept munching grass.

"Then again," Mac continued after a swallow of coffee, "what we got here ain't exactly hardship conditions. Reckon we've endured our share of worse, haven't we?"

Once again Pard showed more interest in eating grass than conversing.

Mac could take a hint. He stayed quiet after that, sipping his coffee, watching the stars start to emerge more distinctly in the cloudless, slowly darkening sky. Thinking.

The words *We've endured our share of worse* kept rolling back around in his head. It was certainly true. On the trail drives he and Pard had worked together ever since he selected the big paint out of the Circle Arrow remuda, they'd been through a lot. Pushing longhorns meant long, hard, dust-eating hours in every kind of weather, over every kind of terrain you could imagine. Once Mac gained the skill and reputation for being a good trail cook, he usually ended up manning and driving the chuckwagon for whatever outfit he was with. Despite that, he kept Pard close by because there were plenty of times when he had to climb in the saddle and help out with wrangling or scouting. On a cattle drive, everybody pitched in and did a little bit of everything.

And then, of course, there had been the journey over to and down the length of California, culminating tonight in this meadow. And along the way there had been plenty of stops far less hospitable than either a soft bed or the relative comfort of this particular campsite.

Our share of worse conditions.

Yeah, there had definitely been a number of those. But there had also been conditions that made for some mighty good times, too. And most of those, Mac was realizing with increasing frequency, had been on the cattle drives he'd joined. It was a hard life, and there were times when every element of man and nature seemed like it was working against you—but within that, within the crew you were part of, there was a tough-spirited sense of camaraderie that gave you assurance you could somehow make it through and finish the job as long as you stuck together. "Riding for the brand" meant something.

Reflecting on this now, thinking back on the things he'd enjoyed about being part of a ranch crew, Mac found himself wondering if it was something he ought to consider returning to. Always before, he'd seen cattle work as a means to an end in order to elude the reach of Leclerc and work his way toward California. But now Leclerc was dead, and it was time to admit that the California dream was a bust. So what did that leave? No sense wasting any more time here, and going back to Louisiana held no appeal.

In between was Texas. That was where he'd hooked up with his first cattle drive. And Lord knew there were plenty of cattle still there and plenty of ranches where a fella with his experience ought to be able to find work. Places where people were "a lot sparser" and the ones who were part of your outfit, who rode for the same brand as you, could be counted on to have your back and not be quick to plant a knife or bullet in it for the sake of a few dollars promised by lies on a piece of paper.

Mac drained the last of his coffee and lowered the cup. Right there, in that moment, he made up his mind. The weeks of feeling disappointed and restless and unfocused came to a halt.

He glanced over at Pard again and said, "Too late to raise any objection now, hayburner. You had your chance to speak up but didn't. So just keep filling your face and enjoy a big, final taste of California . . . because tomorrow we're headin' for Texas."

Chapter 4

There was no mistaking the sound. It was a rifle shot. It came from not too far off, somewhere on the other side of the long slope Mac was riding along. He reined in and cocked an ear, listening for something more. There was no second shot, no other discernible sound except for the soft sigh of the wind.

The single report of a gun could mean anything. A hunter, somebody dispatching a snake or some other varmint, maybe even a snagged hammer falling accidentally on a full chamber. It could mean trouble, too, except trouble usually came with more than just one shot. Or it could be somebody hurt, trying to signal for help.

Whatever it was, Mac tried telling himself, it was none of his business. Only what if it *was* somebody hurt or in trouble? He knew it would eat at him if he didn't at least take a look-see. Might even gnaw hard enough so he'd get partway down the trail, then turn around and come back to make sure. So, he might as well get it over with.

After turning Pard in the direction he judged the shot to have come from, Mac heeled him toward the crest of the slope at a steady but somewhat cautious pace. It was midmorning of another sunny, clear day, and the temperature was rising rapidly. Due west, the Temescals had fallen away to a low, lumpy line on the horizon. The current terrain was mostly rounded, gently undulating hills covered by short brown grass, with few trees and occasional ragged rock outcrops.

At the top of the slope, Mac reined in again and gazed down at the scene in a shallow draw on the other side. There was a wagon there—a chuckwagon, ironically enough. Hitched to it was a single mule in two-puller rigging, standing with its head hung low. A dozen yards away, a second mule, obviously dead, lay sprawled on the ground, with a handful of wrangler types milling near it. Between the men and the wagon, a knot of saddled, ground-tied horses waited indifferently, nibbling at the skimpy grass.

It was a curious sight, yet it didn't take Mac long to reach a conclusion on what had happened. The dead mule, he reasoned, must have gotten injured somehow and so had to be unhitched and put down. That would explain the single gunshot. What the wranglers were likely palavering about now was how best to proceed with only one mule to pull the wagon. The only thing Mac couldn't quite think of an explanation for was why a gaggle of cowboys, complete with chuckwagon, was out here with no sign of cattle anywhere.

Whatever the reason, it didn't seem like a situation that presented any kind of danger, so he gigged Pard forward and on down into the draw. As he drew closer, the cowboys stopped talking among themselves, and five faces turned to silently watch him come the rest of the way.

Coming to a stop once again, this time a few yards short of the group, Mac spoke first, saying, "Mornin', gents. Looks like you've hit a patch of trouble."

One of the men edged forward a half step, indicating he was the one in charge. He was tall and lean, thirty years old, give or take, with curly blond sideburns, a square jaw, and quick, alert eyes.

"True enough we ain't had the best morning," he responded. "Rattler nailed one of the mules. We had to unhitch the poor critter and put him out of his misery."

"Bad way to go, for man or beast alike," Mac allowed.

"What we're hashing over now," the blond man added, "is whether we go on with just the one mule pulling until we reach a town or someplace where we can match him up with another or if we try putting one of our saddle horses alongside him."

Mac lifted his eyebrows. "If you don't mind some advice from a stranger, I'd say you're probably wasting your time, plus risking a kick to somebody's chops, if you try hitching a horse in there."

One of the other men, who looked to be the oldest of the lot and who was stoop shouldered and gray whiskered, with an off-kilter left eye, muttered, "That's the same as I been tryin' to tell 'em."

The blond man regarded Mac closer. "You know mules, do you?"

"Some. I've pulled reins on a few different teams." Mac gestured. "From the seat of a chuckwagon, as a matter of fact."

"So you've done some cowboying, then. You from around here?"

"Only just temporary," Mac explained. "Had me a longtime hankering to see California. So I finally worked my way out here. Now I've saw it and done it, you might say. On my way back East, headed Texas way, more or less."

The blond man grinned. "Reckon that old saying about it being a small world ain't so far off the mark. You see, we're headed back to Texas, too. We ride for the Double T brand north of Odessa. Just got done delivering a herd of cattle to a buyer over on the other side of Temecula."

"You've had a long trip, with still a stretch to go."

"The return will be a mite easier, though, without nine hundred longhorns to push along. My name, by the way, is Jeff Castle. I'm trail bossin' this bunch of dust-biters."

Mac pinched the brim of his hat. "I'm Dewey Mackenzie. Make it Mac."

Castle seemed to consider something for a moment. After casting a quick glance at the men over his shoulder, he said, "Appears to me, Mac, we've got a situation here that might be worth exploring a little farther. You say you've spent time on the seat of a chuckwagon. Does it follow, then, that you've also been a trail cook?"

"Have for a fact. A pretty darned good one, if I say so myself. And anybody from any outfit I ever traveled with and cooked for would back that up."

"Here's the thing," Castle stated. "We're not only short one mule to pull our chuckwagon, but we're also short a cook to grub our trip back home. For reasons I can go into later if you want, the cook who traveled to Temecula with us is no longer part of our crew. Truth to tell, he was a mighty poor cook to begin with. But, even at that, we have sadly discovered he was better than any of the rest of us."

"You can say that again," grumbled one of the other men, Mac wasn't sure which one.

"So what I'm thinking," Castle went on, "is that since we're all Texas bound, and providing you ain't determined to travel alone, maybe you'd be interested in throwing in with us and taking over chuckwagon duties. If you pan out, I'll put you on the payroll. What's more, if you aim to stick with cattle work for a while and don't have another place already in mind for when we get back, I expect a permanent opening could be yours at the Double T."

Mac felt his mouth stretching into a lopsided grin. Call it fate or whatever, but it seemed like the decision he'd arrived at last night had just found a boost of momentum that sounded too good not to take advantage of.

"Mister," he said to Castle, "I say you got yourself a new cook. Let's get that chuckwagon rolling for Texas."

Chapter 5

On the fourth morning, just as day was breaking, the blasted Mexican finally got around to trying what Otis Bradley had been expecting all along. The only surprise was that the sneaky little varmint had somehow gotten his hands on a knife.

When the blade came thrusting down at him, Otis was barely able to meet it with a double handful of wadded blanket in time to smother the lunge and twist it away to one side. It helped that the weapon was merely a punch dagger, its wickedly pointed blade less than four inches. But that would be enough to open his jugular or poke some gut holes that, in the right spots, would bleed him out.

Shoving his attacker off him, Otis slammed the man hard against the jail cell wall his cot was bolted to. The Mexican spewed a string of Spanish curses as he tried to slash his blade clear of the blanket. Otis slammed him into the wall again, then followed immediately with a knee driven into his stomach and then a second time to the groin. That took the fight out of the Mexican. He doubled up, groaning in pain.

Otis shoved the man again, this time hurling him onto the cement floor of the holding cell. The dagger went clattering free of the wadded blanket.

By then, some of the other men in the cell had been rousted and were sitting up on their cots, grumbling and cursing at being disturbed so early. It was a safe bet that more than one set of sleepy eyes brightened at the sound and sight of the dagger suddenly making its appearance.

Before any of them could make a move toward it, though, a lantern flared bright in the hallway that ran outside the front row of bars, and a scowling guard was suddenly standing there, with the snout of his pistol thrust between the iron uprights.

"Everybody freeze!" the man on the other end of the gun barked. "Anybody tries to reach for that blade, they'll grab a load of lead instead."

More low grumbling and cursing could be heard in response, but everybody stayed in their cots.

A second guard appeared in the hallway, this one brandishing a scattergun. "What's going on?" he wanted to know.

"Some kind of fight broke out in there," reported the pistol-wielding guard. "Looks like one of the prisoners got hold of a knife somehow."

"Not *one of* us prisoners," protested Otis, swinging his feet over the edge of his cot. He thrust a finger at the still doubled-over Mexican lying on the floor. "*That* greaser right there is your man! He's the one behind the whole thing."

Otis was a man of only average height who seemed to loom larger. He was pushing forty and also pushing too much of a gut, but with beefy shoulders and arms to off-set it. He had a wide, flat face dominated by bristly eye-brows and a thick-lipped, expressive mouth capable of twisting cruelly when angered.

"I told everybody from the start not to put this Mex in the same cell with me," he continued now. "I warned you he still had it in for me because of the trouble that landed both of us here to begin with and that he'd try to get even the first chance he got. At the very least, it was your re-sponsibility to make sure he didn't have a weapon to use! I might be behind bars, but I still got rights. I want to see the marshal—or, better yet, a judge!"

"Shut up," said the guard with the scattergun, "or the only right you'll get is the right to be clubbed alongside the head until you quiet down."

"He's speaking true, and you know it," declared one of the other prisoners, a man called Ames. "This fella"—he gestured toward Otis—"was attacked, could've been seri-ously hurt or maybe killed. You throw a man in the clink, it's your sworn responsibility to keep him safe while he's in your custody."

There was some muttering assent from others, but none were quite as bold.

The two guards exchanged looks. "All right, every-body settle down," said the one with the pistol. "We'll start by moving Paco there to another cell . . . *after* one of you steps forward and carefully toes the dagger over here, where we can reach it. Then we need to see that everybody's breakfast gets served. After that, we'll have the marshal come around to talk to you about what hap-pened . . ."

*   *   *

Four hours later, Otis and the man called Ames were sitting astride a pair of horses just outside the Temecula city limits, watching the deputy marshal who'd escorted them that far turn and ride back into town.

"Well then. We've been kicked out of jail and kicked out of town," Ames said with a fatalistic sigh. Then, smiling slyly, he added, "But, hell, I reckon I've been in worse situations. And spending another three days in that slammer, which was how much time I was supposed to have left, would have been one of them."

Otis grunted. "I had seven left. I don't favor being put on the run, but all things considered, I guess I gotta agree it's better than sticking out the rest of that time behind bars. And while I'm at it, let me say thanks for speaking up for me back there when it looked like those guards were gonna clamp down on me some more."

"Think nothing of it," Ames replied. "When the marshal came around, he knew his men had messed up bad by letting that Mex somehow get his hands on a knife. I think he took serious my talk about demanding a judge or lawyer or some such. So he saw booting us out and shutting us up as better than the risk of facing the music if we kept running our mouths."

"Whatever the case, I'm still obliged to you for pitching in."

Ames shrugged. "You say you were in for disturbing the peace?"

"That's right. I got ten days for busting up a saloon."

"That's a pretty stiff disturbing the peace charge. I was in for a whorehouse brawl and only got five."

"I should've stuck with whores in a place made for 'em. My row started over a little señorita serving drinks in that saloon. How she was dressed and the way she rubbed herself against everybody whenever she leaned in to put drinks on a table, who could blame me for thinking she was advertising herself for something more? When I tried to take her up on the extra service I thought was for sale, her boyfriend—that knife artist from back in the cell—went all crazy and tore into me. Things turned wild real quick, and in no time the whole joint was a battle-field."

"If that Mex made the first move on you, you had a right to defend yourself. Shouldn't that have left you in the clear?"

Otis made a sour face. "Well. When that beaner got in my face . . . maybe I was the one who threw the first punch . . . And then, too, there was the fella I shot."

"You shot somebody?" Ames echoed. He was a tall, trim, square-shouldered man looking back on thirty, though not by much. His pin-striped trousers, bib-fronted shirt, and yellow silk neckerchief were of considerably better quality than Otis's worn trail garb. The Stetson carefully situated atop his head rode above an even-featured—what some might go so far as to call classically handsome—face. At the moment, in response to Otis's statement, the expression on that face was somewhere between surprised and amused.

"Luckily," Otis expounded, "the hombre I shot didn't press charges. He was a friend of mine . . . well, sort of . . . and the wound only chewed up some shoulder meat. But all the same, I figure the shooting is why the marshal tacked some extra time on me."

"If you don't mind my asking," said Ames, "why did you shoot somebody who was a friend of yours?"

"'Cause he was trying to drag me out of there before things got too far out of hand and also before I'd got any good licks in on that damned Mex." Otis paused, scowling. "I was drunk and mad as hell, and I just generally don't like being pawed and tugged at. So I lost my head and pulled iron on him. I was sorry as soon as I did, but . . . well, it was a little late by then."

"Where's this fella now?"

"On his way back to Texas, I expect. Him and the others." Otis cast a somewhat longing gaze off toward the east before continuing. "I came in with a cattle drive, you see, riding for the Double T from back Odessa way. We delivered near nine hundred head of beeves to a buyer the other side of Temecula. We all stopped off in town to hoorah a bit before heading back. Reckon you'd have to say I hoorahed a mite too hard."

"So the others all took off and just left you behind?" Ames cocked a brow. "I thought cowpunchers from the same outfit—men who 'ride for the brand,' as they say— always stuck together, always looked out for one another through thick and thin."

"Yeah. Well, it appears that ain't always the case, don't it?" Otis cast another brief glance eastward. "I suppose it's fair to say me shootin' Squint—that'd be Squint Morris, the name of the fella I plugged—was a pretty sure way for me to wear out my welcome. But I never really fit in with that Double T bunch nohow, not from the first. They'd all been together a spell before I came on board, and nothing I did ever measured up to suit those ungrateful rannies. I expect it was gonna be just a matter of time before they found a reason to toss me aside, anyway."

Ames regarded him for a long count. Then he said, "How would you like to meet some hombres, friends of mine, who are more welcoming to new blood and would give you a fair shot to fit in?"

Otis returned his look. "What have you got in mind?"

Ames grinned. "First off, I got in mind to get out of this sun. My friends ain't far off. Ride with me. I'll fill you in more as we go."

"Before we get too far along with this," Ames said after they'd ridden only a short way, "I reckon I oughta square up with you on my name. It's not Ames. My real name is Stack Ketchum. Mean anything to you?"

Otis was quick to shake his head. "No, can't say it does."

"You coming from Texas, I didn't figure it would. But hereabouts, especially to the north, it's a name that trips off a lot of tongues. It also appears on more than a few wanted dodgers . . . In other words, me and these friends of mine we're headed for don't exactly stick to the straight and narrow. You're more apt to find us riding the long coulees." The man formerly calling himself Ames but now rebranded as Ketchum cast a sidelong glance over at Otis to see how he was reacting. "Does that shock you?"

Otis just kept staring straight ahead as he rode, his expression showing no discernible change. "Surprises me a little, I guess. Don't know that I'd say it shocks me."

"Good. I didn't think it would," Ketchum said. "Way I read you, you're cut from a similar bolt as me and the boys I ride with. All your life you been trying to play it fair and square, hoping for a toehold to get ahead. But at every turn you run up against some kind of hard edge, never catch a break, while all around you see other so-and-sos grabbing 'em right and left. Am I right?"

Otis grunted. "You ain't far off."

"That's why me and my boys decided to hell with trying to live like that. We started pushing back against those hard edges, pushing *through*, and making our own breaks. We don't bother women or kids. Nor do we take from the little businesses or the small ranchers and farmers scraping to get by. We go after the greedy fellas at the top, the bankers and miners and railroads, and the cattlemen who have more land and stock than it's decent for any one man to claim. They got fat gouging from everybody else, and our aim is to gouge back from them."

"Man, I can't tell you how many times I've thought about doing that very thing," Otis muttered.

"Everybody does," Ketchum told him. "Only not very many have the guts. But now I'm giving you a nudge, helping you make up your mind to go ahead. So how about it? You want to continue with me? If not, say the word and we'll go our separate ways. No hard feelings."

Otis's forehead puckered with deep seams. "Man, it's a tempting offer. I . . . I'm all for it . . . but I ain't ever killed anybody before."

"There's a first time for everybody," Ketchum said nonchalantly. "Tell me . . . back there in the cell this morning, when the Mex's knife fell out of that blanket . . . if the guards hadn't shown up as quick as they did, you wouldn't have jumped at the chance to snatch up that blade and then used it to stab the hell out of the pepperbelly who tried it on you?"

"You bet I would've!"

"There you go. Anybody can kill if and when they need to. Believe me, if some law dog or do-gooder citizen starts pumping lead at you, you won't hesitate to shoot back and not worry a whisker about killing." Ketchum frowned. "What are you worried about, anyway? You already proved you're willing to shoot somebody . . . and he was a half-assed friend."

Otis twisted his mouth wryly, made no response.

"You any better than that with a gun?" Ketchum wanted to know. "Seeing how you didn't do much damage to that particular character, I mean."

"When I'm sober, I hit what I aim at. Best with a rifle, okay with a handgun. But I can't claim to be fast on the draw or anything."

Ketchum waved a hand dismissively. "That fast-draw junk only matters in dime novels and Wild West shows. Grit and a steady hand will get the job done most of the time. Far as I can tell, you measure up, Otis. So say it out plain. Are you interested in riding with me and my boys or not?"

Otis set his jaw firmly. "You're saying things I've been thinking but not doing anything about for too long . . . Yeah, I'm keen to ride with you. And I won't let you down."

Chapter 6

It didn't take long for Mac to find out he felt quite comfortable in the midst of the Double T crew he had fallen in with. Nor did it take long for those same men to find out how fortunate they were for having gained his cooking skills.

"Lord a'mighty," exclaimed Squint Morris around a mouthful of the biscuits, ham, and redeye gravy Mac had served for breakfast the morning of his second day with the outfit. "If I'd known there was eatin' this good to be had while we was puttin' up with the swill Otis Bradley kept shovin' in front of us, I would have been the one to pull iron and shoot him—instead of the other way around—a long time back."

Squint was a veteran wrangler, fifty or so, solidly built, with bowed legs and the rolling gait of somebody who'd spent more of his life on horseback than on foot. His face would have been fresh and handsome at one time, but now, though still evenly featured, it was weathered and deeply seamed to the texture of old leather. The narrowed eyes that earned him his name, pinched tight against years of glaring sun and biting wind, were bracketed by crow's-feet so distinct and sharp they looked like inward-pointing arrowheads.

"I agree Otis probably deserved bein' shot a long time back, for more reasons than just his lousy cookin'. But you can't claim it took vittles this good before you knew how rotten Otis's was."

This response to Squint's remark came from Hank Larabee, the grizzled, walleyed oldster who'd spoken up yesterday to agree with Mac about the inadvisability of trying to hitch a horse with the remaining chuckwagon mule. Larabee was about a half dozen years older than Squint, making him the senior member of the crew age-wise. He, too, was weathered and worn from decades of working cattle, and there was a slight hitch to his walk, which, Mac guessed, probably came from a fall or getting caught by a horn sometime in the past.

"Of course I knew all along how bad Otis's cookin' was. I said that very thing, didn't I?" protested Squint. "And what we rustled up in its place, after we first got rid of him, was about as pitiful. The point I was tryin' to get around to was that too much of that kind of sorry fare could risk ruinin' a body's taster permanent-like. It's a good thing Mac came along, or we might have got to where we wouldn't be able to tell the difference."

Mac, busy stirring his redeye gravy, smiled as he listened to this exchange. He'd already heard a variety of accounts concerning Otis Bradley, not only about his bad cooking but also about what an ill-tempered sort he'd been, right up to and including his shooting of Squint, who still wore a bandage on his shoulder, though the wound didn't seem to bother him too bad. But all of that had been before Mac's time, so there was no point in worrying about it. All he cared about was seeing things continue to go smoothly, and having the prospect of a job already lined up for him when they got to Texas.

"Speaking for myself, I can't hardly see my taster getting so messed up I wouldn't know good cooking from bad. I'd have to be dead and buried not to appreciate the high quality of these vittles Mac is dishing out to us."

This came from Red Pelham, the youngest member of the crew, joining in the banter between the two older men. Red got his name by virtue of the fiery thatch of hair atop his head combined with the permanently sunburned cheeks, which gave color to his otherwise fair complexion. He was only a year past twenty, average height, a bit on the stocky side. He held his own when it came to any duty asked of him and had a fine tenor singing voice that could lull even the most restless herd when he was riding nighthawk.

"Aw, what do you know?" scoffed Squint. "Your taster ain't even all the way growed up yet. Wasn't that long ago you was feedin' on nothing but milk from your ma."

"Leastways I wasn't suckled by some mangy old coyote like you was," Red shot back.

"Wasn't no coyote," Squint said indignantly. "I was raised on rattlesnake milk. That's why I piss poison and my pod rattles when I get my dander up."

"Yeah, and these days that's about all you can get up," Larabee said, joining back in.

Mac's smile widened as he continued listening. This digging back and forth was the kind of thing that went on all the time in a solid, comfortable-with-one-another outfit. It might sound kind of rough and biting to an outsider, but it was all meant in good fun. If anybody went too far over the line and gouged too deep, they were quickly put in their place, and then things got back on track.

Reacting to Larabee's latest barb, Squint rolled his eyes heavenward and then cast an appealing gaze over at Boyd Lewis, who sat silently eating his meal.

"They're gangin' up on me here, Boyd. Ain't you gonna pitch in and help even up the sides?"

Boyd was a smoothly muscled black man with a clean-shaven head and a wiry goatee with sprinkles of gray in it. He was maybe forty, maybe fifty. He moved with the fluid grace of a twenty-year-old, and the way he wore a tied-down Colt .45 holstered low on his hip gave the accurate suggestion that same fluidity could unleather the Colt with impressive speed.

"The only thing I'm gonna help," Boyd replied, "is myself to this fine breakfast. The more you fellas keep yammerin' instead of eatin' your own selves, the more there'll be left for when I go back for seconds . . . which I surely aim to do."

"You are a selfish man, Boyd Lewis," Squint proclaimed, looking disappointed.

"Comes to eatin', you bet I am. When I was a little kid, still on the plantation," Boyd explained, "we ate taters and greens in the mornin' and then, for variety, greens and taters at night. And not overly much of either one. Ever since then, 'most any food you put in front of me, even what we got from Otis, was a step up. So now, with this heaven on a plate Mac has dished out, you think I'm gonna waste my time yammerin' or worryin' about somebody else's taster bein' broke?"

Before anyone else could say anything, Castle reappeared from where he'd been off answering nature's call.

"If any of you are looking for something to worry about," said the trail boss, "try worrying about how soon we'll find somewhere we can pick up a second mule. Having just one to pull the chuckwagon is slowing us down. There are a lot worse problems we could have, but slow is slow. And I don't know about the rest of you, but I'm feeling kind of itchy to get home as soon as I can."

There was a general muttering of agreement.

"Plus," Castle added, "I imagine Boss Tremaine is also feeling itchy for us to bring back the payment for the herd we delivered. So what I'm thinking we ought to do when we get underway again, which needs to be pronto, is for us to fan out wide and be on the lookout for some sign of the nearest town or good-sized ranch that might suit our need."

"Sounds good to me, Castle," allowed Squint, the funning over now. Turning to the others, he said, "Come on, boys. Let's eat up and saddle up. Time for us to go find a mule."

Chapter 7

The woman and girl popped up out of a brush-rimmed dry wash and came running frantically toward where Mac was rolling along on his chuckwagon. The woman was wide eyed and wide hipped, dressed in a simple housedress and apron, which flapped about her legs as she ran; the girl, obviously her daughter, looked to be barely into her teens, her body just beginning to fill out, her face quite pretty. They were Mexican, which meant Mac wasn't able to understand a lick of the woman's excited jabbering.

As the pair drew closer, he reined the mule to a halt, set the brake, and climbed down off the seat. By the time they reached him, he'd also pulled down a canteen, which he promptly held out to them. Both were breathing hard, dust streaked, and dripping sweat in the midmorning heat. The woman eagerly accepted the canteen and then handed it to her daughter before drinking from it herself.

After she'd taken several thirsty gulps, she lowered it and immediately began talking again with animated excitement.

The woman appeared very frightened of something and kept pointing back the way she and the girl had come. Mac could make out the words *bastardo* and *cerdo*, which she used repeatedly. He had a pretty good idea what *bastardo* meant, but *cerdo* was as much a mystery as the rest of what she was jabbering.

Mac held up a hand, palm out. "Try to take it easy. I'm willing to help you if I can, but I don't understand your lingo. *No comprende.* You get what I'm saying?"

The woman frowned and then broke into another outburst. *Bastardo* and *cerdo* got tossed out some more, but nothing that brought any clarity.

Sighing, Mac drew the Smith & Wesson from his waistband. He was going to need some assistance with this, and the crew's agreed signal for anyone coming across something that warranted calling in the others was to fire off two shots. Mac recalled Red Pelham mentioning that he spoke pretty good Spanish. Getting him here to decipher what the woman was saying seemed the quickest way to find out what she was so worked up about.

But the sight of the six-gun alarmed the woman and girl in its own way, causing them to shrink back from Mac. The woman dropped the canteen. Mac had to do some fast talking and hand gesturing—not that they understood his words any better than he did theirs—to keep the pair from bolting.

When they appeared to be mostly calmed down, he pointed the Model 3 skyward and triggered two rounds. This sent the woman into a tizzy all over again. Once more she faced the way she and the girl had come and flailed her arms, wailing in distress. Mac finally realized she was expressing concern that the shots he'd fired would draw the attention of whomever or whatever she and her daughter were running from.

Mac tried a repeat of soothing words and hand gestures to calm her down. But then, just when it looked like he was having a measure of success, he heard the hoofbeats of an approaching horse. Trouble was, they weren't coming from either of the directions in which the Double T men had fanned out but rather from off where the woman and girl had first appeared. Sweeping his gaze beyond the dry wash the pair had risen out of, Mac spotted a horseman taking shape through the waves of heat shimmering above the chaparral.

Mother and daughter gasped in unison.

Their terror was palpable. Sensing it, Mac felt an icy resolve run through him. "Get over here and stand behind me," he said in a low, firm voice. As if understanding his words perfectly, the woman and girl did as he said, moving to a position behind him, with the chuckwagon at their backs.

Mac edged forward a half step and planted his feet at shoulder width. Watching the rider grow closer, he felt reassured by the pressure of the Smith & Wesson where he'd replaced it in his waistband at the small of his back.

As the features of the rider grew more distinct, Mac saw he had some size to him, possessed wide, square shoulders, and sat very straight and rigid in his saddle. Maybe an ex-cavalry man. A Colt .45 revolver rode on his left hip, holstered for the cross-draw. When he'd advanced to within a few yards, his face was revealed to be weathered and built of all sharp angles, with pinched eyes that darted about alertly.

Bringing his mount to a halt, the man hung his gaze on the woman and girl for a long count before cutting his eyes to Mac. Without preamble, he said, "I see you caught up with my runaways."

"More like they caught up with me," Mac replied.

"All the same. I'll take 'em off your hands now."

"Where would that be? Where is it you intend taking them?" Mac wanted to know.

"Where they came from. Where they belong," the horseman answered. "That's enough for you to know."

"Appears to me," Mac drawled, "they got a different notion about where they belong. Leastways, they don't seem anxious to go back where they came from."

"They tell you that, did they?"

"They told me plenty."

The man ground his teeth over that for a minute. Then: "That mean you speak Mex?"

Mac grinned crookedly and gave a slow wag of his head. "Not hardly a lick. But there's ways to understand folks other than just by their words. The feeling I get off these two is that they're plumb scared of something . . . or somebody. You wouldn't happen to have any idea what . . . or who . . . that might be, would you?"

"You want to understand something?" the horseman grated. "Most times the best way *is* by words. So I'll make it easy for you. Read my lips. It's never a good idea to stick your beak in another person's business. Especially when that other person is me. What you need to do is get your wagon rollin' the hell out of here and don't look back. What this is about ain't none of your concern."

Mac frowned in thought a moment before saying, "I always appreciate it when somebody offers me some helpful advice. I purely do, mister. And to show how obliged I am for yours, I won't waste any time taking it. Soon as I can get these gals hoisted up on the wagon seat, we'll roll on out of here, just like you recommend."

The horseman's eyes pinched even narrower, and his left arm subtly shifted back a couple inches, making the Colt on his hip more accessible for a reach-over draw.

"You some kind of joker? A funny man?" he demanded harshly. "You heard me say plain that those two were my property. They ain't going nowhere with nobody but me!"

"Something else I heard plain," Mac replied evenly, "is that no person has the right to call another person their property. And what I can see even plainer is that these gals don't want anything to do with you. I don't know what this is all about, but I can for sure tell that much."

"Too bad you can't tell how not to be so dumb. I warned you about stickin' your beak in my business."

Mac was watching the man's right hand, the way his horse's reins were loosely laced through its fingers. The hand was practically trembling with anticipation, itching bad to let go of the reins and reach instead for the Colt.

"You should know," Mac said, "that those two shots I triggered a minute ago were a signal to some friends riding nearby. When they show up, one of them speaks good Spanish. He'll be able to understand the story these gals have to tell."

The horseman bared his teeth and emitted a raspy chuckle. "Is that the best you can do? The oldest trick in the book? I bet your Mex-speakin' pal is right behind me, sneakin' closer and closer, ain't he?"

"Not just yet. But him and the rest will be here soon," Mac told him.

His teeth still bared in a mocking grin, the horseman said, "Too bad it won't be soon enough to do you any good."

His right hand released the reins and swung for the Colt on his left hip. But he decided to be smug about it— acting too cocky, pulling the iron too leisurely. Not seeing any evidence of Mac's gun, even though he'd just been reminded of the recently fired shots, the rider apparently figured he had time to be showy, milk the moment for all it was worth, maybe intimidate the woman and girl even more.

This worked to Mac's favor. He'd already calculated that if it came to gunplay, he had a reasonable chance of using his Model 3 ahead of getting plugged. There were some very deadly men who wore their guns for the cross-draw, and the fact that they were still alive while others who'd gone against them weren't made a case that rigging one's gun in such a manner could sometimes be effective.

But it was also a fact that the added time it took to reach across your body, clear leather, and then swing your arm back before setting on a target required greater speed in order to compensate for the extra movement involved. Not everybody—not very many, actually, the way Mac figured it—had that greater speed. Which was why he'd reckoned he stood at least an even chance against this blowhard on horseback.

The man's nonchalance, when it came, was a bonus. Before Mac realized it was going to play out that way, however, he pitched to one side and went into a shoulder roll at the first sign of the horseman making a grab for his Colt. After coming up on one knee, clawing the Smith & Wesson from his waistband and thrusting it out at arm's length all in a single smooth motion, Mac didn't hesitate to take the first shot.

The bullet sizzled at an upward angle and struck just ahead of the horseman's left shoulder socket as he was twisting to face Mac full on and only beginning to level his Colt. The impact sent the man into a backward somersault, dumping him out of his saddle. He hit the ground hard, both arms flung wide, and his Colt went skittering through the dust without ever being discharged.

Chapter 8

Relating her words in quick, short bursts, Red Pelham was busy translating what the woman was telling him. "Her name is Viola. Her daughter is Regina. She works as the cook and housekeeper for a rancher named Douglas on a spread off to the northeast. The hombre Mac shot is called Broward. Until a few days ago, he worked for Douglas, too. But he got fired and run off when he was caught trying to take liberties with the girl.

"Apparently, the snake didn't go very far, though. When Douglas and his other hands rode out to round up and brand some strays this morning, Broward showed up back at the ranch. He waited to waylay Regina when she went to gather eggs. Luckily, Viola heard her scream and came running in time to bash Broward over the head with a shovel before he did any serious harm. Then mother and daughter ran away, hoping to hide from Broward or, better yet, catch up with Douglas and the others. They ran into Mac instead."

Gathered closely around, listening to this, were Mac and the other Double T men. Two of them, Squint Morris and Boyd Lewis, were hovering directly over the horseman now identified as Broward, where he remained sprawled on the ground, clutching his wounded shoulder. Boyd's .45 was out of its holster and being held casually at his side, its muzzle mere inches from the back of Broward's head.

When Red paused in his translation, Castle turned his head and glared at the man on the ground. "You got anything to say for yourself, mister?"

"You're damn right. I got plenty to say," snarled Broward. "For starters, I'm hurt and bleedin'. I think the bullet is still in my shoulder, and I'm pretty sure it busted some bones. You gonna just leave me layin' here in the dirt while you listen to the lies spewed by that Mexican cow?"

"Might want to watch that mouth," Boyd drawled, "or your hurt shoulder is apt to be the least of your worries."

Broward sneered up at him. "Boy, I get all the luck, don't I? Ain't bad enough I run up against a pack of meddlers lookin' to rescue a couple damsels in distress, but they got to have a damn darky with 'em, to boot!"

Squint leaned over and swung his big, calloused open hand in two heavy swats—one with his palm, one with the flat of his knuckles—across either side of Broward's face. "That makes two warnin's about watchin' your mouth, bub. I'll be happy to deliver another one or a dozen if the message ain't clear."

"Take it easy, Squint," said Castle. "We ain't in the torture business."

"Why not?" growled Squint. "I know a Comanche treatment or two that'd be just right for this piece of mule droppin's. Any lowlife who stoops to forcin' himself on a young girl ain't gonna stop at just one. But there's a sure way to squash that kind of urge out of a sick critter."

"Who says I was forcin' myself on her?" demanded Broward, a worm of blood crawling out one corner of his mouth. "Look at her, the way she's fillin' out all ripe and ready. You think she don't know it, don't know the effect that kind of thing can have on a man? The way she was swingin' those hips around me all the time, beggin' to be noticed. You damn betcha she knew. Fear of gettin' caught by her ma or old man Douglas is the only reason she squealed about it."

"That don't cut it," argued Mac. "The fear I saw in her eyes when you rode up wasn't no act. Plus, you called her your 'property,' and you was willing to draw on me to stake your claim."

"Only because I saw in your eyes how you wanted her for your own," insisted Broward through clenched teeth. "I see the same thing in all the rest of you buzzards. You want me out of the way so you can have her plumb to yourselves! Ain't that the truth?"

"The truth," Red said, his mouth twisting in disgust, "is that the likes of you makes me want to vomit."

"Some riders comin' yonder," spoke up Hank Larabee, tilting his head to the north. "Got a hunch they might have something to say on this."

Castle's eyes followed the direction Larabee had indicated. "Maybe so. But until we find out what their business is, best we spread out a bit, boys. Ease on around to the back side of the wagon, Hank, and hold ready with that scattergun from under the driver's seat. Red, you keep standing by the gals. Boyd, you stick tight to Broward. He tries to move or speaks out of turn, clunk him with your gun barrel."

Everybody positioned themselves in accordance with

the trail boss's instructions, and then all eyes settled on the dust cloud that marked three approaching riders. The swirling column grew closer until the features of the men contained within it became clearer. Suddenly, Viola cried out in an excited tone, "Señor Douglas!" She and her daughter clutched one another, and each beamed a wide smile.

The riders reined in when they were within a few yards and then held steady until the swirling dust mostly dissipated. At that point, one of the men—sturdily built; fifty, give or take; stern countenance, marked by a mustache and sideburns in need of trimming—edged his mount a couple of additional steps forward.

"My name's Jim Douglas. This is my range. We heard some shooting, came to see what was going on," he stated. Then he turned his eyes to the woman, Viola, and said something more in rapid Spanish.

After waiting for Viola to respond, Red demonstrated that he'd understood the exchange by saying to Douglas, "Yes, sir, the gals are fine and unharmed. By us, that is. Wouldn't have been the case, though, if that low-down skunk"—a jab of his thumb to indicate Broward—"had gotten his way."

Douglas slanted a fierce scowl at the man on the ground. "Griff Broward," he said, spitting out the name like it was a bad taste in his mouth.

"You know this man?" asked Castle.

"To my increasing regret, yes. Up until a couple of days ago, he worked for me. I fired him and ran him off when I found out he was starting to bother the girl. Looks like I should have done more."

"Hard to argue."

"Who shot him?" Douglas wanted to know.

"I did," Mac answered.

"But didn't kill him. Reckon that makes two of us who fell short when we had the chance." Douglas's expression hardened. "Meaning it's time and past time to fix the problem permanent-like."

On the ground, Broward suddenly pushed up on his good arm. The color drained from his face, and a look of alarm gripped it. "What are you sayin'? The only thing it's time and past time for is gettin' me to a doctor! I'm bleedin' and hurt bad, can't you see? I got a bullet in me! If it don't get took care of proper, lead poisonin' is apt to set in!"

Douglas slowly swiveled his head once each way. "No, it won't. Won't have time."

Broward's eyes bulged in horror. "What's that supposed to mean?"

Ignoring him, Douglas made a faint motion, and the two men who'd ridden up with him edged their mounts forward to pull even on either side.

"These are my two sons, Royce and Eddie," Douglas introduced. Royce appeared to be the older brother, about thirty; Eddie was maybe five years younger. Both were square shouldered, clean shaven, even featured. Royce had his father's dark, bristly sideburns; Eddie's were sparser, and his hair was paler in color.

Continuing to address Castle, Douglas said, "I don't know who you fellas are. Where you're from, where you're headed. No matter, travelers are generally welcome to cross my range. Keeping Broward away from my gals makes you all the more welcome and makes me obliged to you. Normally, that would mean inviting you to stop by the house for a meal before letting you continue on your way. But under the circumstances, me and my boys have overdue business to tend to, which I suspect you might want to ride clear of. Law hereabouts is scarce, but that don't mean justice is. It might seem sudden and harsh to the minds of some, but there's a line that has to be drawn and stuck to . . . and when it gets crossed, accounts need to be settled."

"We're heading home to Texas after driving a herd of cattle to a buyer over west of Temecula," Castle explained. "We know about range law back where we come from, too, and understand how a tall tree and a rope are sometimes the only way to hold that line you speak of."

Broward squirmed on his elbow, his eyes darting back and forth between Douglas and Castle. "What the hell are you talkin' about a rope and a tree, you meddler? This ain't Texas! I ain't no rustler or horse thief. I told you, that little chili pepper was beggin' for it, sashayin' her ripe little behind all over the place like—"

He stopped short when Boyd's gun barrel rapped against the side of his head and knocked him off the elbow he was propped on. Broward flopped flat to the ground, emitting a half groan, half curse.

"Hope you don't mind me handin' your man a lick," Boyd said to Douglas. "His whinin' was startin' to get plumb annoying."

"Glad for it. Like I said, I aim to soon end his whining and filthy notions for good," Douglas replied.

"Comes to that," Castle interjected, "me and my crew will go along with whatever suits you. You want us to move on, we will. But if you want us to stick around and maybe lend a hand, we're up for that, too. We heard enough, both before and since you got here, to make it plain this wretch deserves to be scratched off the face of the earth. If nothing else, not knowing how far away your ranch house is, if they'll trust us, we can at least offer a wagon ride for these two gals, who've already had a rough enough go of it."

Douglas's brows pinched in consideration. "That ain't a half bad idea," he allowed. "I don't want them to see what we have to do here, anyway. And since your man planted a bullet in Broward on their behalf, I reckon they'll be trusting enough."

Castle nodded. "Consider it done, then."

Chapter 9

Now that he'd been introduced to Stack Ketchum's gang, Otis Bradley couldn't help feeling some reservation about being part of it. But at the same time, he knew he'd better get over any such uncertainty, and damn quick-like, too. He was in too deep already, and by the sound of things, it seemed clear he was soon going to be sucked in even deeper.

"I had a hunch right from the get-go that Otis would make a good addition to our crew," Ketchum was telling the others. "Let's face it, losing both Slater and Rico on that San Berdoo bank job left us shorthanded for future jobs that might come along."

"That rotten San Berdoo bank. That was a damn snake bite in practically every way there was. We lost two good men, and our haul wasn't much more than what we could've got from a Baptist ice cream social."

This sour appraisal came from Ed Story, a wiry, medium-

sized man with dangerous slits for eyes, which slid restlessly back and forth under a ledge of furry blond brows.

"It was a lousy tip, all right? I've admitted as much,
and I'm sick of hearing about it," Ketchum growled defensively. "When's the last time you mapped out a big
money grab, Ed?"

"I was just saying, that's all. Wasn't accusing or laying
no blame," Story responded.

"Everybody take it easy," advised Jesus Del Sol, a
hard-bodied, hard-faced Mexican/Yaqui half-breed with
a wispy, drooping mustache and a cigarette stub thrusting
from one corner of his mouth. "No matter how or why,
Story's right about that Berdoo bank damn sure marking
a string of bad luck for us. As if the results of the job itself
didn't turn out bad enough, we all let the little brains
below our belt buckles decide to spend part of our paltry
take in the whorehouse where that brawl busted out."

"But the brawl wasn't our doing," pointed out Jack
Needham, a narrow-shouldered hombre with thinning
hair, oddly bent eyebrows, and a quick, toothy grin.

"No matter. We got caught in it all the same," Del Sol
insisted. "I guess you'd have to call it *some* luck that all
of us except Stack managed to make it clear before the
law came barging in."

Ketchum grinned crookedly. "That was because I
nabbed the only pretty gal in the joint. The nags the rest
of you picked out, no wonder you were so quick to bolt.
Me, I had reason for being a little more reluctant to, er,
withdraw . . ."

Story huffed. "Ain't funny, Stack. Wasn't good at all,
you getting slammed behind bars after we'd just got done
losing Slater and Rico. And then when you sent word for
us to not try busting you out—"

"That was the smart way to play it," interrupted Ketchum, his grin turning into a scowl. "Don't you see? We'd already had enough things go wrong. The one thing we had going for us was that our gang was barely known down in these parts. Once I managed to fool those law dogs with a phony name, the last thing I wanted was for you fellas to come hell roaring in and put every badge-toter in the territory on alert. I appreciate the thought of you boys wanting to spring me, I purely do. But I figured me staring at cell bars for a few days was better than the lot of us going on the dodge before we ever even got the lay of things hereabouts."

"That was a gutsy call for you to make, Stack. Now that we know your reasoning behind it, reckon it does make the best sense," said Needham.

"And if it's any consolation," added Del Sol, "while you were cooling your heels in a cell, we weren't exactly living in the lap of luxury holed up in this creaky wooden box that's an oven in the day's heat and a drafty pile of slats in the cold night air."

What he was referring to was an abandoned, dilapidated old farmhouse built into the side of a weedy hill, with a stand of gnarled California buckeye growing close on the upslope. Remnants of collapsed fencing could be seen poking up through the weeds here and there, and near the house was a blown-down pile of timber, which had once been a small barn or shed of some kind. At its best, the place appeared to have been a hardscrabble operation; and what remained—especially the already stifling farmhouse interior under a blazing midday sun—seemed to be accurately captured by Del Sol's description.

On the ride here, Ketchum had explained to Otis how he and the others had first found shelter in the place one rainy night following the jinxed San Bernardino bank robbery. Then, after he ended up in jail, he'd gotten word out to the others to return and wait there for his release. The latter having come sooner than expected was cause for celebration but also for some catching up and explaining.

"So we've all had some unpleasantness to endure," Ketchum said now, summing up. "But the thing is, we *have* endured. Those of us gathered here, that is. Remember, we could be full of lead and buried in a cheap Boot Hill grave like Slater and Rico. We might be uncomfortable and scraping the bottom, but we're still alive. There's always that." He paused, his eyes sweeping each of the faces around him. "And, it so happens, there's suddenly a lot more. Like my pappy used to say, I got some good news about the bad news."

Story frowned. "What's that supposed to mean?"

"It means my time in jail—that would be the particular bad news I'm speaking of, though we all know there's been more—resulted in some things that paint a whole lot brighter picture. For starters, I already told you how I pegged Otis here as a good candidate to help fill out our crew."

Saying this, Ketchum indicated the new man with a flourish of one hand. Otis, who'd been standing by silently watching and listening, suddenly felt the pressure of all eyes on him, and it made him want to slink into a corner.

"But it gets even better," Ketchum went on. "On the ride here, I learned some choice details about Otis's recent past that paint the brighter picture I mentioned. That is, if the rest of you agree that the chance for an easy grab of twenty thousand dollars and change sounds like a nice turn of luck."

"I reckon we'd all be inclined to think that sounds like a real fine change," replied Needham.

"So what's the 'easy grab' that will put this twenty thousand in our hands?" Story wanted to know.

Ketchum gestured again. "Tell 'em, Otis."

And so he did. A bit haltingly at first, still somewhat nervous about the company he found himself in, not to mention what he was proposing to them. But the more he talked and the brighter their eyes seemed to grow with a kind of welcoming eagerness for what he was relating, the steadier Otis's voice got and the more comfortable he felt about his choice to ride along with Stack Ketchum.

By the time he was done, all the faces aimed his way wore satisfied expressions, and there were even a couple of agreeable head bobs.

"So there you have it," Ketchum stated when Otis was finished sharing his experiences with the Double T cattle drive. "Nine hundred longhorns delivered and sold at a price in the neighborhood of twenty-two to twenty-five dollars a head. And now that money's on the way back to Texas, in the possession of five trail-weary cowboys. So we rattle our hocks, catch up with 'em, and give them the choice of peaceably handing over that money some overfed cattle boss ain't hurting for, anyhow . . . or, if they force our hand, they end up giving over the money regardless and taking on the weight of some lead in its place. Either way, I say again, does that sound like an easy grab or what?"

Chapter 10

On Mac's third full day with the Double T outfit, they crossed the Colorado River and rolled into Arizona Territory. The days grew increasingly hotter, the land harsher and the nights clear and crisp. Camaraderie within the group remained high, with plenty of good-natured banter to help pass the time. Their progress, even with the chuckwagon, was steady. Its pace had improved thanks to a second mule, purchased from the Douglas ranch. Mac had his hands full for much of the first day getting the newly paired team to work together. But his practiced handling and liberal use of the kind of salty language that mules responded to best eventually brought them in line.

Though Mac's mule-skinning skills proved adequate, it was his cooking skills that continued to please and impress his new companions the most. And after having been apart from chuckwagon duties for several months, he found himself quickly falling back into the routine with comfortable ease. He'd enjoyed cooking for a crew of wranglers almost from the start, seeming to take to it naturally. But always before he'd seen it as a temporary thing to help him keep on the move, constantly looking over his shoulder for some sign of trouble from Leclerc and his lies, while at the same time hungrily eyeing the western horizon for the promise of California.

Now, with the California promise a washout and his new determination to return to some form of cowboying, taking on this role as a grub wrangler once again suited him fine.

With the job, however, came the responsibility of seeing to it that necessary supplies were stocked in order to serve decent meals. That was where, pretty early on, Mac saw firsthand how his predecessor, Otis Bradley, had failed to measure up. The supplies Mac found available in the chuckwagon were sadly lacking when it came to being able to sustain the crew all the way to Texas or, for that matter, very much farther from where they currently were.

As he dished out supper that evening, Mac made Castle aware of the situation. "There's plenty of beans and bacon," he said. "But if you want much variety beyond that, I'll need at least a few basics, like flour, salt, sugar. Some canned goods wouldn't be a bad idea. And some fresh meat—either beef or even wild game, if anybody gets a chance to bag some—would allow me to whip up some tasty stew."

"Don't see why all that can't be got. Except maybe for the wild game. That's sorta up to what Mother Nature is willing to put in our sights," Castle replied. "I remember this area pretty well from when we passed through with the herd. There's a town not too far off—name of Broken Spoke, as I recall—where you should be able to find the store goods you need. And there are ranches scattered hereabouts, too, where surely we can buy some beef if need be."

Hank Larabee made a sour face. "A crew of cowpokes who ride for one brand buyin' beef from some other brand. Somehow that has a wrong sound to it."

"Didn't you ever buy a cut of meat from a butcher shop? Or order a steak at a restaurant?" said Red Pelham. "You think those always came from whatever brand you happened to be riding for?"

"Ain't never in my life set foot in no butcher shop. I want meat carved from a critter, I do it myself," Larabee told him. "Ain't never ate in no restaurant, neither, except maybe breakfast a time or two after a long night of drinkin'. I go to town, that's generally what it's for—to do some drinkin', not eatin'."

"Speakin' of which," said Squint Morris, eyeing Castle, "if we're gonna visit that town of Broken Spoke to buy grub supplies, there ought to be time enough for a body to duck into one of the local saloons and rinse some of this Arizona trail dust off our tonsils, oughtn't there?"

Castle eyed him right back, cocking one brow sharply. "Well, I dunno. I reckon there'd be time enough, yeah. But can I trust you to behave, and are you healed enough to be up to it? Last time I turned you loose in a saloon, we lost one member of our outfit and you came back with a bullet in you."

"Now dang it, that ain't fair," Squint protested. "You know that was all on that blasted Otis. He's the one who started the fight and then plugged me when I tried to break it up before it got out of hand. What's more, this wing of mine is healed just fine enough for some elbow bendin' to throw down a few belts."

"Comes to that—doin' some elbow bendin' and tonsil rinsin'," Larabee joined back in, "I cast my vote in favor of it, too. I'll even volunteer to nursemaid ol' squint-eye here if that's what it takes to convince you, Castle."

Squint harrumphed. "The day I need to be nurse-maided by the likes of you, you ol'—"

"All right, you two. That's enough," Castle interrupted. "I reckon we can all take time for some tonsil washing when we hit that town. But not too much time and not too much elbow bending. We've still got a long trip ahead of us."

"I'm all for joinin' in," allowed Boyd Lewis. "Just so long, that is, as we don't lose sight of the main reason for stoppin'. And that's for Mac to stock up on grub supplies. I'll trade tonsil wash for some of that stew he spoke of any day of the week."

"You and the way you always think of eating," said Red with a grin.

"I got a lot of empty belly years to make up for, kid. That's just the way it is," Boyd replied, minus any hint of a grin.

"I'll do my part to help make 'em up," Mac assured him. "And first chance I get, I'll serve you a batch of that stew."

"Sounds like we got a plan to satisfy everybody," proclaimed Castle. "By my recollection, we ought to reach Broken Spoke about the middle of the day tomorrow. So there's something you can wrap your heads around when you hit your bedrolls in a little while."

Chapter 11

Because he was awake ahead of anyone else, in order to start preparing breakfast, Mac was the first one to hear the sound. It came from a ways off, though not too far. In any case, there was no mistaking it. Gunfire! It started as a sudden burst of several shots, tapered off briefly, then picked up again and continued sporadically.

It didn't take long for other heads to pop up from their bedrolls. First, Squint, then Castle shoving up on one elbow.

"That what I think it is?" Castle said sleepily.

"Somebody shooting. More than one somebody," Mac responded. "By the sound of it, I judge three or four guns, maybe more, real busy trading lead."

"Hell," grunted Castle, throwing back his covers and sitting up all the way. "How far off you figure?"

Mac answered, "Hard to say for sure. Not more than a couple miles, I don't think."

"I reckon about the same," said Squint, pushing stiffly to his feet.

By now the others were starting to poke their heads up, rousted from their slumber. "What's goin' on?" somebody grumbled.

Scowling as he also stood up, Castle said, "Seems we bedded down near a place where either a war has broke out or folks have a mighty rowdy way of waking each other up come morning."

There was a slight pause while everyone cocked their ears, listening to the ongoing distant reports.

From where he still sat in his blankets, Boyd said, "So now that the noisy rascals have woke us up, too, the next question—which I hate to be the one to ask—is, what are we going to do about it?"

"Not our land, not our concern," declared Larabee.

"But what if it's somebody in trouble? Some unfortunate cuss set on by a pack of owlhoots maybe," said Boyd. "You heard Castle say there's cattle ranches scattered hereabouts. What if it's a rancher fightin' to keep his beef from gettin' run off?"

"Still don't have to be no affair of ours," Larabee insisted. "Ridin' toward the sound of guns is work for soldier boys or lawmen. We ain't neither."

"Mac came lookin' when he heard the shot that Castle put our snake-bit mule down with," pointed out Red. "Ain't you glad he did?"

"O' course I'm glad Mac showed up to join us. But what brung him was one shot. What's going on out yonder," Larabee argued, "is something a whole lot different."

"Then I guess you can wait here to find out what, but it looks like the rest of us are goin' to have a firsthand look-see," Boyd said as he and Red threw back their blankets and came to their feet.

By that time, Castle, Mac, and Squint had already stomped into their boots and were headed to saddle their horses. Larabee scowled after everybody for a long beat, then flung off his covers and reached for his own boots.

"Dang bunch of nosy idjits," he grumbled to himself. "Didn't none of 'em ever hear what curiosity done to the cat?"

With brightening fingers of pinkish gold poking above the eastern horizon ahead of the first sliver of actual sunlight, the Double T riders crossed an expanse of rolling, rugged chaparral toward the continuing sound of the gunfire. Scattered saguaro cacti, tall and murky in the early half-light, extended upwardly bent arms, as if saluting their passage.

As the riders angled south, the land grew choppier, rising and falling in low, sharp-crested hills and dropping away here and there into ragged, twisty arroyos. As they drew closer to the origins of the shooting, Castle signaled the others to slow their horses to a walk. After proceeding fifty or so yards in that manner, he signaled a complete halt. He and Squint dismounted and went cautiously ahead on foot. In one hand, Castle clutched a collapsible spyglass.

Most of the gray was gone from the sky now, and it was only minutes until full daybreak. The gunfire coming from the other side of a rocky ridge popped and cracked, erratic reports from both handguns and rifles.

Mac gripped his Yellowboy and edged forward a bit himself, anxious to find out what this was all about. Red was close on his left, also brandishing a Winchester; Boyd glided ahead on the other side, his right hand hanging loose and ready over the .45 holstered on his hip. Larabee hung back a ways, old carbine cradled in the crook of one arm.

It wasn't long before Castle and Squint returned. Both wore sober expressions.

"What's the situation?" Mac wanted to know.

"Seems pretty clear there was an ambush," Castle reported. "Straight over the ridge is a flat, sandy stretch leading off to the left. On the right, there's a sort of rocky hogback stretching down off the ridge. There are three or four men with rifles up on the high ground. Down on the flat there are three folks pinned down behind scattered boulders. I could see some dead horses laying close by. I figure that the three came riding in on the flat and the riflemen up on the hogback were waiting to greet 'em with lead. They cut down their horses, but the three are making a fight of it—for as long as their ammo holds out."

"I read it the same," Squint agreed.

"So if we was to take sides," said Red, "it'd be with the ones pinned down. Wouldn't we? I mean, nobody likes bushwhackers, right?"

Boyd responded, "Unless maybe it's a case of the fellas in the rocks bein' lawmen—a posse—layin' in wait for three owlhoots on the run. Might be worth considerin' that."

"Might be," allowed Castle. "Except for this. I got a good look through my spyglass, and two of the three pinned down are young women, not much more than twenty. They're with an old man . . . And I didn't spot no badges on any of the riflemen."

"That makes it pretty clear to me," declared Mac.

"That's 'cause you're only a green sprout yourself," countered Larabee. "Trust me, there are female hellcats who can make some of the nastiest owlhoots you're likely to run into."

Squint chuffed. "Yeah, and you'd know, you old scoundrel—because you probably sired a brood all your own."

"Be that as it may," said Castle, "I agree with Mac that the gals over the ridge appear to be on the wrong end of things, and I think we ought to try and help 'em."

"More damsels in distress," commented Boyd, echoing Broward's snide remark from earlier.

"I can't help it. If that's what's put in our path, that's the way it is," snapped Castle. "Here's what I say we should do. Red, you're one of our best shots with a long gun. You go up to the crest of this ridge where Squint and I just came down from. Take Larabee and his Henry with you. The two of you keep a bead on things down over the other side, especially those riflemen on the hogback . . . Me and the rest of the boys will circle around wide and come up behind. With any luck, we might be able to get the drop on 'em before they even know we're there. Unless they force our hand, hopefully we can tame 'em without firing a shot. Then we'll signal the other side in order to put a halt to any more shooting from them so we can go to work on getting to the bottom of the whole story. Everybody with me?"

Squint spoke for the rest, saying, "You're ramroddin' this outfit, Castle. You call the tune. Don't sound like a bad one to me."

The others signaled their agreement by looking on silently, waiting for the final go-ahead from Castle.

"Okay," he said with a curt nod. "Let's get to it, then."

Chapter 12

The brilliantly blazing crown of the sun was rising higher above the eastern horizon as Castle, Mac, Squint, and Boyd spread out at intervals in a long line on the back side of the hogback. On foot, in half crouches, they moved quickly but quietly forward through the sage and prickly pear.

They passed the horses the men they were advancing on had left hobbled, stepping easy so as not to spook the animals and give them cause to raise any alarm. As Mac and the others began ascending the rear slope, an elongated shadow was cast back over them, making them blurred, murky shapes moving within it.

Erratic exchanges of gunfire continued to disrupt what otherwise would have been the peacefulness of early morning. And now, as the Double T men grew closer, they could also hear some harsh words being tossed— along with bullets—primarily from the riflemen.

Somebody hollered, "Give it up, you stubborn old pelican! You rode right into a trap, and now that's just what you are—trapped! You got no horses to get away on, and it's just a matter of time before you run out of bullets and water down where you are!"

From a distance, out on the flat, Mac reckoned, a hoarse voice called back, "We got enough bullets down here for me to have one I mean to plant in your mangy hide, you long-loopin' cattle grabber!"

Mac heard a ripple of taunting laughter from up above.

Then a different voice hollered, "Talk like that only makes you more deserving of a bullet to your own wrinkly ol' hide. That much is already settled. But I'll make you a deal, old man. Hand yourself over now, before this has to drag out into the hot part of the day, and I'll see to it you get put out of your misery quick and clean. What's more, I promise we won't kill those two pretty daughters you foolishly brought along with you. Me and the boys might take our pleasure with 'em for a good long while before we turn 'em loose, but we won't kill 'em."

More taunting laughter, this time even louder and more strident than before.

It was cut short, though, by a sudden burst of three incoming rounds—a handgun, Mac judged—followed immediately by a female voice shouting from out on the flat. "Me and my sister will put bullets in our own brains before we let any of you filthy dogs lay your paws on us!"

Which, after the interruption, only generated more rude laughter.

Mac glanced over at Castle and the others. Mac was on the near end of the line they formed, Castle was next, then Squint, and then Boyd at the other end. They had ascended to within a few feet of the men on top, who were also spread out in a line. By sight and signaling the Double T men had determined there were four riflemen in the rocks along the crest of the hogback—one for each of them. They had positioned themselves accordingly, each coming up directly behind one of the ambushers. The hollering back and forth, intermingled with the shooting and snickering, had helped cover any sound the Double T men might have made on their approach. Now it was just a matter of a couple yards before they could close on their targets.

Castle poised, glancing to each side to make sure the others were keyed on him, before he made the first move. When he did, it was a long, lunging stride up and forward, purposely kicking aside some loose gravel to help make his presence known as he announced in a loud voice, "Everybody freeze! You've got four guns at your backs, and anybody who makes a wrong move will take a bullet!"

Mac simultaneously advanced on his man, an average-sized specimen dressed in wrinkled, dusty range clothes, with a battered sombrero dangling from a chin strap down between his shoulders and a six-shooter in a beat-up holster strapped to one hip. This hombre—like the other three down the line, Mac could see in his peripheral vision—held fast, as ordered.

After a tense, silent moment, the man in front of Castle said, "What's the idea? Who are you varmints to be hornin' in on our business?"

"Don't worry about who we are. Just worry about the guns we got pointed at you," Castle told him. "Now all of you lay your rifles down and ease backward slow, without turning around."

"We got people down yonder shootin' at us!" came a protest.

"Then I'd advise you keep your head down. Do like I told you. Then we'll take care of them next."

The man in front of Mac said, "You claim you got four guns on us, but I only hear one voice. I think you're bluffin'!"

"You got a right to think what you want . . . but you'd be making a big mistake," Mac was quick to inform him in a low, grating voice.

That nearly ended it right there. Mac could feel a grudging resignation pass down through the row of riflemen. He could actually see their shoulders start to sag, as if in defeat, sense they were only a moment away from lowering their guns.

But then, for whatever reason, the trio down on the flat decided to cut loose with a blistering volley, which came ripping and cracking up into the rocks where the high shooters were on the verge of easing back.

This had two disastrous results. First, it caused the ambushers to jerk back reflexively, even though they were already hunkered behind cover. Second, it made the Double T men, who had moved up close to the crest of the hogback, also involuntarily duck away from the unexpected rain of sizzling bullets and rock shrapnel thrown by ricochets. The combined disruption gave the ambushers a desperate chance to try to turn the tables on those who only a moment earlier had the drop on them—and they took it!

Wheeling about in ragged unison, cursing and kicking and swinging their rifle muzzles around like clubs, the bushwhackers lunged back at the Double T men, still jammed close but nevertheless off-balance by the surprise volley from below.

Mac was caught exactly that way. His focus had been jolted away from the man in front of him for only a second. And then, suddenly, the man was spinning to face him, and his carbine lashed around with him.

Mac's Yellowboy was still thrust at an upward angle, still aimed at the man, but his overriding instincts told him the most important thing was to try to duck the impending blow from the rifle barrel hurtling toward his head. So that was what he did, but with only partial success. He managed to pull away from full impact, but he still took a hard glancing blow an inch above his left ear.

Mac was knocked sideways first onto his right hip and then onto his shoulder, grinding down painfully onto a gravelly surface. But the pain shooting through his head and down through his whole left side was worse. At first, he thought he was going to black out. His vision swam, and all sound—the continued curses of other men, thrashing bodies, the reports of more gunfire, from closer now—faded to almost nothing.

Then, with startling clarity, it all abruptly returned. And what it revealed was the shocking sight of the man who'd knocked him down, an unshaven hombre with twisted, yellowing teeth showing in a wide sneer as he loomed over him and started to take aim with his rifle.

But what Mac's renewed clarity also revealed, even through his pain, was that he was still gripping his Yellowboy and it was still angled up toward his attacker. A stroke of the trigger turned the man's yellow sneer into a splatter of bright crimson.

The ambusher's head snapped back but then rocked loosely forward again as his knees buckled under him. He tipped forward and fell, his full deadweight crashing down on Mac.

Mac felt much of the air driven out of him. He tried desperately to squirm free, but the effort was futile. All it accomplished was to set his head spinning again, and this time it kept going, in an endless downward spiral, until he passed out completely.

Chapter 13

"Hold on a minute . . . I think he's startin' to come around now."

The voice sounded familiar but muffled, like the speaker had a blanket wrapped around his head. Mac wished he had a blanket wrapped around his, a nice thick one to cushion the throbbing ache, which felt like somebody was hammering on his skull from the inside. He gingerly tried to move and quickly found it made the rest of him ache almost as bad.

A hand came to rest on his shoulder, and a different voice, seeming suddenly much louder, said, "Mac . . . can you hear me?"

Mac suppressed a groan and then worked his mouth enough to rasp out a reply. "Yeah, I hear you. No need to shout."

Somebody chuckled. "Answer like that comes from the same kind of bustin' sore head as a hangover leaves you with. I know it well."

This time Mac did groan. "If the way I'm feeling was a hangover, at least I would've had a lot more fun leading up to it."

He opened his eyes to slits at first and then slowly the rest of the way, knowing the bright light of day was going to stab like knives. It did, but was more bearable than he'd expected. After he finished blinking his vision into focus, he found the faces of Castle and Squint hovering over him.

Mac groaned again, saying, "If I'm dead, it's plain to see I failed to make it to the upstairs place, elsewise I wouldn't be looking at your two mugs."

Castle grinned. "No, you ain't dead. But the same can't be said for the hombre who clobbered you."

Everything came rushing back then, with sudden and complete clarity. Mac raised himself on his elbows and found he was lying in a grassy patch atop the crown of the hogback. The man he'd shot was sprawled a yard or so downslope. Mac couldn't see his face, but part of the sombrero that had been hanging down his back was pinned under him and part of it, the underside of the wide brim, was sticking up; it was heavily spattered with blood.

Mac turned his head and looked across the top of the hogback. He could see the bodies of two more ambushers, sprawled and still. Beyond them, another was lying on the edge of the rocks. Boyd was kneeling over him.

His eyes returning to Castle, Mac said, "All of ours okay?"

"All except you," Castle answered. "Me and Squint had to kill our men. Boyd shot his but only wounded him. He's in a bad way, but so far hanging on."

Mac frowned. "What about those fools from down on

the flat, who cut loose with all that shooting when we nearly had the situation tamed?"

Squint gestured. "Matter of fact, here they come now. Red and Larabee went to fetch 'em."

Mac pushed the rest of the way to a full sitting position. He felt the strain in his right shoulder, and any movement only worsened the pounding in his head. But there was nothing for it right now. And there remained plenty of other things to be concerned about.

Twisting at the waist, Mac looked down the front side of the hogback, toward the flat where the man and his two daughters had been pinned down. He saw the trio ascending now, nearly to the top, accompanied by Red and Larabee.

The man had some years on him, as evidenced by bristly white whiskers and an unruly thatch of gray-streaked hair. He was of average height, piled on a stocky frame. Making the climb came with added difficulty due to an injured right leg, marked by a bloody bandage wrapped around his thigh.

He was trudging steadily on, however, in a kind of ragged, stubborn limp, aided by a rifle butt, which he jammed down on the ground at his right side with each alternating step, his left arm draped over the shoulders of one of his daughters on the other side.

Even in his own pain, Mac couldn't help but notice how the shoulders the old coot was leaning on flowed down to a trim yet shapely set of female curves that— even clad in a simple cotton shirt, dusty trousers, and boots—would make a fella look for just about any excuse to wrap an arm around them.

What was more, the face that completed the package appeared every bit as fine, even streaked with dust and perspiration and framed by a thick, tangled mane of strawberry blond hair. And adding to this eye-pleasing sight still more was the fact that walking directly on the vision's other side was a second gal equally as attractive. So equal it made Mac think for a moment that the blow to the head he'd received must have left him seeing double.

Finally, though, it dawned on him that the sisters were twins! The realization he wasn't seeing double, after all, combined with the sheer loveliness of the pair advancing in a wash of bright morning sunshine, actually lifted some of his aches and pains.

Upon reaching the top of the slope, the white-whiskered old gent took a moment to gulp a couple of breaths. Then, his gaze sweeping over the bodies sprawled in easy view, he exclaimed, "Thunderation! When you Texas boys take a notion to go rat stompin', you're real terrors, ain't you?"

"This is hardly what we set out to do," Castle replied, frowning. "The only notion we had in mind, after we saw how you and your gals were in a tight spot, was to try to clamp a lid on the shooting until we could find out whatever was behind it all. These hombres forced our hand, and we didn't have any choice but to defend ourselves."

Mac spoke up, saying, "But we darn near had the lid in place if you hadn't cut loose with that volley that busted up our having the drop on this bunch."

The girl who had her father's arm over her shoulders glared at him and snapped, "We'd been trading volleys with this pack of coyotes long before you men ever showed up. We were fighting for our lives! How were we supposed to know anybody else was even up here?"

"That's a fair point," said Red, stepping forward and giving Mac a disapproving look. "But before we talk out the rest of the details, you ought to lower yourself down on one of these rocks, Mr. Hardwick"—this directed toward the old man—"and take a load off that wounded leg. Looks like it's bleeding fresh through that bandage."

The man addressed as Hardwick didn't waste any time taking Red's suggestion. He limped over to one of the rocks the ambushers had been using for cover and lowered himself onto a spot that was weathered flat and reasonably smooth. As soon as he was seated, his daughters pressed close on each side and began fussing over his leg.

"Hold it out straight and prop it up on that other rock in front of you," one of them instructed. "Now that we don't have bullets flying at us anymore, we can take the time to cut away that pant leg and get at the wound so we can do a better job of cleaning and bandaging it."

"Now hold on a minute," protested Hardwick. "Those britches are too good to be hacking away at. They ain't but four or five years old, got a lot of wear left in 'em. And they're already bad enough ventilated where the bullet went in and out. There's no lead in me to worry about, I tell you, just holes where the slug punched through the meat of my thigh."

"That still doesn't mean there isn't the chance for infection to set in," said the other daughter. "You fool around and lose that limb, you stubborn old goat, you won't need the pant leg, anyway."

As a folding knife was produced and the material of his pants was being sliced open, Hardwick looked forlornly at the men around him. "What's a body to do? Ain't bad enough I got to fight off night skulkers bent on robbin' my cattle and throwin' lead at me, I got a pair of pesky daughters gangin' up on me to boot!"

As the girls ignored their father's complaints and concentrated on continuing to tend his leg, Red turned to

Castle, Mac, and Squint, saying, "This is the Hardwick family. The father is Hannibal, and the girls are Sara and Tara. As you can see, they're twins, and I can't rightly say which is which."

"Hell, I can't tell myself half the time," growled the old man. "And it don't really matter, because they're both too dang stubborn to listen to me, anyhow."

This while the girls stuck silently to their task, not even looking up, giving the impression that indifference to their father's lamentations wasn't an uncommon thing.

"They've got a cattle ranch not far from here," Red went on. "Like the other spreads in the area, they've been having a lot of trouble lately with rustlers. The long-loopers swoop in at night and pluck off fifty or so head at a time, small bunches that can be driven away quickly and usually quietly and are sometimes not even missed right away."

"But it don't take long," Hardwick interjected, "before fifty or sixty beeves shaved away two or three times a month start to add up, and you damn betcha that gets to bein' missed! Our Box H spread was never that big to begin with, and it's shrinkin' smaller all the time."

"Last night the rustlers hit the Box H again. Another fifty-plus gone," said Red. "Luckily, because he'd started making night patrols, Mr. Hardwick came along not too long after and spotted the fresh tracks where they'd been driven off. So he went back to the ranch and rousted up his gals. They figured the night was bright enough so's they'd be able to stick with the tracks of the stolen critters for a chance at catching up with the thieves and taking 'em by surprise in order to reclaim their cattle."

"That was a gutsy plan. I got to give you that," allowed Castle. Then he added, "But, at the same time, you'll have to pardon me for questioning your wisdom at involving a couple of young women in it, especially your own daughters."

One of said daughters instantly snapped her face around and favored Castle with a glare much like the one Mac had received. Mac couldn't tell if it was the same girl or if the twins were not only equally pretty but also equal at throwing daggers with their eyes.

In any case, the one who'd turned on Castle said, "For your information, mister, my sister and I can ride and shoot as good or better than most men. Especially the spineless variety they seem to grow too damn many of around these parts."

"What my daughter is tryin' to tell you in her gentle, patient way," Hardwick explained with a rueful smile, "is that she and her sister are the only two ranch hands I got left. I had a couple men, but the rustlers spooked 'em. One got nicked by a bullet, and so both of 'em turned their yellow tails and lit a shuck. They claimed they were leavin' to go make more money workin' for the railroad spur built to connect Broken Spoke with Rimhorn City to the north . . . But I know yellow when I see it, and truth to tell, those two slackers weren't worth much when they was around."

Hardwick shook his head and continued, "You think I liked draggin' my girls along on the chase last night? But if we don't fight for the Box H together, there ain't gonna be nothing left to fight for. And after all the years and hard work that me and them and their ma, God rest her soul, already put in the place, we ain't ready to give up!"

Chapter 14

"Calm down, Pa. You're agitating your wound, making it start to bleed again," said the second daughter, the one who hadn't snapped at Castle. Even their voices sounded alike, thought Mac, so that was no help in telling them apart. The only difference he could see so far was that the sister who'd spoken back to Castle—who was also the same one who'd snapped at him, Mac was pretty sure upon closer study—wore her hair spilling unrestrained from under a flat-crowned Stetson, while the other had hers partly captured in a loose ponytail that also trailed down from a Stetson.

As a result of the girls' ministrations, Hardwick's propped-up leg was now laid bare. The pant leg had been cut away and peeled back; the earlier bandage removed. There were entrance and exit bullet holes in the outer part of his thigh, but luckily the bullet had missed bone. The entrance hole in front wasn't overly big, about the size of a man's thumbnail, but it was red rimmed and leaking a bit, with bruising starting to show on the pale skin around it. Mac couldn't see the exit hole, but he imagined it was messier, as evidenced by frequent drops of blood falling on the rocks underneath.

When the sister with the ponytail asked for a canteen of water to clean the wound, Squint stepped forward, saying, "Right here, miss." He handed her a canteen he'd been holding and then reached inside his vest and produced a flat whiskey flask. Holding that up, he added, "When you get the blood rinsed away, be a good idea to pour some of this into each hole. It'll burn some, but the alcohol will help hold off risk of that infection you spoke of before."

Larabee, who had come up the slope with Red and the Hardwicks but up until then had been hanging quietly back, catching his breath, perked up at the sight of the flask.

"Say now," he said. "You ain't gonna pour the whole thing into them bullet holes, are you? I'm mighty parched from all the hikin' I did to get down off that ridge and then all the way up here . . . I could sure use a pick-me-up."

"The thing for bein' parched is water," countered Squint. "I got another whole canteen of it right here handy. You can drink all you want. Besides, this whiskey ain't just for the wound itself. It's also for soothin' the person carryin' the wound. That would be not only Hardwick but also our own Mac, who I was fixin' to give a jolt to just before the rest of you showed up."

"In that case, I'd say the interruption has lasted long enough," said Mac, holding out his hand. "Hand it over. I'll take that jolt, strictly for medicinal reasons."

Truth to tell, the discussions taking place and the presence of the pretty sisters had kept Mac distracted enough so that he hadn't been overly aware of his lingering aches. Nevertheless, the numbing effect of the fiery liquid flowing down through him when he tipped the flask up for a long swig provided a welcome touch of added relief.

After Mac had his turn, he handed the flask back to Squint, who passed it on to Hardwick. As the wounded man was lifting it for his own long pull, the daughter with the loose mane of hair stood up and pulled her shirt out from where it was tucked in the waist of her denim pants. With the same pocketknife she'd used to slit her father's pant leg, the girl with the ponytail reached over and began cutting a long strip of her sister's exposed shirttail to use for a fresh bandage.

Trying not to gawk too obviously at the two beauties, same as the other men—except for Larabee, who was too busy eyeing the whiskey flask—Red asked, "What happened to Mac?"

"He got conked with a rifle barrel when that volley from below stirred all the bees in the nest up here," answered Squint. Then, nodding toward the nearest dead ambusher, he added, "But he got his payback."

Lowering the flask and having it plucked from his hand by one of his daughters before he got the chance to take another snort, Hardwick squinted up at Mac and said, "I'm plumb sorry our volley caused you harm, son. But like Tara already told you, we had no idea anybody else was up here, let alone anybody out to lend us a hand."

"It ain't that bad," Mac downplayed, reaching up for the first time and tenderly touching the spot above his ear where the rifle barrel had struck. "If you and me took the worst of it, I reckon it beats what could have been."

"Thing I ain't heard yet," spoke up Castle, "is how—if

you and your gals were tracking the rustlers—you ended up waylaid by this bunch."

Frowning, Hardwick replied, "Way I figure it, this bunch and the rustlers are one and the same . . . or least-ways they were, I guess I should say. See, I'm thinkin' the rustlers somehow caught wind we was closin' in on 'em. So they dropped back to surprise us with an ambush in-stead of us catchin' up and bein' the ones to surprise them, like I'd hoped. They cut down our horses right off the bat, and then, even though that made sure we wasn't gonna be foggin' 'em no more, they stuck around to have some sport. Much as I hate to think about it, I expect that was on account of spottin' the girls . . . You heard what they had in mind for them if they'd got past me."

"Well, they didn't. So quit working yourself into a lather over it," said the daughter now holding the whis-key flask. "Besides, you heard what I told them would happen before they ever got that far."

Hardwick frowned. "And I'm supposed to like the sound of that any better?"

"Just drop it already. It never happened." The girl paused, and her mouth formed an impish grin. "But if you insist on fretting, here's something you definitely aren't going to like."

And with that, she poured the first generous splash of whiskey onto the exposed front bullet hole. Hardwick lifted his face to Heaven and howled like he was giving birth to a saguaro cactus. He didn't hold back on some colorful language to go with the howls, either. The way he turned the air blue, Mac reckoned the old man could have held his own in a cussing contest with a string of top mule skinners. Then when the girls rolled him onto one hip and splashed the hole on the back side of his thigh, he did it all over again, and Mac marveled how seldom he repeated any cuss words.

Things finally calmed back down when the daughters started rebandaging the wound. The flask was returned to Hardwick, and he took another big gulp before declaring, "Now, that's where this stuff is *supposed* to go!" Somewhat reluctantly, he held the medicine out to Mac. "Here, you look like you could use another dose, too."

Mac took the flask but didn't drink right away. Instead, feeling the mournful gaze from Larabee's one good eye, he passed it off to him. "Before you bust into tears. You look like you need it worst of all."

From where he'd been occupied with the one ambusher still alive, Boyd came striding over. "Been listenin' to most of what y'all been sayin'. I ain't recommendin' we share any of Squint's who-hit-John with him, mind you, but we're gonna need to decide what we intend to do with that fella over there I shot. He's in a bad way. I got the bleedin' stopped, though, and he might have a chance to make it if we got him to a doctor."

"Why the hell should we?" said Red with uncharacteristic harshness.

Hardwick sat up straighter and looked around to where Boyd had come from. "Wait a minute! Are you saying one of those bushwhackin' dogs is still alive?"

"So far," confirmed Boyd.

"Then we *do* need to get the low-down snake to a doctor," insisted Hardwick. "Don't get me wrong. In the long run, I sure as hell don't care if he dies, though I'd rather see him do it at the end of a rope. But if we can keep him alive long enough to get him to talk first, that could be mighty useful. Nobody's been able to get any kind of clue on the gang behind all these robberies. If we could squeeze something out of this jasper, that could give me and the other ranchers who've been gettin' hit an edge for finally bein' able to run the owlhoots to ground."

"Before anybody worries too much about getting that rustling rat to a doctor, Pa, that's also where we need to take you and this leg of yours as soon as possible," said the sister with the loose-falling hair.

"Where is the closest doctor?" asked Castle.

"Town of Broken Spoke. About five miles from here," Sara said.

"So happens we have a wagon back a ways. We can use it to haul both your pa *and* the wounded rustler to that doctor," said Castle. "And it probably wouldn't be a bad idea for him to have a look at our man Mac's head, as well."

"Sounds like we're about to give Doc Washburn a passel of business," Sara Hardwick said. "Go ahead and fetch that wagon, then, if you please."

Chapter 15

Dr. Isaiah Washburn emerged from the treatment room and stepped out into the front office area of the modest two-story wood-frame building that housed his practice on the ground floor and his living quarters upstairs. He was a middle-aged man showing more than his actual years in a plain-featured, deeply lined face. He wore glasses with round lenses perched perpetually on the tip of his nose, and the sides of the frames where they hooked back over his ears kept wisps of the gray-streaked hair at his temples usually poking out in disarray.

Wringing a white, blood-speckled towel in his hands, the doctor moved out into the center of the office area, where five people were gathered, waiting to hear what he had to say. Mac and Boyd stood leaning against the wall, their loose, relaxed postures belying their impatience for a report; Hannibal Hardwick and his daughter Sara (the ponytailed one), sat in chairs, looking pensive; Curly Strand, the marshal of Broken Spoke, had been pacing slowly back and forth along one side of the room but stopped when the doctor made his appearance.

"The bullet tore through under his left rib cage," Washburn started out. "Far as I can tell, it missed doing damage to the stomach or any major organs. That left tissue and muscle trauma and some bone and lead shrapnel from chipping a rib. I got all of that out, though, and cleaned the wound good, so there shouldn't be any risk of lead poisoning. It still may be touch and go, but barring any internal bleeding I couldn't spot, I'd say the patient has a fifty-fifty chance."

"Can he talk? Answer some questions?" Marshal Strand wanted to know. He was a husky man of about fifty, with weary-looking pale blue eyes and a bulldog jaw bracketed by thick reddish-brown sideburns.

The doctor wagged his head. "Not anytime soon. Tomorrow maybe. You try pushing too hard too fast, you may weaken him at the most crucial time."

"Can I at least bring a few more sets of eyes around just to look at him? My deputy and maybe a couple other fellas I got in mind? I don't recognize the scoundrel, but maybe he'll be familiar to one of them."

"If he's part of the gang that's been hittin' the herds of me and the other ranchers for months now, he's got to have been hangin' around *some* blasted where," said Hardwick. "You'd think somebody ought to know who he is or at least remember seein' him."

"You'd think," grunted Strand. "Like I said, just a matter of findin' the right set of eyes."

"And a set that goes with a mouth willing to speak up," added Mac.

"What's that supposed to mean?" said the marshal, giving him a sharp look.

"It means," explained Mac, "that if the varmint in

there is part of a gang, then anyone claiming to know him could open themselves up to being suspected as part of the gang, too. That's why I'm thinking there might be those—even if they ain't guilty of anything—who might think twice before they'd be willing to speak up."

Strand scowled. "Yeah, I guess it could go like that. I still got to try everything I can."

"Never meant to suggest otherwise, Marshal."

Dr. Washburn scrutinized Mac. "Well, I have to say that smack on the head you suffered doesn't seem to have messed up your ability to reason. I'd still like to examine you a little closer."

"Appreciate the concern, Doc, but I'm okay," Mac assured him. "My aches, head and otherwise, have eased up considerable."

"And you're sure about no dizziness or double vision?"

Mac grinned. "Though I don't agree, mind you, there are those going a long way back who've accused me of acting a little dizzy from time to time. As far as double vision . . . okay, I've got to admit experiencing some of that lately. But only when I look at the Hardwick sisters, and they're too pretty to make me want to be cured."

This brought a brief smile to Sara's lips and a blush to her cheeks.

The marshal harrumphed. "Well, since we can't question that owlhoot in the other room, I don't see a whole lot more reason for us to stick around here. Now that the doc has treated your leg, Hannibal, you feel up to coming with me down to my office? I'd like to record an official statement about what happened out on that hogback this morning. Just take a few minutes."

"Pa needs to get home and settle down so's his wound can start healing," protested Sara.

Hardwick scowled. "Now, daughter, I ain't that bad off. Especially since the doc patched me up and medicated me. And if you think you'll get me home, where you and your sister are gonna expect me to ride a bed for the next week or whatever, I'll tell you right now that ain't happenin'. But as for your statement, Curly, it better not take very long. I'm hankerin' to get back and see if Tara and the rest of those Double T fellas had any luck catchin' up with my beeves that got run off."

Hardwick, Sara, and the wounded rustler were the only ones Mac had brought into town on his chuckwagon; Boyd had accompanied them on horseback. Castle and the other Double T men had stayed behind, hoping to round up the stolen cattle, which they figured must be roaming in the vicinity of where the thieves had dropped back to stage their ambush. Tara had remained with them for the sake of leading the way back to the Box H if they were successful in their recovery.

"Okay. On second thought," the marshal relented, "maybe it would be better if I came out to the ranch sometime tomorrow and took statements there. After all, I should get 'em from everybody who was present at the shoot-out. That would also include you and your sister, Sara. Not to mention the Texas boys who joined in to do the actual killing."

This caused Mac to stop leaning against the wall and stand up straight, frowning. "Killing in self-defense, Marshal. And against a pack of rustling skunks," he made sure to point out.

"I understand that, son. Didn't mean to sound like I was accusing anybody of any wrongdoing," Strand replied. "Truth to tell, I ain't got no jurisdiction clear out there, anyway. Hannibal knows that. But I've still been trying to help him and the other ranchers with their rustling problem as best I can. In case we *do* manage to round up this gang of long-loopers, me having your statements and other reports I've been keeping on the matter might help against 'em if they're ever brought up before a judge."

"I know you got to look at things from behind that badge you wear, Curly. And I appreciate what you've done to try to help with our problem," said Hardwick. "But you, in turn, know how me and most of the other ranchers feel. We catch any of those buzzards who've been strippin' away our beef, we ain't likely to waste a lot of time worryin' about jurisdictions or bringin' in an outside judge."

Strand looked somewhat dismayed. "Like you said, Hannibal, we know pretty well where each other stands. Let's just hope things work out for the best."

There was a moment of mildly tense silence. Until Boyd, speaking for the first time since arriving at the doctor's office, said, "Couple thoughts I'll toss out. Number one, since everybody is convinced there's a 'gang' of rustlers, just how big do you reckon it might be? Seein's how they been stealin' just fifty, sixty cows at a time, that few would take only a handful of wranglers to work 'em. Any chance those four we dealt with this mornin'—the one in the other room and the three dead ones—might account for the whole bunch?"

This brought on a sudden bit of murmuring and muttering and raised eyebrows as glances were passed back and forth between Strand, Hardwick, and the doctor.

"By grab, man," the marshal finally responded. "You may have hit on something. With any luck, that could actually be the case. There are still the buyers of the stolen cattle to consider, most likely Mexican dons across the border, looking to build up their own herds on the cheap.

But unless they're hiring and *sending* the rustlers, they won't pose much of a threat if we're able to dry up their supply source."

Hardwick regarded Boyd. "You said you had a couple thoughts. What else?"

"If the marshal is still lookin' to figure out the identities of the gang members—whether or not there's any more than just the four," Boyd said, "I wanted to remind everybody that three of 'em still ain't been looked at yet. Not by the marshal or his additional sets of eyes, I mean."

The doctor frowned. "Three more? You mean the dead ones? And they're still lying out where they fell?"

"Be surprised otherwise," Boyd drawled.

"Aw, don't look so shocked, Isaiah," said Hardwick. "We had more important things to worry about than plantin' three piles of garbage. Besides, if things had gone their way, it's a damn certain guarantee they wouldn't have gave me or my girls any such consideration."

"Holding ourselves barely above the behavior of the vilest among us is no accomplishment, Hannibal, and you know that," Washburn countered sternly. "Leaving human bodies to the scavengers not only isn't Christian, it's just plain wrong."

Marshal Strand heaved a weary sigh. "Everybody calm down. This man"—a wave of his hand to indicate Boyd—"has raised some good points. Needing to consider just how big this gang of rustlers might be and, toward that end, taking the opportunity to try and identify the ones we've got our hands on. That means the hombre in the other room as well as those three out on the range." He sighed again. "So I'll gather up the fellas I've got in mind to have a look at the one we got here, and then I'll have 'em ride out with me to take a gander at his pals. While we're there, after we've had our gander, we'll load up the bodies and haul 'em back for a burial on Boot Hill. That satisfy you, Doc?"

The tight-lipped sawbones said, "It's the only decent thing."

Next, Strand turned to Hardwick. "Go ahead on home, Hannibal. Good luck on getting your cattle back. I'll be around sometime tomorrow for those statements. Hopefully by then, I might also have news on some identities or some answers out of the wounded varmint in Doc's care."

"I'll be out, too, in a couple of days. To check on that leg," said a somewhat sullen Washburn. "In the meantime, you stubborn old cuss, listen to your daughters at least a little bit and try not to do any more clomping around on it than you have to."

Hardwick cocked an eyebrow. "I'll do that, croaker. If for no other reason than to deprive you of the fun you'd have findin' some reason to want to saw it off."

Chapter 16

"Okay. If nobody else is willin' to say it, then I'll be the one. These folks are in need of some help." Squint Morris paused, eyeing the faces surrounding him in the cluttered, low-ceilinged bunkhouse. "Even if our skirmish earlier broke the backs of the rustlin' gang, ol' man Hardwick and his gals are still left with a mighty tough nail to chew, just the three of 'em tryin' to make a go of this spread with no other hired hands."

"I don't disagree with what you're saying," allowed Red. "But the thing to remember is, if we *did* bust up all or most of the owlhoot gang and the rustlin' and rough-shod tactics stop, then Hardwick ought to be able to hire some ranch hands again. Right?"

Squint shrugged. "Maybe. In time. But another thing to remember is that it ain't like the rustlin' has been hap-penin' night after night. More like a couple times a month, from what I understand. Meanin' it's gonna take a while before anybody can be sure whether or not the gang has been stomped out of business. And the kind of lily-livered rats who skedaddled when the trouble got a little too hot in the first place might not be willin' to come back until things are more certain."

Castle frowned thoughtfully. "Yeah, and the fact we know for sure that at least one of the gang didn't get caught by our guns up on the hogback will only add to the doubt about there possibly being others still left to strike again."

When Castle and the rest of the Double T crew went to try to locate the stolen cattle while Mac and Boyd took the wounded to Doc Washburn, they had been successful in finding the small herd in a grassy draw only about a mile beyond the ambush site. Upon their approach, however, they had spotted a single rider—a lookout left behind, they figured—making his getaway as soon as he recognized they were not his fellow rustlers returning.

Otherwise, the cattle recovery mission had been a success. With Tara on hand to lead the way back to the Box H ranch, they had arrived within a half hour of Mac, Boyd, and the remaining two Hardwicks coming from town. The long shadows of late afternoon were starting to fall by then, so the Hardwicks insisted that the Double T men remain for supper and stay overnight in the empty bunkhouse. There wasn't much resistance to the invitation, especially not with the two pretty Hardwick sisters involved.

Plus, Mac reminded everybody how Marshal Strand—even though he didn't really have any jurisdiction over the incident out on the hogback—meant to come by for statements the following day. What was more, Mac also pointed out, they still needed to make their planned stop in Broken Spoke to stock up on supplies and do some tonsil washing at one of the saloons.

And so it came to be that, with night descended, the Double T men were bedded down in the Box H bunkhouse, hashing over the events of the day and jawing about how things stood with the Hardwicks as well as their own progress on getting back home.

"I don't know where this talk is headed," said Larabee from where he lay belly down on one of the bunks, "but even with only one good eye, it was plain enough for me to see all durin' supper what the aim of certain folks was."

Puffing on a long-stemmed corncob pipe, Squint frowned at him. "What are you drivin' at, you old grumbler? If you got something to say, say it out straight. It's too late in the evenin' for riddles."

Larabee grunted. "Wasn't no riddle to what that old codger Hardwick was anglin' for the whole meal. He hinted at everything short of practically offerin' up his daughters if a couple of you young bucks had showed any sign of bein' interested in stickin' around to help run things around here."

Red's sunburned cheeks flushed an even brighter scarlet at the remark. "That's a heck of a thing to say about a father and his daughters," he protested. "It's not only insulting to the old man, but you make it sound like the girls might even consider being part of such a notion."

"What's the matter? You sayin' you wouldn't be interested in a tasty morsel like either one of those two, no matter how it got served up?" Larabee teased. "Or is it that you ain't got enough confidence in yourself to think you could turn the head of such a pretty filly on your own?"

"Knock it off, Larabee," Mac told him. "I noticed that bloodshot peeper of yours never missed landing on those sisters every chance you got. What I didn't notice, though, was either of them spending any time looking back."

Larabee just cackled, getting a kick out of the game of needling and being needled back. "But there was a time, sonny boy, when the walleyed old rascal you see before you these days wasn't yet so chawed up by hard livin' and hard luck . . . I turned me plenty a pretty head back in the day. Don't ever think I didn't."

"I believe you, Larabee. And I believe you still do," said Boyd soberly. Then, after a second, he showed his teeth in a wide grin before adding, "Only nowadays, they turn their heads *away*."

Everybody got a good chuckle over that, even Larabee.

When it died away, Castle's expression became thoughtful again. He said, "Putting aside any business about his daughters, I'd be surprised if Larabee was the only one who noticed that Hardwick *was* throwing out some pretty strong hints about us sticking around the Box H for a while. In case there was any doubt, he took me aside for a minute as you other fellas were headed out here, and made it real plain."

"How plain?" Squint asked around a curl of smoke.

"He said he'd pay a full month's wages to anybody who'd put in at least two weeks' work. Long enough to help put back in order some of the neglect that's taken place, round up strays he reckons are scattered about, catch up on the branding. Things like that . . . But, as much as anything, hang around long enough to find out if there are any clearer signs as far as the rustling being done, or if it's just simmering out there somewhere, ready to start up again."

Boyd lifted his eyebrows. "He don't expect much out of us, does he?"

"Naturally," said Larabee, regarding Castle closely, "you told him we rode for the Double T brand and already have jobs we need to get back to . . . Right?"

"Of course. That's exactly what I told him," replied Castle. But the statement seemed to hold only tepid conviction, and he had trouble meeting Larabee's eyes when he said it.

Taking the pipe from his mouth, Squint said, "But that ain't necessarily the end of it, is it? The notion of helpin' these folks is naggin' at you, ain't it?"

"Okay, yeah, it is. The old man's plea, thinking about all that needs doing to catch up around here, just him and his daughters . . . made even worse now that he took a bullet to his leg . . ." Castle let his words trail off. Then, scowling at Squint, he added, "Wasn't you singing sort of the same tune just a few minutes ago, when you brought it up to begin with?"

"Yeah, I was. No denyin' it," Squint admitted. "Like I said then—and didn't need nobody droppin' hints or pleadin' with me in order to see it—these folks are in need of help."

"You're both loco," groaned Larabee. "Hell, there's folks all over the world in need of help. But you know what? It ain't our job to go around tryin' to help all of 'em. In the course of just a couple days, we already saved those two Mexican gals and then swatted a pack of rustlers off that hogback. Enough is enough."

"There were lives at stake if we hadn't stepped in," pointed out Red.

"Yeah? Well, there's lives at stake now, too. Ours. Or at least our hides," Larabee argued. "'Cause if we don't haul our smilin' faces back to Boss Tremaine pronto like, complete with his chuckwagon and the money for sellin' his cows, that's what he'll be comin' after—our hides!"

"What about that, Castle? The gettin' back part, I mean," said Boyd. "A couple days ago, when we lost the one mule, you were pretty worried about replacin' him and pickin' up our pace. Now it sounds like you're seriously considerin' tarryin' here and lendin' a hand to the Hardwicks. How can we afford the time?"

"You're right on both counts, Boyd. I *was* pushing before, but now I'm seriously pondering holding on here for a bit." Castle twisted his mouth wryly, gave a shrug. "All I can say is that circumstances have changed. These people—good people, I judge—are in a fix, and it feels like we could do some good by tarrying and helping them out."

"Hard to argue with Christian thinkin' like that," Boyd allowed.

"But what about Boss Tremaine?" asked Red. "We owe him some kind of explanation, don't we?"

Castle's mouth pulled tight. "I'll take care of that. I'll send a wire while we're in town tomorrow. What I'm thinking is this. Boss ain't hurting for this money. He needs it, sure, but he ain't scraping the bottom until we get it to him. And given how we thinned the ranch herd by the nine hundred head we took on our drive, there's enough of a crew left at the Double T to keep handling things while we're away. So us being gone an extra couple weeks ain't gonna put nobody in a bind.

"Leastways, that's how I *hope* Boss sees it. If I explain it proper, I think he'll be understanding. But the last thing I want is to make any hard feelings or put anybody's job in jeopardy. If he makes a fuss, we'll just roll on for home and leave things here to work out how they will."

"That sounds reasonable to me," declared Red.

Squint cut his gaze to Mac. "How about you, bub? You ain't said much of a peep the whole time."

Mac raised one shoulder, let it drop back down. "I got nothing to peep about. I go with the crew. Like Castle said, taking a little time to help the Hardwicks seems like some good we ought to try and do."

"What about me? Ain't nobody gonna ask me what I think?" said Larabee, scowling.

Squint gave a quick response, saying, "You already made your feelin's known, and they're the same bitchin' and moanin' as usual."

Larabee's good eye flared. "Oh yeah? Then how about I give you some relief by crawlin' on my horse come mornin' and makin' dust for Texas. Let the rest of you go on about your good deed doin' and damsel in distress rescuin' without havin' to listen to my bitchin' and moanin' no more!"

Several seconds went by, with Larabee's chin jutted out defiantly against the hard looks he was getting from most of the others. Until Castle released a long exhalation through his nostrils before saying in a low voice, "Okay, if you feel that strongly about it, Larabee, then I guess we'll pick up where we left off and all be starting again for Texas in the morning. I won't bust up our crew, and I won't have just one man heading out alone across the wild country between here and home. The Hardwicks will just have to figure out a way to fend for themselves."

The hard looks aimed at Larabee grew harder.

It didn't take long for the ornery old wrangler to screw his face into a sour expression and push wearily to a sitting position. "Now dang it, Castle, no need to go off half-cocked. How long you and me rode together? You know blasted well I got a bad habit of huffin' and puffin' but not really meanin' anything. And you sure as hell know better, Squint. So maybe I do gripe and moan a little, like you said, but nobody never takes it serious."

"So what are you saying?" Castle wanted to know.

Larabee started to thrust his chin out again but then promptly pulled it back. "What I'm sayin' is that I still think you're all loco . . . But I ride for the brand, and you're ramroddin' our crew, Castle. So if you and the rest of these knotheads think we can do some good stickin' around here for a while, then I reckon I'll be stickin' with you, and you can count on me to do my part."

Castle nodded. "That sounds better. Now let's get some shut-eye. Then first thing in the morning I'll let old man Hardwick know that he's got a bunkhouse full of wranglers working for him again."

Chapter 17

That same evening, while the Double T men were hashing things over in the Box H bunkhouse, another discussion was taking place a dozen miles away in the town of Broken Spoke.

Preston McCall, president of the Broken Spoke Territorial Bank, stood on the back porch of the modest-sized wood-frame house he called home. The dwelling was located in a quiet residential neighborhood only a few blocks from the bank building, which occupied a prominent spot on the town's main street.

As was McCall's habit at the close of business on most days, he ate an early dinner at the Premiere Restaurant before going home, where he lived alone and where he would spend a quiet evening reading, usually for pleasure but sometimes poring through necessary business-related material. Once or twice a week, his attorney—a man named Wincer, also a bachelor—would stop by, and they would indulge themselves with fine brandy and cigars while waging fierce battles on a chessboard.

Other nights, weather permitting, McCall would step out on his back porch prior to turning in and enjoy the cool peacefulness with a pipe of aromatic, top-quality tobacco. He'd been involved in that ritual tonight when a visitor stepped out from the shadows cast by one of the carefully pruned rosebushes bracketing the back-porch steps.

"You know," drawled the visitor, coming forward to lift one foot and then bring it to rest planted on the bottom step, "if anybody was out to rob you or otherwise do you harm—you being a man of prominence and all—you'd make it mighty easy by the patterns you seldom vary from. A couple days of surveillance and you'd be showing 'em what an easy target you make for, say, robbery or maybe kidnapping."

Exhaling a plume of smoke, McCall said, "I quit worrying about making myself a target and taking evasive tactics when the war ended and I left the military, Virg. You know that. Besides, isn't it supposed to be the job of you and the marshal to keep citizens like me safe? And then, too, as a demonstration of why maintaining certain habits aren't all bad . . . I'm not quite ready to be an *entirely* willing target in case somebody gets the wrong idea."

With those words, McCall lifted the left front panel of the silk-lined vest he had unbuttoned for the evening and showed a nickel-plated .38 caliber revolver riding in a shoulder holster.

Virg Lamont, with one foot still hiked up on the porch step and his deputy marshal's badge reflecting a glint of illumination cast by the soft gold glow of lantern light pouring out from the house's windows, grinned up at the man who had been his commanding officer in the late war. Virg stood a sturdy six feet-plus, and entering into his fourth decade hadn't softened him to any notable degree. He walked with a measured swagger, not a bully but neither somebody to trifle with. He had a reputation for being generally easygoing and quick to grin but, when it came to enforcing the law, also for being quick with his fists and adequate enough with a gun.

Responding now to the display of McCall's pistol, Virg said, "Yeah, I guess most folks around town know about your little hideaway. That, and your war record. Reckon those are enough to keep anybody with any sense warned off from attempting anything stupid."

McCall took the pipe from his mouth, and his broad mouth sagged into a frown. He was a heavyset, square-shouldered man of fifty, his bearing very erect, as befitted a man with a military background. His clothing was tailored to his large frame, and his thick, iron-gray, precisely barbered hair was combed straight back above a clean-shaven, ruggedly handsome face.

"Speaking of stupid attempts," he said in a flat tone, "what's the status on that rustling fiasco?"

Virg nodded. "That's what I came by to tell you. I guess that makes one good thing about your habit of stepping out here for a pipe of an evening . . . It allows the chance for us to talk without risk of drawing attention we don't necessarily want."

"Yes, yes. But get to the point. Answer my question."

"Well, so far we've been lucky," Virg reported.

"Lucky? I fail to see how three men dead, one badly wounded, and the cattle they were in possession of now returned to the Box H can be considered lucky."

"I meant lucky in the sense that nobody the marshal brought around was able to recognize any of 'em—just the way you planned it when you assembled all outsiders in the first place—and the wounded fella, Grimsby, so far ain't been in no shape to wake up and do any talking that might let the wrong thing slip."

"What are Grimsby's chances of waking up and possibly talking if and when he does?"

"Doc says fifty-fifty on the waking-up part. If he makes it through the night, supposedly his odds will improve." Virg shrugged. "As far as what he might say if he pulls through, well, your guess is as good as mine. Since he was the leader of the gang, we both know there's plenty he could spill if he took a notion to."

McCall's frown deepened. "And what of O'Leary, the lookout left behind with the cattle while the others went to stage their ill-advised ambush?"

"Right about now he's back at the abandoned mission," Virg reported. "But after me and the marshal and the men we took out to the hogback with us brought the bodies back to town for burial on Boot Hill, I had a chance to sneak a few minutes with O'Leary at that old caretaker's shack behind the cemetery—the emergency meeting place we set up early on, in case things ever took a sour turn."

"What kind of shape is he in?" McCall wanted to know. "Rattled? Or can he be trusted to keep his head long enough for us to regroup?"

"O'Leary will be okay. Right at the moment, he's mostly just glad he didn't get ventilated by those meddling damn Texans. Comes to regrouping and maybe having a chance to get even for those who *did* get cut down . . . yeah, you can count on him for that."

"Good. That's a start." McCall clamped the pipe stem between his lips again and puffed a couple of aromatic bluish clouds out into the night air before adding, "Get word to him at the mission. Send him to make contact with Creo. I want Creo to be at Fran's Place two nights from now. I'll be there to meet with him."

A corner of Virg's mouth twitched up in a brief hint of a smile. "Ah, yes. Miss Fran's Place."

"What's that supposed to mean?" McCall demanded, his scowl knifing through the curls of pipe smoke.

Virg wagged his head. "Nothing in particular. It's just that your occasional, very discreet visits to Fran's are something I hadn't thought of when I mentioned your predictable pattern of habits before."

Miss Fran's Place was a big old former farmhouse located a short distance outside of town. It had been converted into a popular brothel and was run by a transplanted Baltimore woman known only as Miss Fran— though *Madam* Fran was actually more accurate. At any rate, she ran her establishment under very strict rules. Her place and the girls who worked for her offered a sharp contrast to what could be found in saloons or back-alley cribs.

"My visits to Fran's Place," McCall replied without his scowl lessening, "are something you don't need to concern yourself with."

"Duly noted," Virg said with a curt nod. "But as far as meeting with Creo there . . . you figuring to bring him into things on this side of the border?"

"That's the general idea. Now that we've lost Grimsby's bunch, all except for O'Leary, it's the quickest way to continue the rustling without going through a whole recruitment process. Creo and his men have been doing a good job of taking possession of the cattle at the river and handling the sell-offs to the Mexican dons. I'll give him the chance to expand his duties and earnings by taking over gathering the beeves in the first place."

Virg pursed his lips thoughtfully. "You think he'll go for it? Up to now he's kinda made a point of shying away from doing any raiding or robbing on this side of the border."

"For a sweet enough deal, I think he'll jump at the chance."

"How sweet you talking?"

"I think the time is up for making these puny rustling raids of only fifty or sixty head at a time. The only reason I stuck with it this long was because that's how we started out and all Grimsby had enough men to pull off. Also, with each of them being nibbled only a little bit at a time, the scattered ranchers didn't pull tight enough together or get their collective hackles sufficiently raised. And your friend the marshal has never been prodded hard enough to get involved to the point of being willing to reach beyond his jurisdiction."

"What makes you think things are different now?" Virg wanted to know.

"For one thing, Creo has the ability to gather a small army if necessary. Given the right incentive, he could sweep across the border and drive away all or most of a rancher's whole herd. Not merely some piddly fraction."

McCall took the pipe from between his teeth and began making stabbing motions with the tip of its stem to add emphasis to what he said next.

"The first target I have in mind is Hannibal Hardwick. For one thing, his spread is closest to the border. For another, I hear that he and his daughters have recently begun rounding up all their stock and bringing them in closer for the sake of being able to better watch over after his previous hired hands quit him."

"In other words, they've already done most of the bunching work."

"Precisely. Estimates I trust calculate that the full Box H herd numbers between five and six hundred." McCall's eyes took on a brittleness. "What's more, the old blowhard and those Texans who stuck their noses in to help cut down Grimsby and the rest are making noises that claim they broke the back of our rustling operation. I think that earns them the right to a lesson that will teach them how very wrong they are."

Virg regarded the man looming over him up on the porch platform. "You don't mind my saying, you been acting more and more prickly of late, Colonel . . . I mean, Mr. McCall."

During the war, Virg and McCall had formed a bond stronger and more personal than that of just a colonel and his chief lieutenant. So when the fighting ended, they'd headed west together to make their fortune. Both having grown up under dirt poor conditions and disillusioned by the way the army had cast them aside following their participation in the bloody hell of war, they'd jointly agreed not to let concepts like honor and playing strictly by the rules stand in the way of achieving success.

After a pair of fruitless attempts in other places, they arrived in Broken Spoke. McCall's former officer status and impressive display of medals, all legitimate, combined with a quite illegitimate claim of prior banking experience, landed him in the recently vacated assistant director's chair at the Territorial Bank. Within a year, aided by an acting president who wanted desperately to get out of sunbaked Arizona and go back East, he bluffed his way to the top slot.

Virg, in the meantime, settled for a deputy marshal's job, which contented him well enough and provided its own share of side benefits. The two men kept their personal interactions low-key, and the separate but distinct positions they held allowed them to start lining their pockets by slowly but surely squeezing the territory in various ways. The rustling setup was the most overt, though it was only one of many.

Following through on his observation about McCall's prickliness, Virg now said, "I get the notion you got more on your mind than just working up a bigger rustling strike than any before."

"I always have something more on my mind, Virg. You know that better than anyone. And don't pretend you don't have the same."

"The Sea of Cortez." Something akin to a reverent hush crept into the deputy's tone.

"It's there waiting, Virg. And getting closer all the time."

"For true?"

"I wouldn't have said so if I didn't believe it."

The Sea of Cortez—specifically a quiet, exotic spot on its Sonoran shore—was the dream, the ultimate goal, that the two men had set for all their planning and scheming to achieve. A place to spend the rest of their days in peaceful, modest luxury.

"With the tidy nest egg we've managed to build up so far," McCall went on, "I figure we're already well on our way. Add in our cut from one or two of those full-scale rustling raids, and then the biggest egg of all for us to take a cut out of . . . the railroad payrolls, which will start routing through my bank when that spur finally reaches close enough . . . Well, things will start moving faster, and the time will be at hand."

Virg nodded. "We said from the beginning we'd be smart enough not to be too greedy, not to milk it too long."

"That's right. There's a fine line, in the kind of game we're playing, where risk can start to outweigh the chance for added reward." McCall put his pipe back in his mouth and puffed a fresh cloud of smoke. "But we're not quite there yet. I think my escalated rustling idea can provide gain at an acceptable risk."

Virg nodded some more. "I got no problem with that. The only question is getting Creo to go along with it."

"I'm confident I'll have little or no trouble convincing him."

"All right. I'll ride out and send O'Leary to get word to him right after I finish my late rounds tonight."

McCall seemed to consider something for a long moment. Then: "Not meaning to overtax you, but there's also another matter I feel is necessary for you to tend to before the night is over. It involves Grimsby and the matter of risk, as we just discussed. I'm afraid we can't afford to take a chance with him. If he makes it through the night and wakes up at some point, alone, in pain, with a bullet hole in him, and finding himself bombarded by questions from the marshal . . . I find it worrisome how he might respond."

"I was kinda thinking the same thing."

"You have the means to access where Grimsby is convalescing?"

"Got me a ring of skeleton keys that will open 'most any door in town."

McCall puffed some more smoke. "Then I suggest that, in addition to riding out to see O'Leary, you also take time to pay a visit to poor ailing Grimsby . . . and end his suffering."

"Yeah, it's the safest thing," Virg said matter-of-factly. "I'll see to it."

Chapter 18

With the sun a couple of hours short of its noon peak in the morning sky, Mac and Sara Hardwick were on their way to Broken Spoke. The day was warming rapidly and would be like an oven by the middle of the afternoon. Perched once again on the driver's box of the Double T chuckwagon, Mac couldn't help but also be aware of another kind of warmth—that of the lovely young woman sharing the seat with him, their shoulders occasionally bumping together as they swayed and bounced in accordance with irregularities of the ground they were traveling over.

All in all, however, Mac was starting to grow more comfortable in the presence of Sara. More so than with her sister. He suspected this was partly due to having simply spent more time around Sara, yet there was no denying Tara seemed notably less friendly, even a bit haughty at times. The visual difference between the two, however, remained very hard to spot. So this morning's arrange-ment, not only having the two separated to avoid such confusion but especially having Sara all to himself, was very much to Mac's liking.

The change in her attire this morning—from a work shirt, trousers, and boots to a snug-fitting blouse with flower designs on the shoulders and a split riding skirt of maroon corduroy—also presented much to like. As did the ponytail, once again swishing across the back of her neck.

This stroke of fortune had come about due to his repu-tation for being a good cook. It had become increasingly and admittedly evident during last night's supper and again at this morning's breakfast that for all their beauty and wrangling skills, the Hardwick sisters had limitations in the kitchen. A few basics, like stew for supper and bacon and eggs to start the day, they'd confessed, were about the extent of what they could manage. And if one was being all the way honest, the quality of the biscuits accompanying breakfast could be called only barely managed.

All of this was the result, it was explained, of an el-derly German lady named Greta suddenly and unexpect-edly passing away just a few months prior. For many years Greta had served as cook, housekeeper, and care-giver to the frail and long-suffering Mrs. Hardwick. When the latter finally succumbed to her ailments some four years past, Greta had carried on cooking and clean-ing and otherwise taking care of the household. But in the process, blamed equally on their lack of interest as well as the need for them to pitch in as ranch hands, neither of the twins had learned much in the way of meal prepara-tion.

"You'd think it would have been obvious," Sara was telling Mac now, "that the need was bound to arise one day. I mean, Greta was so sturdy and organized and energetic that she might have *seemed* invincible . . . but sadly, of course, she wasn't. When Mother died, she had been so sick for so long it was sort of expected. Even a kind of blessing, like they say, that she was finally relieved of her suffering. But it was so different with Greta. Such a surprise. Such a shock. And then, once she was gone, came the next shock . . . how ill prepared we were in so many ways without her."

"Sounds like she was quite a gal."

"Oh, she was. She never got past her thick accent, and she could be very brusque and impatient at times, but—" Sara stopped abruptly. The fond smile that had been curving her mouth faded, and in its place appeared two spots of bright color on her cheeks.

Looking over at her, Mac said, "What's wrong?"

"What's wrong is how I must have come across a moment ago. Like the worst thing about Greta's passing was the fix it left Pa and Tara and me in, minus any emotion or sadness over simply losing her."

"I didn't take it that way," Mac responded honestly. "You spoke of her real fondly. It was clear you all thought a great deal of her."

"I hope so," Sara said. "I hope she knew how much she meant to us, beyond just the chores she did. The way she cared for Mother all during her long, difficult illness—that alone was something special. And yet I fear that, to a large extent, we came to take her for granted."

"When you have somebody or something you come to count on through thick or thin, that's sorta the way it is,"

Mac allowed. "But knowing you can count on 'em ain't really the same as taking 'em for granted. And, on their end, I expect they know the difference. What's more, in cases like that, it usually cuts both ways."

Sara regarded him. "You sound like you're speaking from experience."

"Reckon I am. On both ends."

"You hear a lot about the loyalty of a ranch crew to their outfit and to each other. 'Riding for the brand' and all that. Although"—and here her pretty face took on a fierce scowl—"that certainly wasn't my pa's experience with those cowardly rannies he had working for him. But is that how it is with you and the rest of the Double T fellas?"

"I believe so," Mac told her. "I can't say for positive, on account of I've only been riding with Castle and the others for a few days. But I've been with outfits where the kind of thing you're talking about was rooted in solid, and this crew has the same feel. If my luck holds and there's a permanent job for me when we make it all the way back to the Double T in Texas, then I guess I'll find out for sure."

"But what about now? Your allegiance to the Double T, I mean. Isn't your whole crew taking a risk by stopping here to help us?" Sara asked.

"Hopefully not. Castle, our trail boss, don't think so. He rode into town ahead of us first thing this morning, after breakfast, to send a telegram explaining the situation to Mr. Tremaine, the ranch owner. Castle thinks he'll understand, as long as we ain't delayed too long."

"I hope so. I hope Mr. Tremaine not only understands but appreciates the fine bunch of men he's lucky to have working for him."

"Reckon we'll find out one way or the other."

"In the meantime," said Sara, finding her smile again, "my family and I certainly appreciate everything you're doing. Right down to you stepping forward to take over the cooking, Mac, and hopefully teaching Tara and me a little something in the process . . . starting with this trip to stock some of the right supplies for our pantry."

Mac grinned. "Take my word, I've been assigned worse jobs. Besides, we were needing to stop and add some chuck-wagon supplies before continuing on, anyway. So this trip will kill two birds with one stone."

"I'm glad for the convenience of that. However," Sara cautioned, "don't be too sure about welcoming the task of cooking for the Box H and giving lessons to Tara and me at the same time. You might come to find out you'd rather be turning a stampede or even dodging rustlers' bullets than trying to ramrod a couple of unbroken kitchen fillies who barely know a frying pan from a soup spoon."

"Now you're starting to worry me." Mac cocked one of his eyebrows to an exaggerated degree. "Are you sure it was the rustlers who scared your pa's hired hands off, or was it really the threat of you and your sister's cooking?"

Sara responded with a musical little laugh, something Mac sensed she had done too little of recently, and it made him feel good that he'd brought it out of her.

But only a short time later, as they topped a low rise and started down the back side, Mac experienced quite a different feeling pass through him at the sight of two riders approaching from the opposite direction. He couldn't say exactly why, but his hackles rose immediately. Maybe it was the way they slouched insolently in their saddles; maybe it was just a general awareness of rustlers and outlaws being in the area. Whatever it was, something told him that an encounter with this pair wasn't going to improve the morning.

And that thought was promptly reinforced when Sara muttered beside him, "Oh, no. Not these two jackasses."

Chapter 19

"Well, well, well. Lookee what we got here, little brother. Maybe it's like the old man has been ragging us about all these years. Maybe there are things that make it worth dragging our butts out of bed before noon once in a while."

"Like the sight of one of the snooty Hardwick sisters purely glowing in the morning sunlight, you mean? Yeah, I gotta admit that makes a mighty pleasing thing for these weary old eyes to feast on."

This exchange was what passed for a greeting once the two horsemen had reined up their mounts smack in the middle of the trail, blocking the way and forcing Mac to pull his mule team to a halt.

At closer range, Mac saw that the pair had the look of typical wranglers, not too far into their twenties, dressed in standard range clothes of a little better quality than most, and exhibiting a notable lack of wear and tear.

Where some wear and tear *did* show, however, was in

the rumpled, bleary-eyed appearance of each—telltale signs that made Mac conclude with a fair amount of certainty that he was looking at a couple of hungover hombres heading to wherever home was after an all-night binge in town.

The one who had identified himself as the older brother, an average-sized, oval-faced specimen with a patchy pattern of whiskers and limp strands of blond hair spilling from under his hat and dangling alongside one eye, spoke again. Though his words were directed at neither Mac nor Sara, his eyes never left them—especially Sara.

"A feast for your 'weary' eyes?" he snickered. "Don't you mean your *bloodshot* eyes?"

His brother shrugged off the attempted wit. He looked to be built a little more solidly, more square jawed, but he was also in need of a shave and also had the same strands of limp blond hair spilling from under his pushed-back hat. With a fatalistic sigh, he replied, "No matter. It don't make the feast any less tasty looking."

To which Sara snapped tartly, "If either of you Barnstable whiskey sops ever saw anything and it *wasn't* through bloodshot eyes, you wouldn't know what you were looking at."

There was a slight pause, and then both Barnstables threw back their heads and cackled wildly. As soon as he caught his breath, the older one said, "Maybe so, honey girl. But the one thing just as certain is that neither of you Hardwick gals can open her mouth without being overly damned sassy. We been neighbors practically our whole lives and ain't never been a time when you and your sister didn't treat me and Brad like dirt."

"That's not true, Leo, and you know it," Sara protested, glaring through narrowed eyes. "When we were little kids, we got along fine. But your fondness for the bottle ruined it. That's when it turned to nothing but crude remarks and disgusting overtures from both of you. Tara and I responded the only way we could."

Leo's sneer stayed in place. "Aw, now, that ain't true. You could have responded way different. You could have gave in and let us show you how much fun some of those 'disgusting overtures,' as you call them, might turn out to be."

"But the good news," chimed in younger brother Brad, "is that it ain't too late to change your minds and still learn. Why, me and Leo have been showed some tricks from the doxies in town we'd be willing to pass on that I can practically guarantee would—"

Mac cut him off, saying, "I think the young lady has made it clear she's not interested in any tricks you'd care to pass on. So, if you'll give us the road, we can be on our way and you can be on yours."

Leo cocked his head back. "Whoa now. Who the hell are you to think you can order us out of the way or tell us anything else?"

"And what gives you any right to be speaking for sassy Miss Sara, who has a plenty sharp enough tongue of her own?" Brad wanted to know.

Sara answered, "This man is a friend of mine. A friend of our family. And what he said is exactly right. Clear the way. We have no time for your vulgar nonsense."

"You hear that, little brother?" said Leo, cackling again. "We been called crude, disgusting, and vulgar all in just a couple mouthfuls. I don't know about you, but I might be on the brink of having my feelings hurt."

"What's more," added Brad, "sassy Miss Sara is making us look bad in front of her brand-new family friend. That might ruin any chance of him being *our* friend, and that don't hardly seem fair."

"You're doing a pretty good job of that all on your own," Mac told him. "Let's call our failure to be friends a mutual loss and leave it at that. Now I'll ask again and even toss in a please. Give us the road so we can be on our way."

Leo's mouth spread in a wide, mocking smile. Leaning forward, resting his forearm across the top of his saddle horn, he said, "Or what?"

"Or I show you the difference between jackasses and mules," Mac replied quietly.

Brad looked puzzled. "Huh?"

In an even quieter tone, Mac told Sara out the corner of his mouth, "Hang on." And then, a moment later, he braced himself in the driver's box, whipped the reins across the backs of his mule team, and shouted, "Yeeahh, you jugheads! Dig in! Go! Show 'em who's got the right of way!"

The mules responded with a powerful forward surge, and the chuckwagon jolted after, its wheels suddenly churning, spitting sand and throwing gouts of dust. The mules gave loud snorts of effort and annoyance but never faltered in barging ahead as urged. The mounts carrying the Barnstable brothers, however, were far less determined when it came to holding their ground. They immediately reared up and swung to either side, chuffing and squealing in surprise and alarm. It was all the men in their saddles could do to hang on and keep from getting pitched to the ground.

Those were the images that flashed by in Mac's peripheral vision to his left and right—Leo and Brad clutching their reins and grabbing their saddle horns in order to prevent being thrown. The sight of this caused Mac's mouth to stretch in a rakehell grin, and at the same time he was surprised to hear Sara emit a wild, reckless laugh as she proclaimed, "The jackasses lose!"

Unfortunately, it was too much to hope for that that would be the end of it. Much as Mac wished it so, he knew better. Which was why, after they'd plowed through the Barnstables and momentarily scattered them, he allowed the mules to rumble down the slope for only a short distance before pulling them to a halt once again and setting the wagon brake.

"What are you doing?" Sara said.

"Jackasses are notoriously slow learners," Mac explained, reaching down to the floor of the driver's box and bringing up his Yellowboy.

"Lord! You're not going to shoot them, are you?"

"Not unless I have to. But I don't think it'll come to that." Mac levered a shell into the chamber. "They're bound to still have some growl and snarl left in 'em, but now that we got their attention and have shown we won't bend to their bluster, I think they'll be agreeable to calling it quits and taking their hangovers on home without too much more trouble."

Chapter 20

As expected, the quarrelsome brothers came boiling up on either side of the chuckwagon, the fire in their eyes burning like hot coals through the clouds of dust that came churning along with them. But something not so expected came also slicing through the dust billows—the whirling loops of lassos that each man had pulled loose from the pommel strap of his saddle and now had raised above his head, widening the loops with practiced wrist rotations.

The Barnstables' intent may have initially been to rope the mules, but with the team already halted, Mac was quick to see that he and Sara might be at risk as substitute targets. No sooner had this thought jolted through his mind than Leo cast the first loop, and it was aimed directly at Mac.

In his overanxious, still hungover rage, however, what Leo failed to take proper note of was the Yellowboy Mac was holding at a ready angle across his chest. This allowed him to lean sharply back in his seat and simultaneously thrust up with the rifle, using it to bat away the descending loop before it was able to close around him.

Sara wasn't so lucky, though. Before she had the chance to take any evasive action, Brad's lasso ensnared her and started to tighten. The girl shrieked in alarm. Beside her, having just knocked away the loop meant for him, Mac twisted at the waist and brought his Yellowboy around with him. Though inadvertent, this placed the rifle muzzle mere inches from the taut rope leading back to Brad yanking on the other end. Mac didn't hesitate. He stroked the Yellowboy's trigger and blew the rope in two.

This caused a rapid chain of results: it freed Sara from the grip threatening to yank her off the wagon, it erased all resistance to Brad straining to make that happen, and with that resistance suddenly gone—like one end of a rope released without warning in a tug-of-war—it threw a furiously pulling Brad so badly off balance that he toppled from his saddle.

Under different circumstances, the latter might have been somewhat comical. But there was too much anger and now humiliation in this current situation for anybody, least of all the Barnstables, to be amused. Sensing this all too clearly, Mac promptly jacked another shell into his rifle and—having seen how capable she was with a gun—handed it to Sara. She flung off the lasso loop and took the Yellowboy eagerly. That done, Mac rearmed himself by pulling the Smith & Wesson from his waistband.

"All right," Mac said, directing his attention toward Leo while Sara was covering a sputtering, cursing Brad as he clambered to his feet, "this has gone far enough. Farther than it had to. Before it gets any more out of hand, I hope you boys can be smart enough to ride off and put it behind you. If not, the next lead that gets thrown will be aimed at more than just hemp."

"I don't know who the hell you are or think you are, mister," said Leo through gritted teeth. "But you damn well ain't the one who says when this is over."

"Fine by me," Mac replied icily. "But if you force it, I'll be the one who guarantees it's over for you."

Quietly from beside him, Sara said, "Mac, there's somebody coming."

Mac took his eyes off Leo long enough to confirm that a lone rider was indeed approaching from the direction of town. He was coming at a pretty good clip, and Mac judged he was likely drawn by the sound of the gunshot. Everybody stayed quiet and watched the rider draw closer. When he was close enough, he became recognizable as Marshal Curly Strand.

Reining up sharp, Strand swept a stern scowl over the scene and then was quick to demand, "What the devil is going on here?"

"What do your eyes tell you is going on, Curly?" Leo responded sarcastically. "This wildcat and her new boyfriend are threatening to plant bullets in Brad and me for only just having a little fun with them!"

"What my eyes tell me is that here are you and your brother in the middle of trouble again," the marshal shot back. "And I can make a pretty good guess what kind of 'little fun' you were trying to have. Some version of the same kind you had last night in town that left Jorgensen's place busted up . . . again . . . and his bartender Paulson with three teeth knocked out."

"Now, we left Jorgensen plenty of money to cover damages," Leo said defensively. "And we told him to have his bartender send his dentist bill for us to take care of, too."

"For your pa to take care of, you mean. Just like he covers all the expenses you two run up," Strand said with a tone of disdain.

"How our family takes care of itself ain't none of your concern, Curly," piped up Brad. "Our debts get paid. That's all you need to worry about."

Strand glared at him. "There are debts and there are debts, sonny boy. The day ever comes when your pa quits shelling out dollars to cover your shiftless hides, you'll soon find out there are those around anxious to collect in a whole 'nother way."

"Is that a threat?" Leo challenged.

"It's a statement of fact. Now shut up for a minute and let me finish finding out the truth of what this is all about." For that, the lawman turned a questioning gaze toward Sara.

"It's like Leo said," she replied in answer to the look. "The little fun him and Brad were having was to block the road and spew vulgar suggestions aimed at my sister and me. Mac told them to stop and tried to get them to show some sense about making way. He tried to be reasonable. When they refused and became belligerent, he whipped up our team and plowed through them, anyway. They gave chase and attempted to lasso us off our wagon. That's when the guns came out."

"We never went for our guns!" protested Leo.

"Only because you never had the chance," countered Sara.

"Who fired the shot I heard when I was coming down the trail?" Strand asked.

Mac said, "I did. I cut the rope that skunk"—he jerked his chin to indicate Brad—"had thrown over Miss Sara."

"Try calling me that when you don't already have a gun drawn on me, bub," snarled Brad.

"All right, everybody knock it off!" the marshal ordered. After pausing long enough to aim a very displeased frown down at the tangle of severed rope near Brad's feet and then at the discarded loop lying on the ground where Sara had flung it, he went on in a tight voice, "I've seen enough. You Barnstables hightail it out of here. I don't want to hear no mewling about it. Just git! And, by the way, you're barred from town for a month."

When Brad tried opening his mouth to protest, the lawman cut him short with, "I can make it longer if that's what you want."

"Button your lip, little brother," Leo cautioned. "Come on. Let's get out of here. We'll let 'em have this round, but that don't mean it's all the way over."

Strand warned, "It had better be. I hear you going out of your way to make more trouble for these folks, we'll pick this conversation back up pronto-like."

The Barnstable brothers wheeled their horses and rode off, soon disappearing in a cloud of dust.

After watching them for a ways, the marshal turned his eyes back to Mac and Sara. "Strikes me that you two ain't exactly strangers to trouble, neither. With or without that pair of fools. If it wasn't for you and the rest of the Double T crew getting ready to move on, Mac, I might have to worry about it becoming a habit."

Mac and Sara traded glances.

Then, after clearing his throat, Mac said, "Not meaning to add to your worries, Marshal, but it turns out us Double T boys won't, er, be moving on. Leastways not real soon."

"What? Why's that?"

Sara took over and explained how Mac and Castle and the others had agreed to stay on for a while in order to help get the Box H back in order and also to watch for some sign of whether or not the back of the rustling gang had truly been broken.

"Speaking of which," Mac said when she ended by mentioning the rustlers, "is that what brings you out our way this morning, Marshal? You said you'd let everybody know if you had any luck identifying the hombres who were killed or if you got any worthwhile information from the wounded man once you were able to question him."

Strand's expression soured. "Yeah, I was riding out with what news I got. Trouble is, ain't any of it good. For starters, none of the men I took out to the hogback could remember seeing any of the dead rustlers before, couldn't shed no light on 'em at all. When we got back to town, though, for a while things seemed more hopeful for that owlhoot in the doc's care. Doc called his condition stable, said he felt more optimistic about his chances of pulling through."

"But I take it something went wrong," said Sara, prodding the lawman to get to the point.

"Yeah, it sure did." Strand heaved a sigh. "Doc said it was an almighty strange thing. By the time he turned in for the night, he felt more confident than ever that the fella would make it to morning and probably be up to doing some talking. Just to make sure, Doc rousted up every few hours and went down to check. Each time things kept looking good . . . until Doc went down about daybreak. He found the patient dead as a stone."

"What happened?"

Strand wagged his head. "Doc can't say for certain. No way to know. Some kind of seizure, he reckons. A delayed shock to the heart maybe. No sign the fella tried to get up and fell or anything. He just stopped breathing.

Another lousy break when it comes to trying to get a handle on those blasted rustlers."

"A lousy break in that regard," Mac muttered. "But at the same time a convenient one for anybody that skunk might have named if he'd lived long enough to undergo some hard questioning."

"Now don't stir up a bunch of unfounded suspicion with that kind of talk," the marshal quickly objected. "The treatment room was locked, neither the door nor window had been messed with, and there was no sign of any funny business. The skunk died from his gunshot wound, plain and simple. The doc said right from the start his condition was touch and go."

Mac held up a hand, palm out. "I was just thinking out loud, Marshal. Don't worry. Ain't my way to run my mouth and stir the pot."

Strand harrumphed. "Good. See that you don't. Now . . . I expect you two want to get on with your business in town, and I need to finish giving the bad news to your pa, Sara. So I'll bid you good day. And if those spoiled Barnstable brats come around giving you any more trouble, you let me know and leave it to me to take care of. You hear?"

"I will, Marshal," Sara promised with a smile. "But I don't expect it will come to that. I think they've learned their lesson, at least for the foreseeable future."

Chapter 21

Stack Ketchum sat his horse atop the hogback where the Double T men had tangled with the rustlers who'd used the spot to stage their ambush on the Hardwicks. Ketchum had no way of knowing these details, of course, nor did the men slouched in their saddles to either side—Otis Bradley on his left, Ed Story and Jack Needham on his right. The remaining member of the gang, Jesus Del Sol, was approaching from a flat area down below, riding up the front slope of the hogback.

By the time Del Sol got to the top, his broad copper face was shiny with sweat and his horse was blowing hard under a shimmering sun near its noon zenith. Before the half-breed Yaqui said anything, he brushed the battered sombrero back off his head, lifted the canteen from his saddle, and tipped it up for a long drink. Then, after gliding to the ground, he poured some of the canteen's contents into his hat and held it for the horse to drink, muttering, "Easy, boy. Not too much."

Ketchum watched patiently for several seconds. When the horse had taken enough noisy slurps, he said, "What were you able to make of it, Jesus?"

Backhanding sweat from his face before clapping the still dripping sombrero back onto his head, Del Sol replied, "I can tell you pretty much everything that happened. Not sure about the order, though, and sure as hell can't say the *why* of some of it."

Ketchum gestured. "Tell us what you can."

"All right. Part of it you already know. We all saw where the bunch we've been following made camp back yonder. I make that night before last. Yesterday morning, early, I judge, they came here to this rise, I'd say drawn by the sound of gunfire from four or five shooters positioned up here."

"What were they shooting at?" asked Story.

Del Sol thrust out an arm, pointing. "They were trading lead with three riflemen nested in some rocks on the other side of that flat down there. Judging by the dead horses just off one side of those rocks, I figure the shooters up here ambushed the three and then had them pinned down for a time."

Needham's oddly bent brows pinched together. "Wait a minute. This is where we followed the wagon tracks from that camp, right?"

"Yeah, that much is true," Del Sol allowed. "But I don't think the wagon came here until later. Maybe to haul away the dead and wounded. Way I read it, something caused Otis's old outfit, the Double T crew, to get crossways of the shooters up here. You can see for yourselves by all the bloodstains and spent cartridges on the ground that there were a lot of bullets flying and hitting their marks. And the rifle fire from below didn't figure in much. There's only a trace of blood down there, except for the dead horses, and then I followed the tracks of five people making their way from those rocks on up to here. Don't know what it means, but two sets of those tracks were made by women—women wearing boots, but women all the same."

Ketchum frowned in thought. "You saying the Double T boys interfered with the ambushers because they were targeting a couple of women?"

"Can't say their reasoning for sure. But it appears to have gone something like that, yeah. Plus, there was some cattle that figured in somehow."

"Cattle? What do you mean?"

Del Sol pointed again. "Off to the south of that flat, I saw sign of some cattle—about fifty or so head—that got driven past there. First, one way, angled toward the south, then back again north and east, the way they first came from. On their way back, I recognized hoofprints of Double T riders driving 'em. Was I to make a guess, I'd say the cattle got stolen but then reclaimed and turned back to where they was took from."

"What the hell sense does any of that make?" wailed Ed Story. "Ambushes, bloody gun battles, stolen cows . . . What would make those Double T rannies stop to stick their noses in? And what kind of boar's nest does that mean we might be headed for?"

"A boar's nest with twenty-two thousand dollars in it, that's what kind!" Ketchum responded heatedly. "Now knock off your damn bellyaching, Ed, and let me think a minute."

Story fumed at the reprimand but stayed quiet.

Ketchum looked over at Otis. "You rode with those Double T boys. Any idea what might make 'em get mixed up in something like this?"

"None," Otis answered with a firm shake of his head.

"I'd figure 'em for being focused on getting that sales money back to Boss Tremaine in Texas, not being sidetracked for very long by anybody else's trouble."

Now Ketchum turned his gaze to the half-breed. "You said something about the wagon hauling away the dead and wounded. What makes you think that?"

Del Sol explained, "The herd of cattle, with Double T riders driving 'em, went to the northeast, like I told you. Back to the ranch they came from, I reckon. But the wagon tracks left here headed more due east. Wouldn't that be about where you been figuring that town of Broken Spoke is, Otis?"

"Yeah. That's the way I remember from when we passed through here on the drive to California," Otis affirmed.

"What you're thinking," Ketchum said, still addressing Del Sol, "is that some gunshot victims from the skirmish here got taken to a doctor in the town."

"Or undertaker," Del Sol added solemnly.

Ketchum pulled an already sodden handkerchief from his pocket, thumbed back the front brim of his hat, and slowly mopped his face with the hanky. When he lowered his hand, he said, "Okay, here's what we're gonna do . . . A dustup like this is bound to have tongues wagging as a result. Especially if there was rustling involved and if the Double T chuckwagon showed up in town, delivering a bunch of shot-up bodies. So, Ed and Jack, I want you two to follow those wagon tracks into Broken Spoke and find out what the wagging tongues have to say. Keep your mouths shut and your ears open, and pick up all the details you can.

"I got plenty of faith in Jesus's tracking skill, but like he says himself, ground sign can only tell you so much. In the meantime, the rest of us will follow the trail of that cattle herd back to what it seems likely will be the ranch they got took from. Since it appears at least some of the Double T riders were in on driving 'em, we'll try to figure out where that stands. We'll have Otis with us to be able to recognize if there are still Double T men possibly hanging around. The main one we want to single out and get a bead on, remember, is the ramrod packing the money belt we're aiming to relieve him of."

"After we scatter and gather whatever information we can, then what?" asked Needham.

"Then we meet back up and plan our next move based on what we've learned," Ketchum answered. "Come evening, we'll join up again. Right here's as good a spot as any. Down in that grove of trees just past the rocks on the back side of the flat. It's out of the way, we're all already familiar with the location, and we can expect it ain't too far to come back to from either the ranch or the town. We'll make night camp in that grove, and then, after we've had the chance to compare notes and make our plan, we'll strike out from there in the morning."

Ketchum paused, scanning the faces surrounding him. When no further questions or comments came out of any of them, he gave a curt nod and said, "All right, then. Let's get to it."

Chapter 22

The first day of the Double T Texans working on the Box H spread went smoothly and productively. It started out with Squint fashioning a crude but serviceable crutch for Hardwick, while Red and Boyd dusted off and otherwise rigged as necessary an old single-seat buggy that they found in a shed. This gave the wounded ranch owner a reasonable amount of mobility to show his new crew around the place. Tara joined in on this also, while her sister and Mac were in town, stocking up on supplies.

Once the lay of things had been made clear, Castle's men split up and began falling with familiar ease into ranch routines and duties they had been away from for some time. It was quickly evident that Hardwick's previous hired hands, even before they turned tail and bolted, hadn't exactly been the cream of the crop. Everything from cracked fence rails to poorly maintained tools to sloppily shod horses to cattle left unbranded was found to be in need. With minimal complaint, other than to curse the shoddy work of fellow so-called wranglers who gave the real thing a bad name, the Double T men merely gritted their teeth and went about making things right.

Just as Mac and Sara were developing a comfort level with one another, something similar was taking place between Castle and Tara. While the latter remained sassier and more outspoken than her sister, she nevertheless also displayed gratitude for the help of the Double T men and respect for Castle's leadership of them. She, in turn, did a good job of living up to her father's brag that she and her sister could rope and ride as well as most men.

What was more, Tara made it clear that such chores weren't something she did just out of necessity but that she actually preferred them over duties more commonly associated to a young woman. A demonstration of this came when it was time to start preparing supper—a task both Hardwick sisters had been encouraged to participate in as a means to improve their cooking skills by learning from Mac while he was available—and Tara obviously avoided going to the kitchen and instead chose to assist in finishing the shoeing of some horses.

Sara *was* present at Mac's side, however, and the resulting supper of baked ham, sweet potatoes, greens, and fresh-baked pie was enjoyed and praised by all. Hardwick himself proclaimed it to be the best meal served at the Box H in far too long.

When supper was finished, the Double T crew was granted the promised overdue trip to Broken Spoke for the sake of doing some "tonsil washing" at one of the town's saloons. Castle assured Hardwick—with a warning glare into the eyes of each man getting ready to depart—that the undertaking would not get out of hand and the men would all be in acceptable shape for work scheduled to be resumed the following morning.

Castle and Mac opted to remain behind. Once the others had ridden off with a unified whoop, and as Sara and Tara busied themselves clearing the table and doing dishes, Hardwick invited Castle and Mac to sit with him out on the front porch and enjoy some post-meal cups of coffee along with the cool evening breeze. The ranch owner was getting around pretty well on the crutch Squint had fashioned for him, but it was clear he was weary from probably overdoing it during the course of the day and his leg was giving him no small amount of pain.

"You know," he said with a sigh as he settled into an old rocking chair that was positioned on the porch for just such evenings, "not all the 'tonsil wash' in the territory is found in town. It just so happens I got a jug or two of home brew right close by. I keep it on hand mainly for medicinal purposes, you understand. But a touch for social occasions ain't out of the question, neither. And you might could even stretch it a mite by claimin' that rinsin' the dust of trail and toil off a body's tonsils is kind of a healthy thing in itself."

Castle grinned. "If you're asking, would we mind a splash of spirits in our evening coffee, I reckon both me and Mac would consider it impolite to turn down such an offer. Plus, if you don't mind my saying, by the way you're favoring that leg, it appears plain enough you could use a medicinal jolt."

"'Bout time somebody noticed my sufferin'," Hardwick declared. Then, turning his head, he hollered into the house for one of his daughters to bring out the whiskey jug from the pantry. Turning back, he scowled and said, "Much as I hate the thought of that sawbones Washburn pokin' and proddin' at me some more, I hope he follows through and pays a visit out here tomorrow to have a look at this wound. Be a relief to hear him say there ain't no sign of mortification. Wouldn't want the old croaker to know I give him too much credit, but he has a mighty good touch helpin' a body's ailments. He made many a trip out here and spent many hours comfortin' my late wife. He couldn't save her in the end—no human hand could've—but he eased a lot of her pain and got her through as best possible."

"If you feel that way, Pa," said Sara, coming out onto the porch, carrying a big ceramic jug with a cork in the spout, "why don't you say something civil to Doc Washburn once in a while? All you two ever do is snarl and growl at one another like a couple of bobcats fighting for the same tree limb."

"Maybe we like it that way. Ever think of that?" Hardwick reached for the jug. "If we was to start speakin' civil to each other after all this time, the shock might be too much for both of us. Besides, now sure ain't the time to be complimentin' the old quack . . . not after he let that shot-up rustler kick the bucket on him."

"Pa! You certainly can't blame him for that," Sara said.

"Didn't say I blamed him. Said I wasn't gonna pick now to compliment him." Hardwick thumbed the cork out of the jug and then tipped a generous amount of whiskey into his coffee cup. After pausing for a moment to consider, he hooked a finger through the loop on the neck of the spout and hoisted the jug for a couple of straight gulps. Lowering it, he smacked his lips in a satisfied way and exclaimed, "Waugh! Who needs a doctor, after all?"

"You do," said Tara, emerging out onto the porch with a handful of neatly folded white cloths in one hand. "But before Doc Washburn gets here tomorrow, we're going to change that dressing. Now. Overhearing all this talk of doctoring and such reminded me that we probably should have taken time to do it earlier today."

Throughout the afternoon, Sara had remained dressed in the split riding skirt and blouse she'd donned for the trip to town. While helping Mac prepare supper, she had donned an apron, which she'd removed when it was time to eat. Tara had washed up and changed to a clean shirt for supper but had otherwise stuck to the trousers and boots she still had on now. Mac, for one, was glad the sisters helped differentiate themselves by their choice in attire, and the bottom line was that it did nothing to detract from the loveliness of either one.

In response to Tara's announced intent, Hardwick argued, "Oh, nonsense. If Washburn is gonna be here tomorrow, there's no need to bother with this dressing now. Besides, don't you have dishes to finish doing?"

"The dishes are soaking. We'll go back and finish them when we're done here. Now lift that leg and prop your heel on the porch rail."

A scowling Hardwick passed the jug to Castle, saying, "Here. Take this and drink quick, before they think to try wastin' it by pourin' some more on my wound."

Castle took the jug and added to his and Mac's coffee from it. After copying Hardwick and sampling a couple direct swallows straight from the spout, he lowered the jug with a bug-eyed expression and exclaimed, "Who-ee! Too much of this popskull and you could forget about sending for a doctor, right enough. You could bring in an undertaker, and he wouldn't even need any embalming fluid to complete his work."

Hardwick chuckled. "Makes me wonder what passes for drinkin' liquor with you Texas boys. Though I'll admit this batch did come out a bit stout."

"Stout?" echoed Castle. "I'm just glad the rest of my

men escaped to the safety of some watered-down bar whiskey in town."

By then the sisters had uncovered their father's leg from the strip of blanket they had wrapped around it to keep his previously split pant leg closed and the bandage protected as he'd gone about his activities during the course of the day. When the dressing was removed, the wound appeared to be doing well, with no sign of inflammation or infection.

"See there, you old crab?" said Sara. "Despite all your fussing and bellyaching, everything looks pretty good. We'll put on a nice fresh dressing for tonight so it will be that much easier for Doc Washburn to treat tomorrow."

"Good," grunted Hardwick. "Now let's just hope I survive his treatment better than that wounded rustler did."

Catching his breath after a swallow of his potently laced coffee, Mac said, "I don't think you have much to worry about at all, Mr. Hardwick. I got to agree with Castle. If you can survive regular doses of what comes out of that jug, a little ol' bullet hole ought not be no threat."

Hardwick cocked an eyebrow. "You too, eh? I'm thinkin' that if I ever go to Texas, I better remember to take along my own whiskey, else I'll end up drinkin' what sounds like not much more than strong tea the pair of you seem to be used to."

"If you're so fond of that jug juice, Pa," said Tara, pausing as she started to wrap a fresh cloth over his wound, "maybe we *should* pour another dose on here before we get it all wrapped. After all, if that weak Texas whiskey we used yesterday did so much good, maybe a generous splash of your brew will have it all cured by the time the doc gets here to have a look."

"Just never mind that, and keep wrapping," her father

insisted. "We wouldn't want to do anything that might cause the sawbones to make a trip for nothing."

After a cautious sip of his coffee, Castle said, "Hopefully, the doc will have another piece of business to take care of when he shows up. That telegram I sent to our Double T ranch boss was carefully worded to explain our reasons for wanting to tarry here a bit. Boss Tremaine's a reasonable fella, so I think he'll understand.

"Since we knew Dr. Washburn was scheduled to be coming out here tomorrow, I left word with the telegraph operator to give any reply to him and then alerted the doc, too. But if it turns out Boss Tremaine answers different than I think he will, you folks may have to be the ones to understand in case we need to cut our stay shorter than we're meaning to."

Hardwick frowned. "If Tremaine wants his crew back without losin' a lot of time that's of no benefit to him, I reckon I couldn't find fault. I sure hope he's reasonable like you say, though. But no matter what, we're almighty grateful for all the help you've already been, right up to and including young Mac facing down those Barnstable chowderheads earlier today."

"Sara and I have handled Leo and Brad Barnstable a dozen times all on our own," Tara sniffed.

Sara shook her head. "But not like they were today, sis. I've never seen them so vulgar or menacing. Thank God Mac was there." Her gaze came to rest and lingered on Mac as she added, "Let's all hope Doc Washburn shows up tomorrow with a good reaction when he sees Pa's leg and is carrying good news from the ranch owner in Texas."

Chapter 23

"That's one of the damnedest things I ever heard of," declared Stack Ketchum, the frown lines in his face deepened by the pulsing glow of the fire burning at the center of the night camp, where his gang had reassembled. "So first, this pack of Double T cowpokes take time out from plodding along on their way back home to break up an ambush they happen to run across but really ain't no skin off their noses. Okay, maybe I can *kinda* understand that, seeing how there were a couple gals involved on the side getting the worst of it. And at least one of 'em, I gotta admit based on the peek we got from checking out the ranch where they returned the cattle to, is almighty pretty. But now, on top of that, word has it the whole crew is gonna stick around for a while and help the old rancher and his daughters on account of all the rustling problems their Box H spread has been having. Have I got it right?"

"That's the talk in town," replied Ed Story. "We heard

the same thing everywhere we went. The old rancher's name is Hardwick. His daughters are twins, so if the one you got a look at is pretty, reckon that means the other one is, too."

Ketchum's frown deepened even more. "I don't give a hang about that! What I care about is what those Double T hombres are up to and what it means for the money they're supposed to be packing around with them." He turned his head and aimed a blazing glare at Otis. "Are you sure the trail boss of that bunch still has the money with him?"

Otis's head bobbed up and down. "He did the last I knew. Was wearing it in a money belt around his waist, under his shirt. I heard him say more than once that's how he intended to take the money back and deliver it. As far as I know, unless something changed after they booted me out, all that still holds true."

"And when you put my spyglass on that ranch, you could make out the trail boss among the others? Looking okay, looking still in charge?" Ketchum asked.

"Looked fit as a fiddle from what I saw. They all did, all the men I rode with. The only one who wasn't there was the black fella named Boyd. He must've been the one who drove the chuckwagon into town."

"Yeah, that goes along with what me and Ed heard," allowed Jack Needham. "Folks said a black hombre and another Double T man named Mackenzie brought in a wounded Hardwick to see the town doc. Also, one of the ambushers, who was shot up pretty bad, and a couple folks mentioned Mackenzie got hurt some, too."

Otis shook his head. "I don't know no Mackenzie. He must have hooked up with the outfit after I was out of the picture."

"Wait a minute," said Del Sol, taking a cigarette stub

from the corner of his mouth and flipping it into the fire. "You saying that wagon showed up in town with only two or three wounded men? The bloodstains on that hogback up yonder say there was a hell of a lot more damage done than that and not to just two or three unlucky bullet stoppers."

"Don't worry. Your sign-reading skills ain't failing you," Story was quick to assure him. "Three more of the ambushers, or rustlers or whatever you want to call them, died up there under Double T guns. Their bodies didn't get brung in until later. And a fifth man got away when they went after the stolen cattle."

"Must be some pretty rough cobs in that Double T bunch," remarked Needham. "Cutting down four bushwhackin' long-loopers and running off a fifth without receiving barely a scratch themselves. They might be a passel of do-gooder Robin Hoods, but their goodness appears to have some grit mixed in with it."

"What's a Robin Hood?" Del Sol asked with a puzzled look.

Needham smiled tolerantly. "It's the name of a person, amigo. While you grew up being taught useful things, like how to track and read sign, us less fortunate brats were having to hear about things like this old English scoundrel who—"

"Knock off that pointless talk," snapped Story. "We got more important things to hash over than yarns about some nancy boy Englisher who ran around in tight pants and hid in the woods most of the time."

Needham looked ready to snap back, but Ketchum interrupted before he could say anything. "Hold on a minute. I'm in no mood to spin tales of Robin Hood, either. But mention of his name makes me think of something that could fit this current situation and might actually explain it in a way that makes more sense."

All eyes turned to him, and as the men waited for him to say more, their expressions were expectant.

"Don't you see? What was Robin Hood first and foremost?" Ketchum asked rhetorically. "An outlaw, right? I mean, never mind all that 'rob from the rich and give to the poor' crap. Before he could give anything away—and you can bet the truth of the matter was that plenty, if not all, of what got took stuck to the paws of him and his gang—he first had to do the robbing. Making him an outlaw, like I said. What if this trail boss . . . What's his name again, Otis?"

"Castle," came the answer.

"Uh-huh. So, what if this Castle *does* have a little Robin Hood in him, but not so much the do-gooder part? Maybe he got so easily distracted from delivering what's in that money belt back to Texas on account of he never meant to take it all the way, anyhow."

Otis shook his head. "That don't sound like the Castle I knew. He's about as on the level as a body can be. Yeah, maybe his outfit dumped me back in Temecula, but I mostly had it coming. Hell, I shot one of the other Double T riders."

"It's mighty easy for a fella to be on the level when there ain't no temptation luring him otherwise," Ketchum argued. "Real temptation, I'm saying, like about twenty thousand dollars' worth. That much money strapped around a fella's waist has *got* to make him think thoughts besides simply handing it over at the end of the trail back in Texas."

"Okay, I can follow your line of thinking that far," said Story. "But how does it figure into him being willing to stop off and help these folks here in Arizona? If Castle is planning to hang on to the money—either as a split with his men or all for himself—wouldn't he be in a hurry to go ahead and make his play rather than get bogged down with a whole new piece of business?"

"Not if he saw the new piece of business as a way to fatten that money belt even more. Nothing fuels greed like larceny. Once you stick your toe over the line, it's a lot easier to slide the rest of the foot after it." Ketchum paused to smile wolfishly. "If Castle already has designs on keeping the Texas rancher's money, is it so hard to think he wouldn't spot the vulnerability in Hardwick's situation? Now that he's wangled his way onto the old man's good side, maybe he smells a way to make a profit from there, too. Maybe by siphoning off some direct cash, or maybe by cleaning out the rest of the Box H cattle herd for a quick sale across the border."

Needham's distinct eyebrows butted together to form a scowl. "Now, I ain't saying none of that can't be possible, Stack. Maybe even reasonable. But, golly, that's puttin' a powerful lot of—what ya call it?—speculation into it, don't you think? And even if it's accurate, does it make any real difference as far as what we're about?"

"Why don't it?" Ketchum demanded.

"Because it don't change our target from being what's in that trail boss's money belt. Does it? What if Castle's got some other scheme cooking? You ain't thinking we should wait around to see if it pans out, are you? The easy grab of the cattle-drive money those cowboys are headed back to Texas with is what we set out for from the get-go."

There was a tense span of nothing but Ketchum and Needham trading scowls. Until Del Sol broke the silence by saying, "You're the boss, Stack, so you know we'll go along with whatever you say. But Jack's got a fair point. Whether Castle does or don't have something else cooking, the money belt is there for sure . . . and it *is* what we came after."

Ketchum released a long, slow exhalation out through his nostrils. "I guess you're right. It is a fair point. Whatever else Castle and his bunch might be up to, I reckon we ought not lose sight of the easy grab we started out for."

Story nodded. "I gotta go along with liking the sound of that better."

"And better yet," said Del Sol, "is the fact we can get it over with quick and clean. Since we know right where Castle and his money belt are settled in, we can hit that Box H ranch right now, tonight, and relieve him of packing around all that extra weight."

"Not quite so fast," Ketchum objected.

"Why not?" Story wanted to know. "Hit hard and light out, like Jesus is suggesting, is always what's worked best for us. Hitting that ranch while nobody there has any reason to suspect we even exist—what could be easier? Hell, that's even better than if we'd've caught up with 'em on the trail, out in the open."

"Ain't a matter of being easy," Ketchum insisted. "I'm thinking about being sure where the money is."

"It's where it's always been. Around the waist of that trail boss. Why would it all of a sudden not be?" Story asked now.

"Because Castle's situation is different now. Wearing that money belt while he was on the trail, in a saddle and on the move, that was one thing. But keeping it strapped on all day while he's doing ranch chores and such?" Ketchum wagged his head in response to his own question. Then he continued. "No, in a case like that, I'd see it more likely he'd take off the belt and stash it somewhere safe until he was ready to be on the move again."

"Okay," said Needham. "In that case, we put the trail boss under the gun, maybe slap him around a little if we have to, and force him to spill where the money's stashed. That don't change a lot as far as still going in after it."

Ketchum grunted. "Ain't you the one who pointed out those Double T boys have shown they've got some grit? We go in like that, we won't be going against a bunch of soft-handed store clerks or bank tellers. Seems a safe bet we'll have to trade some lead before it's done. What if a slug takes down Castle and it turns out he don't have the money belt on him and nobody else knows where he stashed it? Where will that leave us?"

Nobody spoke for several seconds.

Finally, it was Del Sol who again broke the silence. "Nothing is ever a sure thing, Stack. We hit that ranch and the money is there—like we have every reason to believe it has to be—then I say our odds are damn good for riding away with it."

"You're probably right," Ketchum conceded. "But why not take a little extra time and turn the odds from good to certain?"

"How we gonna do that?" Del Sol asked.

Ketchum slowly turned his head and settled his gaze on Otis. "Because it so happens we have an old friend of the Double T crew, who, with the right spiel to lay on them, ought to be able to wangle his way back into their good graces long enough to get an accurate picture of what we need to know . . ."

Chapter 24

"There you go, you old rascal," announced Doc Washburn, leaning back from tying off the fresh dressing he had just applied to Hardwick's leg. "I don't know how, but that mangy old hide of yours is healing up faster than a green sapling with a scrape on its bark."

"Clean livin' and pure thoughts, sawbones. That's at the core of it," Hardwick replied somewhat smugly. "Don't try takin' too much credit for any magical healin' powers on your part."

"Father! That's an awfully rude thing to say after the doctor was good enough to come all this way to check on you," scolded Sara.

"Don't bother on my part, gal," said Washburn. "If the ornery old cuss was anything *but* rude, now that would worry me. In fact, I suspect his orneriness—far more than any purity of thought or deed—is probably doing him some good when it comes to his healing."

"The main thing, whatever the contributors," summed

up Tara, "is that the wound is doing well. Let's just settle for that."

"I ain't arguin' that ain't good news," allowed Hardwick. "But we don't have to settle for it bein' this mornin's *only* good news. The telegram Doc brought from the Double T ranch owner in Texas—statin' his agreeableness to his boys remainin' here with us for a while—rates right up there, too."

From where he stood nearby on the sun-washed front porch of the main house, where Hardwick had once again positioned himself in his weathered rocking chair, with his leg propped up on the rail to present it for the doctor's attention, Castle said, "I told you Boss Tremaine was a reasonable sort. I'm just glad he lived up to my expectations. And considering the opportunity laid out by your other visitor this morning, the timing couldn't hardly be better."

"What other visitor was that?" inquired Washburn.

"Yeah, this old ranch has been a regular hub of activity this mornin'," declared Hardwick as his daughters began closing up his split pant leg and re-blanketing it. "'Bout an hour before you showed up, Isaiah, a buyer from that railroad spur reachin' down from the north came by to see if I was interested in selling a hundred head of beef to help feed their work crew."

The doctor nodded. "Uh-huh. As they get closer, they've been making buys from a number of ranches in the area. They're spreading their money around, trying to be fair, giving everybody the chance to make a sale. And from everything I hear, they're paying pretty decent."

Hardwick's head bobbed also. "Yeah, the price he offered was that. And the other thing about it, if he'd come around a week earlier with the same or even a better offer—back when it was just me and the girls keepin' this place afloat—I probably would've had to turn him down because the three of us wouldn't have dared leave everything for the sake of drivin' the beeves to the railhead where they're wanted. But now, with Castle and his men here, some of them can wrangle those critters easy as pie. I'll go out with 'em soon as we're done here and help choose the hundred I want to send. They can start off first thing tomorrow to get 'em delivered."

"Sounds to me," Washburn said, "like these Double T boys have brought some overdue luck to the Box H. First, by busting up that ambush you got caught in, then by agreeing to stick around awhile to help get things around here back in order, and now being on hand so you can take advantage of this stock-selling opportunity."

"It ain't nothing any other decent person wouldn't do," Castle spoke up, uncomfortable with too much praise being heaped on his and his men's contribution. "Not like we're putting ourselves out overly much or going to any special strain. Punching cows and seeing to chores around a ranch is what we do pretty much wherever we are. We're just stopping off here to help some good folks caught in a bind. And it ain't like Mr. Hardwick and his daughters weren't managing without us. Some tough breaks were starting to pile up against them, that's all."

"I never suggested that Hannibal and Tara and Sara weren't doing a valiant job of keeping the Box H going," the doc responded quickly.

Grimacing as he lowered his leg after his daughters were done wrapping it, Hardwick said, "But the tough break of me gettin' us caught in that ambush was something we dang well might *not* have been able to manage. Not without you and your men steppin' in, Castle. And not many people—not even decent ones—would have been so quick to go against those rustlers' guns on our behalf. Now, if you'd just quit callin' me Mister all the dad-blasted time, I'd be even more grateful!"

Washburn chuckled. "Leave it to you, Hannibal, to grouse about someone feeling obliged to show you a little bit of respect."

"I don't mind bein' respected. I just ain't comfortable bein' called Mister. Makes me feel like I'm puttin' on airs or some such."

"Nobody would ever accuse you of putting on airs, Pa," Tara said dryly.

As Washburn began loading medical items back into his bag, Sara said, "Can you take time for a cup of coffee and some fresh-baked biscuits before you have to hurry off, Doc?"

Before the doctor could reply, Sara gave a little laugh and added, "Wipe that look of terror off your face. I'm not threatening you with biscuits baked by Tara or me. Yet another benefit of having the Double T crew in our midst is that one of them, Mac—you've met him before—is a very good cook."

"All right. I can't deny some coffee and a biscuit sounds inviting. And that is in no way an admission I would feel differently if the cook was you or your sister."

Sara laughed again. "You lie gallantly, Doc. Put your bag in your buggy. Then come back to the porch and pull up a chair. I'll go fetch a tray."

Otis Bradley sat his horse just back from the crest of a grassy slope looking down on the Box H ranch. It was from here, with the aid of Stack Ketchum's powerful spyglass, that Otis, Ketchum, and Jesus Del Sol had reconnoitered the ranch at some length the previous evening. Even with daylight starting to dim, the glass's strong lens had given clarity to distant details, people, and movement. Far more so than now, in the brightness of early afternoon, as seen only by the naked eye.

There was once again activity down there, even more so than last evening, but Otis couldn't clearly distinguish the individual features of those involved. Not that it mattered, really. Otis knew full well who they were. Just as he knew his assignment was to go down there and face them.

He didn't like it much, but he liked even less the thought of crossing Ketchum. Ever since being drawn into Stack's gang, Otis had felt moments of reservation and regret. There had also been moments of exhilaration, a sensation of being daring and unrestrained, but those had come few and far between.

The plain truth was that deep down, Otis Bradley was no outlaw. Yeah, he had always been sullen, was often belligerent and hot tempered, but the thought of robbing and riding outside the law and living on the dodge had never crossed his mind . . . until he fell in with Stack.

But that was where he was now, no doubt about it. Not only that, but in too deep to see any way out. If he tried to make a run for it, flee from the gang and leave this whole business behind, Otis feared that devil Del Sol would track him down and he'd be made to pay in a real bad way for attempting to run out. It was the same risk if he went to Castle and the others with the truth—the real truth. That was certain to result in a bloody confrontation, and if Otis's betrayal was somehow discovered by any of the outlaw gang, his life wouldn't be worth a handful of dirt.

No, if he had to betray anybody, his safest bet was to stick with Stack's plan and for it to be the Double T crew. He didn't like it, but Otis couldn't see any way out. He'd been sitting there in his saddle for too long already, trying to work up the courage to ride the rest of the way down. For all he knew, Stack and the others were watching him from a distance even now. He could almost feel their eyes on him.

Damn.

Otis cursed himself for having gotten in so deep. And he knew that going on down the slope and facing the Double T crew would amount to plunging in even deeper.

Yet he had to go ahead with it.

Damn.

Otis batted his heels against the sides of his horse and gigged the animal the rest of the way up over the crest and down the other side. . . .

Chapter 25

Mac had heard plenty about Otis Bradley, none of it very favorable. But now, watching the man squirming on a backless stool in the middle of the Box H bunkhouse with a pack of scowling Double T riders crowded in close around him, Mac couldn't help feeling a twinge of sympathy for the poor slob.

"Look," Otis was saying in an anxious tone, his eyes shifting restlessly from one to the other of the frowning faces looking down on him, as if searching desperately for one that showed some sign of sympathy. "I know I didn't do you fellas right during the time I rode with you. I was surly and ill-tempered most of the time, and on top of that, I was a lousy cook. I lied about that part right from the get-go, about being an experienced grub slinger, on account of I was on hard times and needed a job so bad."

"Well, you sure ain't lyin' now, not when you say you was lousy at it," grumbled Squint Morris.

"I know, I know. I admitted as much, didn't I?" wailed Otis. "And I also know that you, more than anybody here, Squint, has every right to send me packing and maybe even beat the tar out of me—or worse—for taking a shot at you like I done."

"You did more than take a shot *at* him, you blubberin' tub," snarled Larabee. "You plugged him!"

"Yeah, yeah. I know that, too. But it didn't amount to much more than a bullet burn, and you look like you healed up okay. Right?" Otis's eyes pleaded with Squint. "Like I already told you, I'm sorry as sorry can be. You gotta believe me. Please. And try to understand that I was never really shooting at *you*. I was drunk and in a red haze in the middle of that brawl and—"

"Save it," Castle said, cutting him off. "You already gave that spiel, and if Squint wasn't willing to hear you out on the rest of what you say you have to tell us, your backside would already be bouncing in a saddle, making dust away from here. So get to it. What's this bad trouble you say you're in, and what about it is also supposed to be cause for concern to the rest of us?"

Otis had shown up an hour or so earlier, riding into the ranch compound with a forlorn look on his face and a plea to make amends with his former coworkers, starting with Squint Morris, the Double T man he'd shot out of blind anger during a saloon brawl. He had also claimed to have some "critical information" that he sought to share with trail boss Jeff Castle.

Inasmuch as both Castle and Squint, as well as Boyd Lewis, were off culling out a batch of cattle with Hannibal Hardwick when Otis arrived, the first ones to greet him were Larabee and Red Pelham. Mac also happened to be out by the corral with them at the time, but he had no recognition of the man until he heard the other two call him by name.

They were plenty quick to call him other things, too, so it wasn't exactly a warm welcome. In fact, the first inclination of Red and Larabee—especially the latter, whose habitually sour mood was running even more sour than usual due to the hangover he was fighting after washing his tonsils a bit too aggressively during the crew's visit to the Broken Spoke saloons the previous night—was to run Bradley off without ever giving him a chance to even see Castle or Squint. After a thorough tongue-lashing, however, they relented in favor of letting the other Double T men have a say for themselves.

What resulted was the confrontation now still underway after the matter was taken out of the brutal afternoon sun and into the abandoned Box H bunkhouse.

The initial hurdle was Squint, who had a right above anyone else to set the boundaries as far as further dealings with Otis. While his first reaction at the sight of the man was understandable anger, Otis's instant outpouring of apologies and pleas for forgiveness succeeded in holding the old wrangler at bay long enough for him to be willing to hear more of what the former cook claimed about being in personal danger and also having "critical information," which he implied had a bearing on the safety of the others, as well.

At Castle's prodding, the time was now for Otis to give some specifics on those claims.

The former cook started out by saying, "It all stems from an hombre—an outlaw—by the name of Stack Ketchum. Being from Texas, like me, none of you probably ever heard that name before but—"

"I have," Mac interrupted.

All eyes turned to him. "As I was making my way down through central California," Mac explained, "I heard mention of that hombre plenty of times. He heads up a gang of owlhoots who tear things up pretty good. Bank robberies, stagecoach robberies, cattle rustling . . . The way I heard it, they've stuck their grubby paws into about everything except an honest day's work. Like I said, though, that was farther up, north of Temecula."

"Yeah. Yeah, that's the thing," Otis said almost eagerly, grateful for the unexpected verification of at least this much of his story. "You see, Ketchum was in the same Temecula hoosegow where I got thrown after that brawl and shooting. But because him and his gang had never operated that far south before, the local law didn't recognize him. He was serving out a short stretch for disturbing the peace, same as me, under a phony name."

"Then how did you know who he was?" asked Castle.

"Because he told me. On the sly. Ketchum friendlied up to me, see, after that damn Mexican—the same little bastard who started all the trouble in the saloon—got thrown in the same cellblock with me and then tried to finish his beef by coming at me with a knife he somehow snuck in. When I managed to fight him off, that's when Ketchum thought he saw in me the makings of somebody who'd make a good addition to his gang."

Otis wagged his head, as if in remorse, then continued. "In the beginning, I gotta admit I kinda liked the idea. I was feeling pretty bitter about everything and everybody at the time. Between the deputies who arrested me and the jail guards when I got tossed behind bars, I got shook down to nothing in the way of money or belongings of any value. So I already knew what I had to look forward to when I got out. And you fellas were already long gone. Not saying I blame you, but all the same, it was one more part of a pretty gloomy picture . . . And then there was Ketchum, offering something different. Maybe better."

"Hard to see how jumping to the wrong side of the law can seem like a better idea," remarked Red.

"Depends on where you're at when you face considering it," responded Otis. "Besides, I never said I *did* jump to the wrong side of the law. I said I was tempted to."

"So get to it," said Squint peevishly. "You've told us a real heart-tuggin' tale about how low you were feelin' and how a bad hombre was tryin' to lure you lower . . . but where's the part that brought you here, and what kind of new danger are you in, and what about it might mean trouble for us?"

Otis slowly dragged a hand down over his face, wiping away sweat and collecting his thoughts for a reply. Then: "Okay. What it came down to, after Stack had confided all this stuff to me and I'd agreed to join his gang, was that I would be getting out a couple of days ahead of him, so I'd wait, and then when he was out, we'd ride together to meet up with the rest of his men. Only once I was on my own . . . well, I chickened out. Ain't no other way to say it. Hell, I'm no outlaw. Never wanted to be, not really. What I realized was that when Stack took a liking to me and started opening up to me, I . . . I was too scared to tell him no, I wasn't interested. But with me having those two days before I'd have to face him again and live up to the promises I'd made . . ."

"You took off," Squint finished for him. "You ran away from Ketchum and came running to us. But that still don't explain why and what—"

"I think I can answer the rest," Castle interrupted. "I have a pretty good hunch how it all adds up. During the time you were primed to become a bad man and join Ketchum's gang"—here his eyes bored into Otis like hot coals—"you told him about us, didn't you? How we were headed back to Texas with a fat purse of money we got for the sale of the herd we'd just finished delivering. That information was your bona fides for fitting into the gang at a prominent level. Right?"

Otis's chin dropped, and he couldn't meet Castle's blazing stare.

The trail boss continued. "But when you showed yellow and ran, that left some serious loose ends you had to worry about. For starters, Ketchum revealed too much to you about his operation to risk you running around being able to blab about it. Especially after you showed your lack of backbone by bolting on him. On top of that, you also realized you had set us up as juicy targets for a pack of hard cases, who'd likely want to still come after the money. So by showing up here now, you're looking to gain some safety for yourself by us allowing you back in the fold in return for the warning about what's headed our way. Is that about the size of it?"

Otis continued to hang his head, staring down, avoiding every eye. In a husky, barely audible whisper, he said, "Yeah . . . Yeah, you put it all together, Castle."

"Why, you low-down, belly-draggin' skunk," snarled Larabee. "You think there's a chance in hell we'd allow you back in our midst after you sicced those curly wolves on us, on top of already pluggin' one of our own in the past!"

"Now hold on a minute," protested Red. "I ain't nohow saying I'm ready to take this jasper home to meet my sister, mind you, but he *is* owning up to the wrong he's done, and he rode all this way to give us warning. As for plugging Squint, that's Squint's call to make, and he already gave some allowance for it."

"*Some* allowance," Squint was quick to say. "But I'll

go along with Red on the part about Otis catchin' up to give warnin'."

"Only, as much as anything, that's due to him lookin' for safety in numbers to protect his hide after crossin' Ketchum," pointed out Boyd.

Bolstered by hearing a couple of voices speaking up tentatively on his behalf, Otis lifted his face and said, "It's true I'm hoping for the safety that would come from being surrounded by you fellas. I already admitted as much. But it's also true I could have rode off in a whole different direction and banked on Stack and his gang coming after this outfit and the money rather than chasing me down. That might have been my safest bet of all when you weigh the value of my hide against what Castle is packing around his waist. I thought about doing it that way, I truly did. But after I'd been tempted by the owl-hoot way once and turned my back on it, that didn't seem a whole lot different. So, whether you believe me or not, my remorse or guilt, or whatever you want to call it, over setting you fellas up the way I did got the better of me. I decided that warning you about Stack and his bunch was the only thing I could do to try and square things."

Nobody spoke for several beats.

Until Red said, "How would those owlhoots even know where to find us?"

"Thanks to me, they know where you're headed. Remember?" Otis replied dully. "And the route you've been taking is the straightest, most logical way. Plus, since there's been no rain over any of the ground you've covered so far, the wheel tracks of that chuckwagon are pretty plain."

"You said Ketchum wasn't due out of jail until a couple days after you. You figure that's about how much of a lead you got on 'em?" Castle asked.

Otis pursed his lips for a moment. "About that, I reckon. Yeah. It took me most of a day to make up my mind what I was gonna do. But by the same token, it would've taken Stack a while to add up that I'd rattled my hocks and then to gather up his men. Once I started, though, I came at a pretty good clip. So yeah, I think it's reasonable to figure I still got a couple days on 'em."

Things got quiet again, everybody frowning in thought.

This time it was Larabee who broke the silence. "I can't hardly believe it, but it appears to me that some here are maybe willin' to swallow what this scoundrel is dishin' out. Not so much about the hard cases who might be comin', I don't mean, but about him earnin' his way back in with us."

"He went to considerable length to catch up with us and to admit his wrongs face-to-face. For all he knew, he might've been met with a bullet, considering how he left things with Squint," Castle pointed out. "I'm having trouble seeing any gain for him if this is some kind of trick."

"So, we thank him for his trouble and send him packin'. Then we watch our backs," insisted Larabee. "If we bring him in with us again, you can bet I for one will damn sure be watchin' my back even closer."

Castle mulled some more. Then, turning to Squint, he said, "You got the biggest reason to be leery about this rascal. You say run him off, I will, and that'll be the end of it. If you want to give him some consideration, I'll put it to a vote and let everybody have a say."

"Do the vote," Squint said without much hesitation.

And so they did. Larabee and Boyd cast nay votes; Squint, Red, and Castle were willing to take a chance on the ex-cook. Mac abstained on the grounds he had no basis to form a reasonable opinion on either the man or the history of the situation regarding him.

When it was done, Castle pinned Otis with a hard stare and declared, "All right, you're back in. But if you're up to anything, if this goes bad in some way as a result, you'd better make sure it goes bad all the way. Because if harm comes to any of my men and there's even a piece of me left, I'll ride, walk, or crawl if need be to hunt you down."

"It won't come to that, Castle. I swear," Otis promised in a slightly husky voice. "I'm dealing straight with you."

Chapter 26

At first light the next morning, Castle, Red, and Tara Hardwick started out driving a hundred Box H cattle north to the railhead. A fair amount of discussion had preceded this. The plan initially had been for Squint to accompany them also. But the arrival of Otis and the information he brought with him had changed things. It had been decided instead that as many guns as possible should remain behind at the ranch in case Stack Ketchum made an appearance sooner than calculated.

Before anything else, however, a meeting with the Hardwicks had been necessary.

"The idea was for us to stick around awhile and be of help to you, not bring added trouble," Castle had told the old man and his daughters after explaining to them about the Ketchum gang. "Me and my boys don't have much choice. If that pack of curly wolves is gonna try and act on the information given to 'em, all we can do is stay ready for if and when they show. But that don't mean here is where they have to catch up with us. If we go back on the move toward home—like we were doing, and how they're expecting to find us—that'll draw them right on past the Box H, and there'll be no risk of you folks getting caught in it."

Cocking one shaggy brow, Hardwick had replied, "Lucky I've taken such a likin' to you, Castle boy, or I might find noises like that comin' out of your piehole insultin' enough to make me take this cane of mine and wallop you alongside the head with it. After the way you fellas have stuck out your necks for the sake of me and my daughters, you think for a minute we'd repay you by duckin' for cover and sendin' you on your way just because some ornery polecats *might* be on your trail? You don't have a very good idea what us Hardwicks is made of, do you?"

After that, once it had been made clear the Hardwicks were willing to run the risk of getting caught in whatever the potential arrival of Ketchum and his hard cases might bring, they went ahead with plans for carrying out the cattle drive and other work around the Box H that was already on tap.

Initially, there was some discussion of Castle also dropping out of the drive since he, as the one packing the money belt, which was the alleged robbery target, ought to be on hand to help defend it in case the gang showed up before he got back. The need for this was promptly objected to by Hardwick, who insisted he wanted Castle to head the drive.

Additionally, Castle revealed that while he was in town the previous morning to send his telegram to Boss Tremaine, he'd been confident enough in getting the go-ahead for him and the others to remain for a while that he went ahead and deposited the cash from the money belt in the local bank for safekeeping, rather than continue to carry it around on his person.

The drive had gone ahead with its slightly trimmed wrangling crew. It was estimated they would reach the railhead on the following day. Since for such a relatively short trip, the wranglers would be getting by on saddle rations and thus would have no chuckwagon to slow their return, it was further estimated they might make it back by late the second night. If not, then early the following morning.

In other words, within a time frame sooner than it was expected Ketchum's bunch could show up, if they came at all. And in the event they did, the Double T's best guns—Boyd, Squint, and Mac—would be on hand to serve as a reception committee.

After breakfast had been served and the drive had departed, Mac and Sara had shared kitchen duties to complete the post-meal cleanup and get the dishes done and put away. Their comfort level with one another was increasing steadily.

This was also true, though in a more subdued way, for Castle and Tara. The latter's continuing avoidance of the kitchen kept her more in Castle's company, while Sara's genuine interest in learning to be a better cook placed her more in Mac's presence, and this may have partly accounted for these pairings. But a physical attraction between the parties involved was also clearly in evidence.

In any case, both Mac and Sara had agreed that their time in the kitchen needed to be more limited over the next couple of days so they could help with a bigger share of the ranch work due to the absence of those who had gone on the cattle drive. Toward that end, Mac was planning some simpler upcoming meals, which would be quicker to prepare and easier to clean up after. This morning's spread, meant to give the wranglers a hearty send-off, would be the last on that scale for a while.

After emerging from the bunkhouse now, his cook's apron traded for the bridle and saddle he carried hoisted on one shoulder, Mac headed for the horse corral where Pard was trotting back and forth restlessly at the sight of his approach.

The early sun hanging in a clear cobalt sky was already a blazing white-hot ball getting stoked for the real heat it would be pouring down by the middle of the day. Across the compound, in a separate fenced-in area, three or four dozen head of unbranded stock had been segregated during yesterday's roundup of beeves to take to the railroad.

Mac could see Squint, Boyd, Larabee, and Otis preparing to get the critters' overdue marking done. Larabee was stirring up a bed of glowing red coals for the branding irons, while the other three were doing some last-minute repairs to the squeeze chute, which would be needed to hold some of the larger animals. From the seat of his buggy, Hardwick was overseeing the operation.

Stepping inside the corral where Pard was ready and waiting, anxious because it had been too long since he'd been put to use as a mount, Mac wasted no time starting to slap on his gear.

"I know I haven't been paying much attention to you of late, old friend. I promise to try and do better, okay?" he murmured to the paint. He'd just finished tightening the cinch strap when Sara came out of the house and walked over to lean on the outside of the corral rail. She had changed her attire to dungarees, work shirt, and a flat-crowned Stetson, which was perched above her ponytail. Mac recognized this as the way she'd been dressed the first time he saw her. No matter, she looked mighty fetching whatever she wore.

"No need for me to saddle up, since it appears we have plenty of riders and ropers for the limited number of cattle," she said, glancing over at the holding area. "Looks like I'll be swinging a branding iron."

Mac grinned. "I bet you swing a mean one."

Sara returned his grin. "Better than I swing a frying pan. But that's going to change. Just you watch."

Mac led Pard out of the corral, and they walked over to Hardwick's buggy. The old man was wearing a disgruntled expression when they reached him. It softened for a moment when he glanced down at his daughter but then hardened again when his eyes returned to the work being done by the Double T men.

"Look there," he grumbled. "All or most of those cattle should have been branded long before this. And the disrepair that squeeze chute was in . . . Those two lunkheads I used to have workin' for me wasn't worth spit even before they turned yella and ran off. And I oughta have my tail kicked for not payin' closer attention. I was too busy worryin' about rustlers to pay attention to what was goin' on—or *not* goin' on, as was the case—right under my doggone nose!"

"Just forget those no-accounts, Pa," Sara advised him. "We're lucky they're gone and even luckier to have Mac and Castle and the others here putting things back in order now. Once they've moved on and the problem of any more rustling is resolved, you'll be able to hire new help, and you'll know to make sure they're better quality."

"You can count on that," Hardwick grunted. Then, abruptly, his mood seemed to change, and he switched his attention to Mac, saying, "Something else has come to mind that I'm hopin' to count on where you're concerned, Mac lad. Seein's how some castratin' is gonna be called for with part of these critters here this mornin', do your cookin' skills include knowin' how to work up a batch of prairie oysters?"

The question lifted Mac's eyebrows.

Before he could reply, Sara exclaimed, "Pa! What a question to ask. And what a thing to even think of!"

"It's exactly the right thing to think of at a time like this, and a plumb sensible question to ask," her father insisted. Then, turning his attention back to Mac, he said, "You see the problem? I'm surrounded by delicate little offspring who don't appreciate good eatin'. Even if they could cook, neither this one nor Tara would have anything to do with such a thing. They even turned ol' Greta against makin' any for me! I ain't had a plate of proper-cooked oysters since their ma was healthy enough to fix some. For the both of us, I might add. She wasn't too good to enjoy 'em right along with me."

Sara frowned. "I'm not speaking ill of Ma, or you, either, you stubborn cuss. But disgusting is disgusting. I don't care who thinks otherwise."

"I don't want to get in the middle of anything here," Mac said cautiously, understanding how many folks— even some seasoned wranglers—didn't take to the notion of eating bull testicles, more commonly called *prairie oysters*, even though they were quite tasty when properly prepared. "But to answer your question, Mr. Hardwick, yeah, I've had occasion to cook a few batches of prairie oysters. Reckon I can make you some if you want."

"I do indeed."

"Well, there's one cooking lesson I won't be around for," Sara announced somewhat haughtily.

Before either her father or Mac had a chance to say anything to that, Squint came ambling over from the repaired squeeze chute. "We're ready to get started, Mr. Hardwick," he said, "just as soon as Larabee gets some dope mixed up to slap on the ones what need to be nutted."

Hardwick nodded. "Good. We were just talkin' about that."

"Uh-huh, I overheard. Mighty good eatin', them prairie oysters," Squint allowed.

Sara rolled her eyes, and Mac had to turn his head away to keep her from seeing his grin. In so doing, he spotted three riders approaching in the near distance.

"Looks like visitors on the way," he noted, thinking there was something vaguely familiar about the way a couple of them sat their saddles.

He got his answer a moment later, when the others turned to look and Hardwick was quick to mutter, "Neighbors. But not necessarily welcome visitors. It's Frank Barnstable and those two sorry sons of his."

Chapter 27

The three horsemen reined up next to Hardwick's buggy on the side opposite from Mac and Sara. Frank Barnstable sat a tall Appaloosa stud between his two sons. He was a well-built man of fifty with a ruddy, heavy-jowled face bracketed by bristly white sideburns. He wore a cream-colored Boss of the Plains hat and a corduroy jacket trimmed in leather at the lapels and cuffs.

"Morning to you, Hannibal," he greeted in a rather gruff voice.

"It's mornin'," Hardwick acknowledged. "I note you didn't say *good* morning, and by the look on your face, I'm figurin' you didn't come in particularly good spirits."

Barnstable snapped off a quick nod. "You're figuring it right. We've been neighbors a long time, Hannibal. We were among the first to settle here when there wasn't much else but cactus and Apaches. You and I've never been especially close, but we've always gotten along okay."

"You didn't ride over here to give me a history lesson, Frank. If you got something stuck in your craw, I'd be obliged if you commenced spittin' it out. As you can see, we're in the middle of tryin' to get some work done."

What could also be seen, by the way Barnstable's already ruddy face flushed an even deeper shade of red, was that the rancher wasn't used to being spoken to that way. Mac had no trouble spotting this, even though he was already occupied trading glares with Leo and Brad, who'd begun giving him the stink eye the minute they rode up.

"Okay. You're damn right I'll spit it out," Barnstable responded, his tone a bit gruffer still. "While the two of us may have tolerated each other well enough, the same hasn't been true of our offspring. From what I've heard, those girls of yours have often gone out of their way to be rude and standoffish to my two boys. I've never said anything before, because I figured that was something that oughta be worked out among the four of them. Plus, I believe a gal has the right to refuse attention if she chooses, and I know that my boys can be, er, sort of on the rambunctious side."

"That's an understatement if there ever was one," piped up Sara.

"See how she is, Pop?" Leo was quick to say in response. "And she's the quieter twin . . . at least I think she's the one."

"Keep still. I'm handling this," his father barked out the side of his mouth. Then, ignoring Sara and keeping his eyes on Hardwick, he continued, "But my boys told me of an incident day before yesterday that takes things to another level. I expect you've heard a version of it, as well. Only I took the time to go into town and confirm it with the marshal. As a result of the incident and some other matters, he confirmed that my boys—extremely unfairly, in my opinion—have been barred from going into town for a month. And it was all brought to a head due to your daughter and one of these Texans you've brought into the mix of things."

This time it was Squint who couldn't hold back from adding a comment. "Ain't so sure I like the way you said '*these Texans*,' mister," he drawled, easing forward from where he'd been standing off a ways from Mac and Sara.

Barnstable finally took his eyes off Hardwick and sent a hard glare in the direction of the veteran wrangler. "Nobody was talking to you, fella. And I don't much care what you like or don't."

Emboldened by seeing his father start to get his hackles up, Brad sneered, "That's right. We ain't got nothing against Texans . . . as long as they stay in Texas."

Barnstable rebuked him even more sharply than he had his brother. "Shut up! I said I'm handling this."

"Whatever it is you think you're handlin', Frank, you'd better get to it before this gets the rest of the way out of hand," Hardwick advised in a flinty tone. "And a good way to hold it together is to keep your pups from any more yappin'."

"There was yappin' from your side, too!"

"Difference is, they *are* on my side. They're here because I want 'em to be, and this is my property. I'll cut you some slack because we've been neighbors for a long time, like you said. But Leo and Brad are long past bein' welcome on my land. The 'incident' you speak of? Yeah, I heard all about it. That was the last straw. Time was, not so long ago, I would've been showin' up at *your* place to pay *them* a visit. But the marshal came by to put it to rest on the spot, so I decided to stand down."

Barnstable scowled fiercely. "I already told you my opinion that the marshal did a piss-poor job! Okay, maybe the barring-from-town part had more to do with a saloon brawl the previous night than the trouble on the trail with your daughter. But that's my whole point for being here. The trail incident was left totally unaddressed by the marshal! And that . . . that Texan who was there got away with taking a shot at one of my sons!"

Now it was Mac who couldn't keep quiet. "That's a damn lie!" he said loud and clear.

"Are you calling me a liar?" Barnstable demanded in a roar.

"I'm saying the claim I took a shot at one of your boys is a lie. What would you call somebody spouting it as fact?"

"Both of my sons stand behind that claim."

"Then they're lying to *you*, Mr. Barnstable," said Sara. "I was there. I saw everything. Yes, Mac drew his gun and fired a shot—but it was only to cut the rope of the lasso Brad had thrown around me and was trying to jerk me off the wagon with."

"What? What lasso?" Barnstable sputtered. "I never heard anything about—"

"More lies, Pop!" Leo insisted. "You gonna believe them over us?"

Sara thrust a finger, pointing, and said icily, "Maybe Brad can explain the frayed end of the lasso coiled right there on the side of his saddle. And if you want further proof, maybe you'd like to see the loop end of it, which is lying on the floor of the chuckwagon driver's box, where I threw it down after I was free of it. It has a frayed end, too, matching the one on his saddle to mark where Mac's bullet blasted the lasso in two."

Barnstable leaned over suddenly and yanked Brad's coiled lasso from his saddle. He shook it vigorously, loosening the coil, spilling it down onto the ground, until the only thing he was holding in his fist was a frayed, broken end of rope. He stared at this with blazing eyes for a long beat and then slowly lifted the fiery gaze and fixed it on Brad.

"You . . . You roped a girl and *tried to drag her to the ground*?"

Brad paled, and his eyes took on the look of those of a trapped animal. "You don't understand, Pop. There's more to it. That damn Texan rammed us with his wagon and team of mules!"

"That's right," Leo added desperately. "He could have knocked us from our saddles, maybe broke our necks. Or maybe toppled our horses and broke one of their legs."

"We had a right to retaliate!" wailed Brad.

Barnstable's lips were peeled back as he grimaced as if in disgust. "Retaliate by roping the girl and dragging her to the ground like an animal you were fixing to hog-tie and brand?"

"It wasn't like that!" Brad said.

"No, it wasn't anything like you two lying pups have been telling me all along, was it?" Without warning, Barnstable lashed out with the length of rope he was still gripping in one hand, aiming to strike Brad with it.

The young man leaned far back in his saddle, avoiding the blow, and wheeled his horse sharply away in a quarter turn. "What the hell, old man! You got no call to do that!" he hollered.

"Pop! Brad!" cried out Leo. "For God's sake, stop it!"

For a split second, Brad seemed to hesitate. As if his brother's words had had some impact. But then he twisted in his saddle, and all at once his fist was filled with a six-gun he was aiming straight at Mac.

"This is all your fault," he yelled. "We should have doubled back on the trail that day and finished you right then and there!"

Everything went still and quiet. The only thing that moved was the air starting to shimmer faintly in the day's building heat.

And then, from over in front of the branding-iron fire, where he stood with his feet planted wide on either side of the pan of castration dope and with a Henry repeater aimed from one bony shoulder, Larabee called in a clear, steady voice, "You can go ahead and pull that trigger if you really want to, sonny boy . . . but if'n you do, your pa and brother will be takin' home what's left of your head in a leaky gunnysack."

Chapter 28

Another stretch of tense silence followed Larabee's words. Brad's eyes slid off Mac and slowly drifted to look over at the old man aiming a rifle at him.

Mac broke the tension, saying in a low voice, "Last time I was the one holding a gun on you, Brad. You said if I wasn't, things would be different. Well, now you're the one with the gun. But I don't think things are different in quite the way you hoped."

Brad's eyes came back to Mac. "You go to hell."

"Remains to be seen," Mac said. "But in the meantime, how about this? I don't figure you deserve to have your head blown off just yet, but neither do I think you ought to get off simply slinking away with your tail between your legs again. What do you say to tossing aside the shooting iron, climbing down off that saddle, and you and me settling our differences sort of in between the two?"

"He's got near twenty pounds on you, Mac," cautioned Squint.

"Yeah, but it's all mouth. Hot air and gut wind don't worry me."

"Don't let him talk to you like that, Brad," urged Leo. "Show that damn Texan!"

Brad looked around and searched his father's face, as if seeking some sign of support or approval there. But all he got was a stony stare that refused to meet his gaze. Brad turned back to Mac and hesitated just a second before he flung his gun to the ground, sprang from his saddle, and went barreling around the end of Hardwick's buggy. Mac rushed to meet him.

At the rear of the buggy, they slammed together like two charging bulls. Brad immediately swung a wild right cross, which Mac managed to duck with little trouble. Then, hooking his left arm around Brad's torso, he used the momentum and body-twisting motion of the young hothead's missed punch to propel him in an effort to ram his face against the back panel of the buggy.

Brad turned his head at the last moment so that he took the impact of the collision on his cheekbone rather than getting his nose mashed. He hit with a solid thud, anyway. And before Brad could pull back, Mac slammed a forearm on the back of his neck, driving his face against the buggy once more.

Brad buckled at the knees, partly from being somewhat stunned, partly as a defense against getting his face rammed yet again. With his center of gravity lowered, he kicked backward, hard and desperate, and plowed into Mac at waist level with enough force to double him over and jolt him off balance. This pushed Mac into an awkward backpedal and allowed Brad the chance to straighten up and get turned around.

The two men faced each other with balled fists raised and ready. They quickly closed again. Brad promptly threw another wild right. This time when Mac ducked under it, he immediately fired a right of his own, a quick hook to Brad's ribs. The punch hit with a satisfying pop, but Brad absorbed it better than expected and Mac was too slow pulling away. Brad instantly lashed out with a counter-punch of his own, his right again, whipping the arm in reverse and driving the back of his elbow against the side of Mac's head.

Mac was sent into a quarter spin and had to do a ragged side step to maintain his balance. But that was as far as he went. He braced himself and was ready when Brad followed his arm whip and came turning back the rest of the way. As soon as he was around far enough, Mac drilled a hard left to Brad's gut, causing him to bend forward into an uppercut that hammered home under the point of his chin.

Brad staggered backward, arms windmilling, and likely would have gone down if he hadn't fallen against one of the buggy wheels. Mac waded after him.

Supported by the wheel, Brad met him with a flurry of flailing punches. But they lacked any real power. The rancher's son was obviously hurting. His eyes were glazed, and he was breathing raggedly, possibly from a cracked rib. Mac took a couple of glancing blows to his shoulders and one to the side of his head, blocked two others. He got in a left jab and a right hook, both smacking solidly. Brad sagged a bit, relying more and more on the wheel to hold him up.

Mac backed off slightly, still keeping his fists raised. "Had enough?" he said, also sucking for air.

"Not by a damn sight," Brad rasped.

And then, lowering his head, he shoved himself off the

wheel and charged at Mac in another desperate bull rush. More than anything, it amounted to a barely controlled forward stagger. But the unexpectedness of it and the weight of his swarming mass had an impact, nonetheless. Mac was driven back. The top of Brad's head butted him high on the chest and then rammed upward into his throat. Gagging out a curse, Mac twisted away.

Brad's momentum continued to carry him forward in a drunken lurch. Getting his feet replanted, Mac hammered a punch to the side of Brad's face as he stumbled past. Brad's knees buckled sharply, and his forward movement was halted. Stepping closer, taking his time now, Mac drew back his fist, measuring, and put everything he had into a straight right to the jaw. It was finally enough to knock Brad into a full-out sprawl.

He lay there, not moving, one cheek flattened to the ground and little clouds of dust puffing up with each exhalation of his labored breathing. Mac hovered over him, fighting to catch his own wind, hoping like hell the fool would stay down.

"That's enough. Don't hit him anymore." Frank Barnstable's voice was quiet and sounded strained yet was still commanding.

Mac turned his head and looked at him. Barnstable sat very rigid in his saddle, eyes fixed on his battered son. His expression was flat, unreadable. Without shifting his gaze, he said quietly to Leo, "Go help your brother to his feet."

Leo slipped from his saddle and hurried to do as bid. He stepped wide around Mac, eyeing him with a mix of wariness and displeasure. After dropping to one knee beside Brad, he got a grip under his shoulders and lifted him to a sitting position. Brad's head lolled for a moment, but then his face lifted. He blinked, starting to come out of his daze, and his breathing began to level off some. Leo spoke to him in a low, encouraging tone.

Abruptly, Sara stepped forward. She reached to seize a canteen that lay on the buggy seat beside her father. Looking up at him, she said, "This *is* water, isn't it?"

Hardwick blinked innocently. "This early in the day, what else would it be?" He paused and shrugged. "Well, there might be a little touch of pick-me-up added in."

All the same, Sara took the canteen and handed it to Leo, saying, "Here, give him a sip of this. Careful with it, though."

Brad took a couple sips, coughed a bit, then gulped another swallow. His eyes seemed to brighten, and he sat up a little straighter. Leo handed the canteen back to Sara with a grateful nod. Then he helped his brother the rest of the way to his feet, and they started back to their horses. Brad walked with increasingly steadier steps, though he leaned on Leo some and kept one arm hugged to his left side, where Mac had landed a blow to the ribs.

Everyone continued to watch silently as Leo helped Brad back onto his horse, stooped to retrieve the gun that had been tossed to the ground, and stuffed it in his waistband before swinging once more into his own saddle.

When both of his sons were mounted, Frank Barnstable said quietly to them, "You boys go on back home now. Brad, have your ma tend your cuts and have a look at those ribs. I'll be along in a spell."

As the brothers rode off, Barnstable's gaze made a slow sweep over the Box H crew now spread before him. His eyes paused for a brief tick on Mac, then came to rest on Hardwick.

"Apologies don't come easy to me, Hannibal. I expect you can relate to that," he stated in a flat, clear tone. "But what happened here this morning . . . I regret. I particularly regret my part in it, in not taking time to get my facts straight before throwing blame around."

"Mistakes get made, Frank. The only difference is, it gets harder and harder for old mossbacks like us to admit 'em," Hardwick replied.

Barnstable's mouth stretched in a grimace. "A little bit ago I called my boys rambunctious. That's the excuse their mother and I have been making for the past few years." He shook his head. "Too long. I see now it's an excuse that's gotten out of hand. Some changes need to be made."

Hardwick met his grimace with a crooked smile. "Changes are always happenin', and more are usually always needed, Frank. Like you said at the outset, we ain't never been overly close, but we've been neighbors for a long time. This mornin's bruises to body and pride will fade, and then neighbors is what I reckon we'll go on bein'."

"Fair enough." Barnstable gave a curt nod and almost managed a hint of a smile, too. "I'll be seeing you around."

After the rancher had wheeled his Appaloosa and ridden off, Sara stepped up beside Mac and held out her father's canteen. "Could you use a pick-me-up?"

Mac arched a brow skeptically. "If that's got some of your pa's home brew in it, it might be more of a knock-me-down."

"You just won a knock-down, drag-out fight, but you're scared of a stiff drink?" Sara said impishly.

"Fella's got to know his limitations."

Sara's expression turned stern. "Seriously. Are you okay?"

"From the fight, you mean?" Mac shrugged. "I kind of have to be, don't I? Like you just said . . . I won."

Moving up close behind them, Squint said in a gruff tone, "Good to hear. That settles it, then. If you're okay . . . and if you're done showin' off for your girl and the rest of us . . . we've got brandin' to get on with."

"All right, grumpy. Lead the way. I'm right behind you," Mac assured him.

As they turned and headed for the holding area, Hardwick called after them, "Don't forget about them prairie oysters!"

Chapter 29

Otis Bradley was experiencing a curious mix of emotions. During the course of the day, as he'd helped Squint and the others with the branding and additional chores around the Box H, he'd actually found himself feeling reasonably comfortable and almost like he was fitting in a little bit. Certainly better than his previous fit, when he'd tried to pass himself off as a cook. It wasn't that he had a lot of experience as a ranch hand, either, but he was strong and he'd always been pretty good with his hands, so getting the hang of the chores Squint gave him to do wasn't hard, and he seemed to get them done satisfactorily.

In a cockeyed kind of way, the morning confrontation with the neighbor Barnstable and his two sons had also worked in Otis's favor. Him being on hand to stand *with* the Double T crew against a belligerent outsider, even though his role had been little more than that of a silent bystander, somehow had seemed to bring him a little more fully into the group. Even the perpetually sullen Larabee had treated him somewhat better afterward—which was to say he had ignored him rather than grunting and bitching at him every chance he got.

Not that any of the others had shown signs of treating him as a backslapping buddy just yet. Basically, they had tolerated him and spoken to him civilly when it was necessary. The main exception was Mackenzie, the new cook and newest member of the crew. It was partly this, Otis guessed—that is, Mac's own newness, meaning he wasn't yet a full veteran of the group, either, although he appeared quite popular—that made him a bit friendlier and more open than the rest. Still, even he had shown signs of restraint.

All in all, as the day drew toward a close, Otis felt it had gone as well or better than expected. He'd wangled his way back in and served his purpose by finding out what he'd been sent to learn. Now would come the next phase. Passing the information on to Stack and then . . .

Otis didn't know *what then*. Increasing concern over what it might be had been taking the edge off all that had gone well during the day. Ever since he'd heard that Castle had deposited the cash from his money belt in a Broken Spoke bank, Otis had been worried how Stack would react to the news. Even though the gang had talked about being experienced bank robbers, they'd also spoken of their most recent attempt at it turning bad. Having the "easy grab" of taking twenty thousand dollars from a handful of cowhands now suddenly turn into another bank job in order to get at it . . . Otis dreaded the thought of what the reaction to that would be.

No matter, he'd be right in the middle.

Otis's mind churned as he tried to imagine what alternative plan Stack might come up with. No chance in hell he'd simply ride away and consider it a prospect gone sour. Most likely, he'd want to go for the bank. And Otis would be dragged along. Making him not only an outlaw but also a bank robber—the most fiercely hunted and, when caught, the most harshly punished of all lawbreakers.

Otis could barely suppress an audible groan. Once again, he told himself he wasn't cut out to be an outlaw. And once again, he reminded himself that, regardless, he was getting pulled deeper and deeper in.

Damn.

He was scheduled to meet with Stack later tonight. From there, Otis had a sinking feeling this whole thing was only going to get worse. . . .

With the shadows of late afternoon starting to thicken within the grove of trees just off the base of the hogback, Stack Ketchum and his men began to feel some relief from the day's heat. They were also experiencing a growing sense of restlessness.

"Otis has only been at that ranch for a night and a day," Jack Needham was saying as he absently swirled the last quarter inch of tepid coffee in the tin cup he was holding. "You think that's enough time for him to have found out where the trail boss is keeping the money?"

"A night and a day?" echoed Ed Story from where he was leaning against a tree trunk, with his hat tipped down over his eyes. Thumbing the brim of the hat back and sitting up straighter, he added, "I swear, it seems like we've been holed up in this baked-over corner of stinkin' Arizona for at least *a week* and a day!"

Ignoring Story's lament, Ketchum responded to Needham, saying, "Yeah, I think there's a good chance Otis will have found out something useful. He's got some slickness to him. If he didn't, he wouldn't have been able to wheedle his way back in with that Double T bunch to begin with."

"Yeah, I got to give him that," Needham allowed. "I'll give him credit for guts, too, to go in attempting to run that bluff you and him put together."

Jesus Del Sol gave a disdainful grunt. "You could call it guts, I guess. Or you could look at it as Otis being more afraid of saying no to Stack and the rest of us than of going back to face his old pals. Ain't any of you ever seen his eyes when he thinks nobody is looking? He's been practically scared to death being in the company of hardcase hombres like us ever since Stack brought him back from jail. I'm sorta surprised he ain't tried to jackrabbit away from us by now. But, then again, it's his fear holding him back, I reckon."

Ketchum frowned. "I don't know about that. Yeah, I suppose Otis is a mite skittish, starting to ride the long coulees for the first time. But as far as I can see, he's taken to it just fine. He'll be there for our meeting tonight, and I'm betting he'll have some worthwhile information."

"I hope you're right. This 'easy grab' is turning into a damnably long, drawn-out chase," pointed out Story. "It's about time for it to pay off and put some money in our hands."

"What time is it you're gonna meet with Otis?" Del Sol asked Ketchum.

"Between midnight and one in the morning. Out by the privy in back of the bunkhouse. That's when he'll get hit by a sudden need to go answer nature's call. When he's sure the coast is clear and nobody's paying attention, he'll signal me."

Story chuckled and then remarked sarcastically, "Ah,

the romantic life and bold adventures of a Wild West outlaw. Funny, though, in all those dime novels about Billy the Kid and Jesse James, I don't recall ever reading about any midnight rendezvous behind some outhouse somewhere."

"Maybe I should send you ahead to stand lookout from *inside* the privy."

Story shrugged. "Go ahead. It couldn't be worse than having to squat in the weeds out here in rattlesnake heaven. I never figured on living forever, but I'd kinda like to go out in a bigger blaze of glory than getting nailed by a rattler while I was—"

"Knock it off," Ketchum growled. "I swear to God, Ed, if money could be made off griping and complaining, you'd be richer than some A-rab sultan with so many diamonds and rubies on hand that he tucks the spare ones in the belly buttons of all his wives."

"That'd be all right," Story allowed. "But right now, for starters, I'd settle for my share of that twenty thousand."

Creo Davies claimed to be a descendant of the French pirate Jean Lafitte, most famous, at least in the States, for aiding Andy Jackson in turning back the British at the Battle of New Orleans. In the citywide revelry that followed this victory, Lafitte had a one-night dalliance with a married Cajun belle, alleged to be Creo's grandmother. Brief though the dalliance was, according to entries found in a secret diary discovered after the aged belle's passing, it resulted in a pregnancy that traced down to Creo.

With no further verification than those obscure diary

entries, Creo's mother—a woman whose bad luck with men and life in general left her despondent and worn down and old before her time—had clung fervently to a belief in this familial connection to fame and notoriety. She passed it on so convincingly to Creo that he had embraced it boldly and loudly for as far back as anyone could remember. And as he'd grown to manhood and gained his own notoriety as a ruthless bandit while scouring the border regions of northern Mexico and southern Arizona and New Mexico, anyone harboring doubt about his heritage had learned to keep quiet about it if they valued their life.

So enamored was Creo of his pirate bloodline that he displayed trappings in his daily attire of what he imagined a privateer from early in the century looked like. This included a wide silk sash, bloodred in color, worn around his waist. A low-slung gun belt was buckled over this, but it did little to detract from the prominence of the sash or the bejeweled handle of a dagger thrusting up from within its folds. Additionally, he wore a gold hoop earring in one ear and a tight-fitting head wrap, also of bloodred silk, with its knotted tails dangling down the back of his neck from under a wide-brimmed sombrero.

This was the apparition before Preston McCall now, slouched casually in a plushly cushioned armchair in a select, well-appointed private chamber of Miss Fran's establishment. As a recurring customer and a man of prominence in the area, McCall was afforded specific accommodations when arranged in advance.

For his part tonight, he was dressed far less colorfully than the man he was meeting with, though a crisp, precisely tailored business suit of slate gray presented his status well enough. Like Creo, he occupied a plush chair, and both men were enjoying frequent pulls from glasses of fine brandy in between puffs on aromatic, top-quality cigars, all provided courtesy of the house.

Across the room, leaning against the wall and looking on silently and somewhat forlornly, stood the man called O'Leary, the lone survivor of the Grimsby rustling gang, which had been hitting ranches in the area for some months.

"I gotta tell you, McCall," Creo was saying as he blew a fat smoke ring from his cigar, "that meeting directly with you is a whole lot better than the powwows I used to have with Grimsby. When him and me got together, it was usually in some dusty canyon or on a sun-blistered slab of rock out in the middle of nowhere. Now this"—he made a circling motion with his cigar to indicate their surroundings—"is a lot more like it."

"During the late war," McCall replied, "I quite had my fill of meetings and strategy sessions in conditions not too dissimilar to what you describe. Often with bullets and cannonballs filling the air close by. Too close. When I put that behind me, I vowed to make the change as thorough as possible."

"Yeah, I heard you was an ex-military man." Creo smiled slyly. "In my line, I've done a fair piece of business with bullets flying through the air around me, too. But never cannonballs. Don't sound like something a fella ought to be sorry for missing out on."

"No. Indeed not." McCall took a sip of his brandy. "Your line of work, as you might have guessed, is what I asked you here to discuss."

"I was hoping so," Creo admitted. "When I heard what happened to Grimsby and his men, all except for O'Leary here, I was naturally sorry for them. But then, to be honest, I was also sorry for myself and my men. Sorry for the business I thought would no longer be available. When O'Leary showed up to say you wanted to have this meeting with me, however, I took that as a sign that perhaps not all was lost."

"In fact," McCall told him, "not only is nothing lost, business-wise, that is, but if you are open to what I'm about to offer, then there is more to gain."

Creo made a gesture with his cigar. "By all means continue."

McCall took an unhurried sip of his brandy and then laid out his plan in quick, concise details. These included his idea for Creo and his men to handle things on both sides of the border and to increase the size of the raids, taking larger quantities of cattle each time. The bandit's eyes grew brighter the more McCall talked, and especially bright when he mentioned the first target, the Box H spread, having between five and six hundred head ready to be driven off.

When McCall was done, Creo leaned back deep in his chair and said, "I am very interested in what you are proposing. Up until now I have not crossed the border into this area, because Grimsby was already at work here, and because he and you had the wisdom to involve me for the part that needed to be done south of the Rio Grande."

"But you *are* willing to work this side of the border, aren't you?"

"*Sí*. I have many times, in other places. But only where it suited me because the opportunity was worth the risk."

"That's understandable. I feel the same." McCall steepled his fingers. "What I bring to this operation—while you and Grimsby have done the physical parts, the riding and wrangling—is to minimize the risk by having my finger on the pulse of the area. I closely monitor what the local law is thinking. I can report when attention is particularly heightened. I know which ranches are most strongly guarded, which ones are more vulnerable, where pockets of prime beef are bunched and ready to be plucked. I've even paid off a few individuals to look the other way at key moments. And my bank serves to discreetly turn payments made by the dons in pesos or raw gold into more widely accepted and easier to spend U.S. dollars."

Creo gave a faint nod. "I'm well aware of the role you play in all of this. I'm also aware that you take a healthy percent of the profits—more than half—for your trouble."

"I'm not in the habit or the mood to haggle," McCall stated. "I don't know what Grimsby might have told you, but the fact of the matter is that I gave him thirty-five percent of whatever sales you negotiated with the dons. How you and he split that, I never knew or cared."

"Let's just say it was agreeable to each of us."

"Uh-huh. And it was you who set the selling price with the buyers."

Creo's eyebrows pinched together. "Are you suggesting I somehow shaded the price in my favor?"

They locked eyes for a long beat. Until a corner of McCall's mouth quirked upward. "If you didn't, you wouldn't be worth the pirate blood you claim runs in your veins. In your place, I sure as hell would have. Two or three cents difference per head, sliding your direction ahead of the balance dropping into the pile set to be divvied three ways . . . could add up to a nice extra profit in time."

Creo continued to aim an uncertain frown his way, saying, "Sounds like you might have some pirate blood running in you, too, banker man."

"Wouldn't surprise me," McCall conceded. "So, one

pirate to another, here's my offer. Forty percent to you from a per-head selling price that I set the bottom limit on. You make a deal for anything over that, you keep the difference in addition to your forty percent and no skin off my nose."

The uncertainty faded from Creo's face. "It sounds to me like two pirates just reached an agreement."

At that, O'Leary, who had been standing silently off to one side, pushed away from the wall and took a step closer. "Wait a minute. Where is that supposed to leave me?"

Creo rose smoothly from his chair. McCall remained seated but turned his head, looking clearly displeased at the interruption. "What kind of question is that? Where do you expect this matter should leave you?"

All at once O'Leary's posture seemed to freeze in an awkward way and his eyes became those of somebody who suddenly regretted something he had just said or done.

"All I meant . . . er, mean . . . is that I'm wondering what, uh, kind of spot there's gonna be for me in this new operation? Certainly, meaning no disrespect to your outfit, Creo, but I don't see how I'd fit very good riding with you and your boys on account of, well, most of 'em speak the Mexican lingo . . . and, uh, I don't. Not hardly at all."

Creo nodded sagely. "*Sí*, O'Leary, I also share a concern for your treatment going forward."

"You do?"

"*Sí*. Though my concern has nothing to do with a language problem. For me, it is more a matter of trust and superstition." Creo glanced briefly over at McCall before continuing. "You see, I have a superstition about riding with anyone who has the mark of a loser—either all on their own or as part of a group. What's more, I've always had trouble trusting anyone who somehow manages to emerge as the lone survivor of a conflict that claims the lives of all others."

O'Leary's face flushed with anger, and he took another step forward. "Now wait a minute! I was left behind to watch over the cattle herd while Grimsby and the others went to spring their ambush. I was nearly two miles away when those Texans snuck up on 'em from behind. It was all over before I even understood what happened. Only sensible thing for me to do then was to take off in order to save my own skin. You believe me, don't you, Mr. McCall?"

After taking an unhurried puff of his cigar, McCall responded, "Never had reason not to. But then, Grimsby was the one, not me, who always dealt with you. And as for this current issue between you and Creo—which you brought on yourself—it appears once again to be something I am not a part of."

"Well, that's a hell of a thing!" O'Leary exclaimed. "I rode for you all these past months, along with Grimsby and the rest, doing your dirty work and living hidden away between jobs like a bunch of lepers or something. And now, just as soon as things take a bad turn, you're ready to toss me aside and hand everything over to this . . . this—"

Creo cut him off, saying in an icy tone, "Choose your next words very carefully, amigo . . . else they be your last."

But O'Leary was too angered to take heed either of the warning or of the fact that Creo had glided up directly in front of him. In fact, when he responded by snarling, "How about you kiss my backside, you phony pirate!" their faces were close enough that the spittle spraying with his words made Creo blink.

Unfortunately for O'Leary, that wasn't Creo's only reaction. In mid-blink, the bandit leader's right hand blurred in a series of well-practiced lightning-fast moves. It reached across his waist, seized the bejeweled handle of the dagger carried in his sash, pulled it free, and then made an upward thrust that plunged the wickedly pointed tip straight into O'Leary's heart.

O'Leary's mouth opened and closed, but no sound came out. His eyes widened with surprise and a moment of pain. But only a moment. He was dead that fast. As soon as Creo pulled back the dagger, his victim crumpled to the floor, a lifeless heap.

Creo leaned over long enough to wipe clean his blade on O'Leary's shirtsleeve. Then, straightening up and returning the dagger to his sash, he looked over at McCall.

"I regret having to do that. I hope you agree he was a man of little value."

"I suppose." Still in his chair, McCall gave an indifferent shrug. "Same can't be said for the carpet he's bleeding all over, though. Comes to facing Miss Fran about that . . . you're on your own, amigo."

Chapter 30

Mac had fixed another hearty but basic supper that evening at the Box H. Boiled potatoes, greens, and ham hocks. From the cattle castrating done earlier in the day, he had taken the removed testicles and also made a batch of prairie oysters, which he had served in a large wooden bowl, with a cup of hot sauce on the side. Hardwick had wasted no time digging in and had been almost as quick to heap praise on Mac for how good they were. Squint and Larabee had also partaken of some. Mac probably would have, too, except they were mostly gone by the time he'd sat down at the table—not to mention his wanting to avoid the disapproving scowl he'd seen Sara aim at the others.

Due to this request of her father's being included in the meal, Sara had been unavailable for most of the meal preparation. She'd helped serve it, however, steering wide of the bowl of oysters, and then had remained to help with the cleanup afterward.

It was while she and Mac were washing and drying the dishes that she said, "I suppose I owe you an apology for skirting my duties earlier and not showing up for my cooking lesson."

Mac shook his head. "I got no apologies coming. I agreed to show you and your sister what I could if and when you were available. In case nobody's noticed, she ain't hardly been available at all. But you have. You've taken a genuine interest, and you've caught on quick to a lot of things. So when you didn't come around earlier, I just figured you must've had something more important to—"

"Oh, pooh! Quit making excuses for me," Sara said. "You know darn well I skipped helping you with tonight's cooking because of those stupid oysters. And what difference did it make? You made them, and everybody ate them, anyway. I guess Pa was right when he said he had a couple of offspring who are nothing but delicate little flowers."

"I've seen both you and Tara ride and rope and even shoot," Mac replied. "You're all woman, Sara, and a woman ought to have some delicateness to her. But there's a lot more to you than just that."

Suddenly Mac was once again aware of the warmth of Sara's shoulder touching his. And when he looked over at her, she was gazing up at him with a look in her eyes like he hadn't seen before. "Did you really mean that, Mac? Do you really see me as a woman?" she wanted to know.

All of a sudden Mac felt the need to swallow, and when he did, his Adam's apple seemed to have grown to the size of a saddle horn.

"Well, of course I see you as a woman, Sara," he said, a touch of huskiness in his voice. "How could I help it?

Not just a woman, but—as if you didn't know—an almighty fine and pretty one."

Spots of color appeared on each of Sara's cheeks. "I guess I know I'm pretty. Folks have been saying that about me and Tara for a long time. And being told you're attractive and shapely and so on, that's nice . . . But it ain't the same as knowing a man sees you as a woman."

Mac had no idea how he should respond to that, so he said nothing and just kept scrubbing harder at a burnt-on spot he was trying to get off the pan he was washing.

But Sara wasn't ready to let up. She said, "Earlier today, after you fought Brad, your friend Squint made a remark about 'showing off for your girl.' Why did he say that?"

"How in blazes am I supposed to know? Surely you've seen how fellas in a wrangling crew like to needle each other a little whenever they get the chance. Mostly in a good-natured way. I guess Squint was doing that, trying to embarrass me. But I hope you don't think he said what he did due to me making some kind of improper claim about you and me around the bunkhouse or some such."

"No, I know you wouldn't do something like that." Sara kept gazing at him in that bright, probing way. "But would the notion of having folks think I'm 'your girl' be such a bad thing?"

Mac stopped his scrubbing and met her gaze. "Certainly not, Sara. Any fella with eyes and a brain and red blood running through his veins would just about bust with pride to have you for his girl . . . But if that same fella had a measure of honor and decency in him, then he oughta figure he should also have something more he could offer a girl like you before he had any right to try and push himself on her."

"If the girl felt the right way about the fella, then it wouldn't take much pushing," Sara countered. "And a man and a woman caring for each other strongly enough could build 'something more' together . . . like my ma and pa did right here, to make the Box H."

Once again, Mac didn't know what to say.

And once again, Sara wasn't ready to let up. "I know there's a lot else going on right now that needs attention. The rustling trouble, the hard cases supposedly on their way to try and rob the Double T money, your outfit needing to get on back to Texas . . . But none of that is any call to try and hold back feelings or to not speak out about them. You *are* a man of honor and decency, Dewey Mackenzie. I could see that right off. Almost as fast, I began feeling a fondness for you. And if that isn't plain enough, you lunkhead, I'm saying that all you have to do is push just a little bit for the sake of my pride and I would welcome being called your girl."

On his way back to Broken Spoke under a cloudless night sky, just outside the city limits, Preston McCall saw a lone rider appear in a pool of moonlight on the trail ahead. The banker's immediate reaction was to slow the pace of his horse and slip one hand under the lapel of his jacket to the revolver resting in its shoulder holster there. A moment later, however, he recognized the features of the rider and the deputy's badge on his chest glinting in the moonlight. McCall relaxed.

"Evenin', Colonel," greeted Virg Lamont.

The two men closed the distance between them and then reined in their horses.

"Looks like my timing was pretty good for catching

your return from Miss Fran's. I won't ask all the details of your visit. Some things are strictly personal, right?" Virg showed his teeth in a knowing smirk. "But I reckon the meet with Creo is as much my business as anybody's. So how did it go?"

"It went all right. Pretty much as expected," McCall responded. "One minor snag, though. Creo and O'Leary got their hackles up with one another. O'Leary is no longer with us."

Virg's smirk went away. "Damn. Bad enough the toll those Texans took, we're being kinda hard on the hired help ourselves lately, ain't we? First, I finish the job on Grimsby, and now you're telling me that O'Leary, the only one of our old crew who was left, has bit the dust, too."

"It was unexpected and unfortunate," allowed McCall, frowning. "But nothing all that major. The more important thing is that Creo is keen to take on a bigger role in the expanded rustling raids. So keen, in fact, he claims he can have the necessary force of men ready to hit the Box H by tomorrow night."

Virg let out a low, impressed whistle. "That's moving mighty fast."

"Things *are* moving fast, Virg. Faster and better than we dared hope." McCall's eyes gleamed with excitement in the murky light. "A big raid first thing tomorrow night, on top of the unexpected windfall of a deposit in my bank by that Double T trail boss, combined with what we've already accumulated . . . Man, I'm starting to wonder if holding out for the start of those railroad payroll deposits is even necessary."

Virg's jaw dropped. "Are you serious?"

"I don't know." McCall dragged a palm down over his face and then repeated, "I don't know. But, like I said, it's got me wondering. Thinking . . . You remember, during the war, how there were times when we'd go into battle with the most meticulously laid-out plans? Only then, once the fighting was actually underway, all or part of those plans—for no clear reason—would somehow start to feel wrong."

"I wasn't involved in a whole lot of high-level planning, Colonel," Virg reminded him.

"Well, I was. Take it from me." McCall scowled. "Usually I followed orders, stuck to the plan. A couple of times, though, when my gut feeling got too strong, I decided on another course. And each of those times I avoided disaster that would have cost many lives for our side, likely including my own."

"I'm glad if it worked out for the best," Virg said. "But I, uh, I'm not sure I follow what it's got to do with our situation here in Broken Spoke."

"It's my gut feeling, Virg," McCall explained. "We've had our plan in place here for some time. It's been solid, and we've stuck to it up to now. But these recent developments . . . the big deposit from the trail boss, my new idea about larger rustling raids . . . you see how they might signal that it's time to alter our plan some? The risk of us getting found out increases the longer we keep at it, while the added gain of waiting for a railroad deposit grows less important. It's a fact worth considering that greed, not accepting when enough is enough, has brought about the downfall of operations like ours more than any other factor."

Virg cocked his head to one side. "Are you saying you think it's time we settle for what we got, tighten our cinches, and ride on?"

"That's the feeling taking stronger hold in me, yes," McCall told him. "Especially with the addition of that

Texan's deposit, we've amassed a tidy sum during our time here, Virg. It would hardly be a paltry settlement. On the Sonoran coast it would enable us to live quite handsomely."

"What we've been aiming for, right?"

McCall sighed. "But since the big raid by Creo is already set in motion, we naturally need to wait and see how that pans out. Afterwards, I suggest we step back, give some hard consideration to where we stand, and then make a decision on how we proceed. What say you?"

"We been talking about the Sea of Cortez for a long time," Virg replied. "You give the word, I say I'm ready to go have a look, Colonel."

"A bank! How the hell did that trail boss's money end up in a bank?" wailed Ed Story.

The flickering glow of the campfire cast shifting patterns of light and shadow across Stack Ketchum's face, making his glare look all the more menacing.

"I know you ain't ever had much experience putting money *in* a bank, Ed," he growled, "but the way it gets there is that some folks do a thing called making a deposit. It gives 'em peace of mind believing their money is safer in a bank vault than being carried around in their pocket or in a glass jar buried in the backyard."

"Very funny," Story grunted. "But the joke's on them, considerin' how there's always the chance of scoundrels like us around. Right? That's why you'll never catch me handin' over my cold, hard cash to somebody else for the takin' care of."

"That still don't explain why, though," said Jack Needham with a puzzled frown. "In the case of this trail boss, this Castle character, I mean. After hauling cash in a money belt all the way from California, what made him all of a sudden decide to slap it in a bank clear out here in Nowhere, Arizona?"

"Far as Otis could find out, he never really gave much of a reason," said Ketchum, squatting down to pour himself some bitter brew from the coffeepot that had been simmering on the edge of the coals while he and Del Sol had been gone for the behind-the-privy meet at the Box H. "Otis reckons that since the Double T men decided to stick around and help the old man and his daughters, Castle must have figured it was smarter to put the cash in the bank rather than to keep carrying it on him. Especially since he's currently off heading a small trail drive to deliver some Box H beef to the incoming rail spur crew."

"Speaking of Otis—where is he?" asked Red. "Since he found out what you sent him in for, why didn't you bring him back with you?"

"Because with everything shifting around the way it has been, I decided it was better to leave him in place so he could report in case something else takes an unexpected turn." Ketchum paused to try a sip of the coffee he'd poured. He made a face but then went ahead and drank some more, anyway. "Besides, we got no better need for him. Not right now. After tomorrow will be another matter."

"What's gonna happen after tomorrow?" Story wanted to know.

"Simple." Ketchum took another drink of the grimace-inducing coffee. "First, we're gonna spend a chunk of tomorrow scoping out the town of Broken Spoke and its bank. Then, unless we see something that's a real show-stopper, we'll reel Otis back in tomorrow night, and bright and early the following morning we're gonna hit that bank."

Story groaned. "We came all this way for an 'easy grab' . . . and now it's turned into a grab from a damn bank?"

Del Sol spoke for the first time since he and Ketchum had gotten back to the campsite. "We're the kind of scoundrels who do that sort of thing. Remember?" he remarked dryly.

"Yeah, I remember," Story snapped back. "I also remember a bank in a place called San Berdoo. Way I recall, that worked out about as lousy as anything we ever tried."

"Ain't none of us can argue against that," allowed Needham. "But neither can you argue, Ed, how we hit other banks in the past and had some pretty good luck. Yeah, plenty went wrong at Berdoo—we lost two good men, and our haul was pitiful. But this time we'd be going in knowing that, at the very least, there's twenty thousand waiting in the pot."

"Plus, whatever else the local businessmen and other ranchers have tossed in," added Ketchum. "No, it ain't the grab we came after. But it's what's in front of us now, and it ain't necessarily bad. The added difficulty should be balanced out by the added take."

"If there ain't *too much* added difficulty."

"That's what we'll determine when we scope things out tomorrow." Ketchum scowled. "Come on, Ed. You know how this works. Have I ever asked anybody to stick their necks out if the setup looks in advance like a bad deal? Mine will be on the line, too. You said yourself, we came all this way. You telling me you're ready to turn your back on it just because some pissant bank in a dust bucket of a town is now part of the picture?"

Story hung his head for a minute. When he lifted his

face, his eyes were blazing in the reflected campfire flames. "No. I ain't ready for that, not by a damn sight. Thinking about that Berdoo job got me a little overcautious for a minute, but I'm okay now. Let's have a look at that dust bucket tomorrow and come up with a plan for busting their lousy bank wide open!"

Chapter 31

The following day at the Box H began with another round of basic chores and previously neglected repairs. In the middle of the morning, Doc Washburn came by to examine Hardwick's leg. When he was done, he put on a fresh dressing and pronounced the wound to be healing well enough so it wouldn't be necessary for him to return unless summoned due to a serious change. As he had other outlying patients to call on, the medic lingered only long enough for a cup of coffee and then was on his way.

Toward noon, everybody's attention became focused on the corral where a handful of unbroken horses had been gathered from the Hardwicks' remuda. Boyd Lewis, in Castle's absence the best bronc stomper on the Double T crew, had decided it was time to ride the rough off a few of the ornery cusses. With Squint and Larabee helping to single out the ones he wanted to try, he was bent on showing who was boss.

In their time, the two oldsters had each broken their

own share of broncs, but too many years and too many fractures and torn muscles had brought acceptance that these days riding the hurricane deck was better left to youngsters with their bones and gizzards still intact.

Once again Hardwick was looking on from the seat of his buggy, which was parked near the corral rail. Mac and Sara, who would have to be going inside soon to work up a noon meal, were leaning on the rail, also looking on for the time being. Over in the doorway of the horse barn, Otis was mending tack but keeping an interested eye on Boyd's progress, as well.

They all watched as Boyd fought to stay astride a bucking, whirling, snorting steeldust determined to unseat him.

"Stick with 'im, Boyd!"

"Ride 'im down! Give 'im what fer!"

The encouraging shouts coming from Squint and Larabee rang with so much exuberance that anybody looking on who didn't know better might think they'd never been part of such activity before.

At the rail beside Mac, Sara said, "How about you, cowboy? You going to do some bronco busting?"

Mac lifted his eyebrows. "Can't say it's something I had any plans for."

"Not even to show off some more for your girl?"

Mac's eyes darted to Sara's father, a short distance away. But Hardwick was concentrating so hard on what was going on inside the corral that he hadn't overheard the question. Mac lowered his voice to reply, "We ain't gonna start that again, are we? Especially not here."

Sara grinned impishly. "What's the matter with right here? Besides, it's already started. Did you forget about that kiss?"

Last evening, when the dishes were done and put away

and Mac and Sara had been preparing to part for the night, she'd suddenly thrown her arms around his neck and planted a warm, sweet kiss on his lips. And no, Mac certainly hadn't forgot about it, not for one second since.

In answer to Sara's question concerning it now, he admitted as much while still keeping his voice low. "Not hardly. You sure know how to mess with a fella getting a decent night's sleep."

The impishness leaving her expression, she said, "It works both ways, in case you'd like to know."

Once again, Mac would have had trouble coming up with a response, but he was saved from needing to try by the commotion as Boyd suddenly lost his battle to stay on the steeldust. He sailed through the air, arms and legs flailing, then hit the ground hard. As he rolled through the dirt, the steeldust scampered away, kicking its heels high and emitting a throaty sound that might have passed for a horse laugh.

Squint and Larabee hurried to the fallen man and hovered close, partly to prepare to help him back to his feet and partly to make sure the horse didn't come trotting back around to display its annoyance, the way some rank critters were known to do. But the steeldust seemed content to stay on the far side of the corral and just strut somewhat haughtily back and forth.

"Is he okay?" Hardwick called from his buggy.

"There's a few places on him right at the moment I expect smart some," Larabee called back. "But give him a minute to catch his breath, and yeah, he'll be okay."

"Dang right I'll be okay," Boyd grunted as the two oldsters pulled him up by his arms. "Soon as I get my wind back, I'll be okay enough to climb on that hammerhead again, and this time I aim to take the sassiness outta that strut of his."

"That's a real spirited outlook, son, and I'm proud of you for it," said Squint. But as he was speaking, his gaze was drawn off by something to the north. After a moment, this caused him to add, "But you might have to put it off for a bit. Appears we got company comin'. And unless I'm mistaken—which I ain't, on account of I been watchin' Castle sit a saddle for a long time now—it's him, Red, and Miss Tara returnin' from deliverin' those cattle."

The others turned their heads and looked in the same direction as Squint. They saw that, sure enough, those he'd named were approaching along the edge of the main herd, which was scattered across the nearby grassland.

"Tarnation!" exclaimed Hardwick. "They made mighty good time."

Nobody said anything more until the trio had closed the remaining distance and reined up alongside the corral. The horses were blowing hard; the riders were dusty and weary looking but smiling, clearly relieved to be back home. Squint, Larabee, and Boyd had come over to lean on the corral rail opposite Mac, Sara, and Hardwick up in his buggy. They, too, were smiling. Only Otis, who stayed in the barn doorway, looked on without expression.

"The railhead had reached closer than we figured," Castle explained, thumbing back the brim of his hat and sleeving a smear of sweat off his forehead. "We delivered their beef, took the payoff, and kinda pushed to get back as pronto as we could."

"*Kinda* pushed?" echoed Tara. "I had to keep looking back to make sure we weren't being chased by Indians or some such." There seemed more mischief in her tone than genuine annoyance.

"You made it safe. That's the main thing," declared Hardwick.

"Safe and with a little something to show for our trouble," Tara told him. She pulled a plump leather pouch from her saddlebags and tossed it to her father. "There's the price you agreed on. What's more, the buyer said ours was some of the best stock he's taken in so far, and to tell you he'd be coming around for more before too long."

Hardwick nodded. "That sounds good to these old ears."

"How about those hard cases Otis spoke of? Any trouble while we been away?" Red wanted to know.

"No. No trouble from those hard cases," Larabee answered. "Which ain't to say we didn't still have a few touches of excitement, though."

"How's that?" said Castle.

"Well, let's see now," Larabee drawled, running his fingers through the whiskers along the underside of his jaw. "Yesterday, young Mac there took a strange notion he had too much meat on his knuckles, so he went to work skinnin' some of it off on the jaw and teeth of a neighbor fella who was obligin' enough to stop by for a visit. And then, just a little bit ago, ol' Boyd here up and decided he wanted to learn how to fly. He got off to a pretty good start, too, launchin' hisself from the back of that steeldust prancin' around over yonder. Just before Squint spotted you folks ridin' in, Boyd was sayin' how he was hankerin' to get in some more practice on stayin' up a little longer. Seems you're lucky to be in time for more of the show."

Twisting his mouth wryly, Boyd responded, "Very funny, you old buzzard. Maybe I oughta throw you up on the back of that steeldust and see if you can flap those scrawny arms of yours hard enough to stay in the air any longer."

"Wouldn't be no contest," Larabee scoffed. "If I clumb on that hammerhead, he'd right away just start walkin' around easy as pie. You see, I broke so many broncs when I was younger that word spread all through the horse ranks everywhere for no critter to even bother tryin' to throw me on account of I was certain to ride 'em down flat. If any saw me comin', they just naturally turned gentle without a fight. Sad to say, that took all the fun out of bronc bustin' for me and everybody else, man and horse alike. The only way I could save it was to spread new word amongst the nags that I was callin' an end to my bustin' days and lettin' things go back to the old, more challengin' ways."

When the old wrangler paused to take a breath, Castle was quick to remark, "Well, it's plain to see one thing. Certain folks sure didn't lose their knack for spinning whoppers while we were away."

Everybody shared in a good chuckle.

Then Mac said, "And my skinned knuckles haven't cost me the knack for working up a noon meal, either. Which I was fixing to go do when y'all rode up. Coming off a long haul on the trail, I expect you'd appreciate me getting on with that."

"Now you're talking my language," Red assured him.

"Fine as that sounds, Mac, I have to say that I want a hot bath even more," announced Tara. "Save me a thick sandwich for afterward, please, but first, I have to heat some water to soak away some all-over dust and more than a few aches in places I'll refrain from mentioning."

Red countered that with, "A wash of my hands and face is all I need to be ready to eat."

To which Castle said, "Reckon I see it about the same as Red." With a teasing little smile aimed toward Tara, he added, "We'll do our best to *try* and save you that sandwich, though."

Sara stepped over and took the reins of Tara's mount, saying, "Come on, sis. I'll help you heat the water and get a bath ready." Glancing back over her shoulder, she said to Mac, "I'll be in to help you in the kitchen as soon as I can."

Chapter 32

It was a very long afternoon for Otis Bradley.

On one hand, the return of Castle and the others from their trail drive was a welcome thing. It diminished the risk of them showing up later with a last-minute surprise or some new development that would require Otis having to get word to Stack Ketchum sooner than planned, in case the news was something that might require new consideration by the gang leader.

As it stood, Otis was scheduled to rejoin the gang sooner than he wanted to, anyway. Tonight after midnight he was to slip away once more, making a final break from the Double T crew, and meet with Stack and the others at their campsite. If their interim reconnoiter of the town of Broken Spoke and its bank had gone well, the tentative plan, as roughed out by Stack, was to head out from there at daybreak and rob the bank as soon as it opened in the morning.

With Otis in the thick of it.

Damn.

If Otis wasn't cut out to be an outlaw, he sure as shootin' wasn't ready to be a bank robber. The notion of that—and the possible repercussions—scared the hell out of him. The only thing that scared him worse was the thought of double-crossing Stack . . . and that human blood-hound Jesus Del Sol. If there was ever a crueler joke than naming that cold-eyed half-breed after the son of God, Otis shuddered to think what it might be.

The only thing that got him through the balance of the day without his anguish becoming obvious enough to draw attention was that his assigned task of mending tack kept him mostly apart from the others. It helped, too, that the rest of them all had their own chores. And much of their attention following lunch returned to bronc busting, with Castle and Boyd taking turns on the hurricane deck.

Glancing over at this activity from time to time, Otis couldn't help thinking how the struggle going on inside him—being tossed back and forth by regret and indecision—wasn't all that different. . . .

While Otis was going through his turmoil, elsewhere on the Box H spread, there were some spirits soaring considerably higher. Mac was brought up to date on this shortly after he and Sara started to prepare supper that evening.

"It's supposed to be a secret, but I'm going to bust if I don't tell somebody," Sara abruptly declared in the midst of peeling a pile of potatoes.

Mac gave her a dubious sidelong glance, then said, "Those taters will likely turn out better if you don't bust all over 'em, so I reckon you'd best go ahead and tell me what it is you're talking about."

Sara's eyes grew bright with excitement. "You don't have any idea? You haven't noticed anything different in the air this afternoon?"

"Can't say I have. It was blazing hot again, just like every other day in these parts."

"There's nothing different about that."

Mac frowned. "I just said so, didn't I? You're the one who was gonna bust if you didn't spill something . . . so now you're gonna make a riddle out of it?"

"Oh, all right." Sara tossed a quick glance over at the kitchen door, as if making sure no one was there. Then: "It's Tara and Castle. You haven't noticed anything about the way they're acting?"

Mac's frown grew puzzled. "Well, I've noticed 'em, yeah. I mean, how could I not? They're back. They're prancing around amongst us again. I don't understand what—"

"Boy, you can say that again," Sara declared, cutting him off. "You don't understand, because you're a man. If it ain't something to fight, shoot, or eat, then not one of you notice a blasted thing! I'm talking about the way Tara and Castle are acting *toward each other*. You haven't noticed that at all?"

Mac's puzzled look stayed in place.

Sara heaved an exasperated sigh. "What I'm telling you is that they've fallen for one another. In a romantic way. Is any of this sinking in?"

"Are you sure?" Mac asked.

"Very. I spotted it right away, and then, as soon as we were alone, I got Tara to admit it."

"Does Castle know?"

"What a question! Of course he knows," insisted Sara. "How much plainer do I have to say they have romantic feelings *for each other*? Like I said, I spotted it right off. When I questioned Tara about it, she tried to hem and haw a little at first, but as twins, we know each other too well. When she finally quit trying to dodge the question, she admitted everything, and I've seldom seen her happier. Are you sure Castle never indicated anything to you?"

Mac shook his head. "We haven't been around each other that much since he got back. Besides, him and me ain't really that close. If he said anything to anybody, it'd more likely be to Squint."

"He's probably keeping it a secret for now. Like Tara would have, too, if I hadn't pried it out of her."

"If they truly have those feelings, why the secrecy?"

"Since it all happened so sudden, they want to be a little surer between themselves before they broadcast it too much," Sara explained. "Also, as you're aware, there happens to be a few other things going on right now."

Mac took the time to choose his next words very carefully. "Did you, er, tell your sister about us?"

Sara shot him one of her penetrating looks. "*Is* there an us, Mac?"

He had to look away. "Doggone it, gal . . . You know there's something going on between us. There's been some things said, and . . . and that kiss last night was mighty special. Don't think for a minute I didn't want to throw my arms around you and not let it end . . . but like I told you from the first, I . . . I . . ."

She stopped her potato peeling and lifted one finger, then pressed it to his lips. "Never mind. Hearing you say you didn't want that kiss to end is enough for now. I can be patient. I know you think you don't have enough to offer me, which is ridiculous but at the same time kinda charming. So there's no rush, and no, I didn't say anything to Tara about us. Not yet. But in the meantime, it wouldn't be a bad idea for you to pay closer attention to Castle, and maybe some of his willingness to go along with his feelings will rub off on you."

Chapter 33

It was time. Actually, a little past time.

The midnight hour was nearly over, and though Otis lay listening to the variety of snores and rhythmic breathing that filled the bunkhouse shadows surrounding him, he hadn't slept a wink. Too many thoughts roiled inside his head. A prominently recurring one was the notion to go out and saddle up the fastest horse in the Box H remuda and ride it as hard and far as possible away from this whole mess.

But he knew he didn't have the guts to do that. He didn't have the guts to do anything but follow the plan Stack Ketchum had laid out for him. Follow Stack . . . and hope to hell it didn't ultimately lead to standing over a trapdoor with a hangman's noose around his neck.

Slowly, Otis sat up on the edge of his cot and pulled on his boots. Then, clad only in boots and baggy long johns, he shuffled quietly out the back door, as if headed for the privy. Outside, he paused to let his eyes adjust to the wash of star and moonlight and to listen for any sound of stirring behind him that might indicate his departure had drawn the attention of somebody. Satisfied at hearing nothing, though wanting to make extra sure, he went ahead and paid a brief visit to the outhouse.

Upon emerging from the shanty, he crossed to one side and stepped behind some thick bushes. Earlier, he had hidden a blanket-wrapped bundle of spare clothes and his personal belongings there. After quickly dressing the rest of the way and rewrapping the bundle to carry with him, Otis started toward the horse barn and the larger corral out back where the remuda of broken mounts milled.

He'd taken only a few steps, however, before he froze.

Something felt wrong. No one had followed him out of the bunkhouse, yet he was seized by a sense that he wasn't alone out here in the night. There were the nearby horses and cattle, of course, but this was something different. Something that didn't belong, something that somehow seemed . . . threatening.

Otis's gaze traveled in a wide, slow arc, starting with the main house, off to his left, and then wrapping around to his right, and ending at the bunkhouse as he craned his neck and looked back. Nothing. No movement, no sound anywhere within the shadows or splotches of deeper black or bands of silvery moonlight. But he still couldn't shake the uneasy sense of some other presence being out here with him.

Had Stack maybe come to fetch him back to the campsite? Eager for that to be the answer to whatever was increasingly spooking him, Otis was almost ready to call out an inquiring whisper.

And that was when he finally spotted movement. Lots

of movement. It was quite a way out, spread across the pasture beyond the far corrals and headed steadily closer. For a moment Otis thought it was a mass of cattle on the move, for some reason advancing toward the buildings. But that didn't make any sense. Also, they were being too quiet for that many cattle stirred into motion.

Suddenly, it quit being quiet.

It started with a single word, issued harshly, like a command. *"Fuego!"* Then the word was repeated, moving rapidly down a row of voices echoing it. And in conjunction with the spread of the word, pumpkin-sized balls of flame—lighted torches—began glaring to life in a line several yards long. In the flickering illumination thrown by those torches, Otis was able to make out the features of mounted men with their faces set in grim expressions.

Before he could overcome being stunned by this sight, another harsh command rang out, and the line of torch-bearing riders instantly broke into a charge at full gallop! Part of them veered toward the main house, part came straight forward, and the rest branched in the direction of the horse barn and corrals.

Otis found his voice, even though the cussword came out in a half-strangled squawk. Then, as he wheeled and began running back toward the bunkhouse, he hurled warning shouts strong and loud out ahead. "Wake up! Wake up! Fire! Wake up! We're under attack!"

Inside the bunkhouse, the Double T men were jarred awake by Otis's shouts. The unmistakable fear and panic in his voice made them quickly shed any grogginess. Feet hit the floor, and hands immediately filled with shooting irons.

Just as Otis burst back through the door, Red was striking a match and getting ready to light a coal oil lantern hanging on a nail. "No!" Otis warned. "Don't light that! Don't give away our—"

Before he could finish getting his words out, a shattering hail of gunfire came hammering against the outside of the bunkhouse, blasting out window glass and pounding puffs of dust and spraying needlelike splinters from the wood-framed adobe structure. The men who had only moments earlier clambered to their feet now threw themselves to the floor on their bellies and went elbow crawling to press against the wall that was being hammered. They squirmed frantically into positions below and beside the blown-out windows, cursing and gripping their guns in frustration, as more sizzling, slamming bullets poured in, keeping them momentarily pinned down.

"What the hell's going on, Otis?" demanded Castle. "Is that Stack Ketchum and his gang out there?"

"I don't know who they are," Otis hollered back. "But no, they ain't Ketchum's bunch! There's only a handful of them. That pack of banshees out there now, from what I saw, look to number three dozen or more!"

"He's right," reported Boyd after venturing a quick peek through a cracked window frame. "There's a whole mess of rascals out there. Thirty or forty, at least. They're hittin' like guerrilla raiders from back in the war years— up to and includin' bringin' along torches!"

"Yeah. When they started lighting their torches is when I first spotted 'em," Otis confirmed.

After bobbing up long enough to thrust his Remington muzzle over a windowsill and trigger off a round, Larabee dropped back and cackled, "There's one of the dirty so-and-sos who ain't gonna fling his torch our way!"

"Watch out, you old fool, or you ain't gonna be around to care *what* they do with their dang torches," Squint scolded him.

Bullets continued hammering the bunkhouse, but more and more of the Double T men were beginning to return fire, not making it so easy for the raiders to pop away without paying a price.

Mac had his Yellowboy propped next to him, but for the moment he was doing most of his shooting with the Model 3 handgun. It was easier to thrust it through an opening, fire, and pull back, as opposed to doing the same with a longer gun. And the raiders had moved close enough now to be obligingly within range.

"I don't know what all they got in mind, but some of those torchbearers are swinging toward the horse barn!" Mac called to no one in particular yet everyone.

"It's clear the dirty dogs got in mind to blast and burn everything in their path," declared Squint. "We probably can't save the horse barn, but we can damn sure save our own hides!"

He stroked the trigger of his long-barreled Colt, and one of the raiders who had ridden in close and was reaching back with one arm, getting ready to throw his torch at the bunkhouse, was knocked out of his saddle.

Gunsmoke was starting to roll chokingly thick inside the bunkhouse, and there was little letup from the slap and whine of incoming rounds. The roar of guns and the rumble of hoofbeats mingled with the shrieks of horses and the shouts and curses from men, creating a din so intense it almost had a physical impact of its own.

From his end of the bunkhouse, Boyd called, "There's more of those torch-swingin' devils branchin' out on this side, too! They're headed for the main house!"

Castle's head snapped around, and even in the smoky murkiness, his face showed instantly pale and tormented.

"The old man and the gals are ready for 'em, though," Boyd added excitedly. "I hear the crack of their guns, and there goes one of the raiders—no, make it two—bitin' the dust!"

By then, Mac had already pushed away from his window. Jamming the Model 3 back into his waistband and sweeping up his Yellowboy, he moved purposefully toward the bunkhouse exit that faced the main house, saying, "Somebody's got to go lend a hand, or they'll be overrun!"

He was suddenly aware of a grim-faced Castle striding silently beside him.

"Do what you got to," Boyd told them, tossing the words over his shoulder as they glided past behind him. "Move quick. Stay low. I'll cover you best I can."

Chapter 34

Outside, things were even wilder and more frantic. The air was filled with the buzz of bullets, like swarms of deadly mosquitoes, and the very ground trembled from the churning hooves of the mounted horses being spurred this way and that. Illumination thrown down by the moon and stars was regularly blotted out by billowing clouds of gunsmoke and dust kicked up by the horses.

Yet through this swirling haze another eerily stuttering light was starting to show as the torches flung at the horse barn started to take hold and burn higher and brighter.

Mac had never participated in a battle of the recent war, but minus any cannon blasts and with fewer combatants involved here tonight, he imagined it must have felt similar. Close enough, at any rate, to make him damned glad he *hadn't* seen combat.

But that didn't mean he had any reservations about charging out into the thick of this attack, the way he and

Castle were doing now, for the sake of trying to reach and help protect the Hardwicks. Most importantly for him, Sara—just as he knew Castle was undoubtedly more driven by his feelings for Tara.

The layout of the Box H ranch headquarters amounted to a sprawl of buildings and corrals spread across a flat, mostly sandy expanse of ground speckled with a few patches of grass and a smattering of bushes. In other words, not much in the way of natural cover between the bunkhouse and the main house some fifty yards away. There was a well housing of piled stones at about the halfway point, and a broken-down old buckboard twenty feet short of that. Nothing more.

Mac and Castle paused for a moment in the outer recess of the bunkhouse doorway, long enough for Castle to thumb fresh cartridges into his Remington revolver, making sure it had a full wheel.

"I say we make a run one at a time," said Castle, his voice breathy. "I'll go first. You help cover me as far as the buckboard. You come next. I'll cover you. Then we do it twice more, hopscotching to the well housing and lastly the house."

"You make it sound so easy. What could go wrong?" said Mac. Then he added, "Go ahead. Start it off."

Castle broke into a run an instant later. What he and Mac were attempting caught the raiders completely off guard. Castle made it to within a few feet of the buckboard before any of the attackers took notice of him. When one did, he issued an excited shout, barely noticed in the surrounding turmoil, and raised his rifle to draw a bead on the target that had caught his eye.

To his misfortune, this instantly made *him* the target of both Mac and Castle. In all the commotion, the almost simultaneous crack of their shots didn't attract much notice. But the double punch of slugs tore into the raider and knocked his carcass to the ground.

Seizing the opening this created, Mac shoved away from the bunkhouse and made his own run for it. He ran bent forward at the waist, hugging the Yellowboy to his chest, and then zigzagged slightly as he closed on the buckboard. Bullets chewed the ground inches behind his heels, and one higher round passed close enough to singe the hairs on the back of his neck. Ahead of him, he saw Castle leaning out and rapid-firing shots at something, but he didn't turn his head to look and see what it was.

When he was within a few feet, Mac threw himself into a shoulder roll and came skidding in behind the buckboard. He quickly got himself turned around and into firing position, the Yellowboy raised and ready. "So far, so good," he panted. "Are you rested up for another dash?"

"I reckon I am," Castle answered through gritted teeth. "But take a closer look out there. I think they're starting to fall back. And look farther past the burning barn. Something more is going on out there."

Mac squinted through the stinging smoke and dust, trying to make out what Castle was talking about. There were still plenty of guns going off, and the air was still being ripped by bullets. But he also began to see the rest of what the trail boss was describing. Several of the mounted raiders did appear to be wheeling around and fading back. Turning away from the bunkhouse and from the main house, as well.

Though, in both cases, men still with burning torches lingered long enough to heave them like fiery missiles in a last-ditch attempt to do more damage. A couple paid with their lives, but a couple others succeeded in lobbing their torches end over end and landing them menacingly close to where they had fuel to ignite.

Momentarily diverted from this, Mac's gaze went scanning beyond the inferno that had once been the horse barn. Out there on the wide-open grassland, something was moving. A mass of bobbing, writhing shapes cast in alternating shadow and splashes of yellow gold from the high-reaching flames. It was the Box H cattle herd . . . being driven into a near stampede!

"They're taking the cattle!" Mac exclaimed. "They're rustling the whole bunch!"

"That's what this is all about," Castle replied, teeth still clenched. "It's been a rustling raid all along! The shooting, the burning, the running off our remuda . . . That part was meant to cripple us, leave us shot up and fighting fires and then on shank's mare so we can't give chase anytime soon."

"That makes 'em as clever as they are ruthless." Mac's eyes narrowed as he watched the lumpy mass of cattle pick up speed as it moved away and grew blurrier. "They'll be in Mexico before we ever get started after 'em."

"Let the buzzards run," said a grim-faced Castle. "No matter how late a start we get and no matter how far they go . . . Mexico or halfway to hell . . . I won't stop until I catch up. And that's a promise!"

The dawn of a new day laid bare the full extent of loss and damage suffered by the Box H as a result of the previous night's raid. It wasn't pretty.

Since nobody associated with the ranch had suffered serious injury, however, it could have been worse. Red's right cheek and a portion of his forehead were peppered with numerous small cuts from flying glass. Castle had suffered a shallow bullet burn across the back of his left thigh during his run to the buckboard. A variety of burns and blisters all came from fighting the fires left in the wake of the torch throwers.

The horse barn had been a lost cause even before the last of the raiders rode away. The only thing left to fight there had been to prevent the flames from spreading out onto the pasture grass and to keep the smoldering attached corral rails from all burning down.

More urgent had been the three smaller but no less hungry fires ignited by the torches stubbornly thrown at the very end of the raid—two against the outside of the main house, one at the bunkhouse. Both blazes had required frantic dousing by water and dirt before they could get out of hand.

While the ranch defenders had made it through in decent physical shape, the exchange of gunfire had taken a considerably heavier toll on the raiders. As the murkiness of night lifted, six bodies could be seen sprawled across the open ground in front of the bunkhouse and main house.

For a little while, one of them had some life left in him. Long enough for him to glare defiantly up at Castle and Hardwick and the others as they gathered around him.

When asked his name and who was behind the raid he'd been part of, the man bared his blood-outlined teeth in a sneer and said in a thick Mexican accent, "I ride with Creo Davies . . . I hope you go after him. I hope you catch him . . . Because if you do, I know he will avenge me . . . by cutting the black, stinking gringo heart out of each and every one of you!" And then his entire body was racked by a single great shudder, and he, too, was dead.

Drawing back from this, a somber-faced Hardwick said, "Creo Davies. I've heard of him. A bloody, notorious bandit from south of the border."

"Isn't he the one who fancies himself some sort of pirate?" queried Tara.

"Pirate?" echoed Castle, standing close beside her.

Though no one had as yet given any indication of having noticed, as soon as the raiders were turned away and the coast was clear, both of the Hardwick sisters had come running out of the house and had thrown themselves into the arms of the two men who'd braved a hail of lead crossing mostly open ground in an attempt to try to ensure the twins' safety. The embrace between Mac and Sara had been somewhat subdued, but there had been nothing of the kind when it came to the other two. And for the duration of the night, even when beating down fires, they'd seldom been more than arm's length apart.

In response to the question of Creo Davies being a pirate, Hardwick further explained, "It's got to do with him supposedly bein' some kind of kin to Jean Lafitte, the old buccaneer who sided with Andy Jackson at the Battle of New Orleans. This all stems from nothing but the claims of Creo himself, mind you. But, true or not, he appears to buy it whole hog, right up to halfway dressin' like a pirate, accordin' to stories from those who've supposedly seen him."

"Well, what he did here tonight ain't far from the way yarns are told about how those old pirate raids went," noted Mac. "Sweeping in—on ships, instead of horses—and ripping and tearing and burning until they got what they wanted, then leaving everything in plundered ruination behind 'em."

"No denying they hit us hard and tore things up pretty

bad," allowed Castle grudgingly. "But they didn't bring the Box H to ruination. Not yet."

"No, they didn't," Mac agreed. "Hadn't been for Otis, though, and his need to slip out and, er, answer nature's call . . . well, it could have gone a whole lot worse. Without the warning he was able to give, we wouldn't have known those skunks were anywhere near until they came through the doors of the bunkhouse and main house with their torches and guns blazing full bore."

Castle grimaced, as if in sudden pain. "Yeah, and blast me for not thinking to post a lookout to begin with. Otis had already given us one other warning about Stack Ketchum and his gang possibly closing in on us. I should have had us on guard for that, if nothing else."

"Don't go layin' the whip on just yourself. The rest of us knew the same thing and didn't suggest it, neither," said Squint. "What's done is done. The thing now is to be grateful Otis *did* give us that second warning and we was able to come out of this scrap no worse than we did."

"But that's only true if we catch up and bring those cattle back," Castle insisted stubbornly. "Otherwise, the Box H *is* looking at ruination."

Hardwick gave him a sidelong look under pinched brows. "I admire and appreciate your determination, lad. But you make fetchin' back those beeves sound almighty easy. I purely wish that was the case. But the plain facts, just for starters, are that we ain't got horses to saddle up and take out after 'em. And even if we did and we rode out right this minute, they got more'n a four-hour start on us and by now are already in Mexico."

"They ain't the only ones who know how to cross the border," Castle countered.

"Plus," Hardwick pointed out, "by rough count they got upwards of thirty guns. And that's guns in the hands of rough customers who know how to use 'em. Sure, we got lucky and thinned out a few here, but there was still more out there drivin' the cattle, ones we never even caught full sight of." The old man wagged his head sadly. "Much as I can't afford to lose that herd, what I can't afford even more is to send a handful of good men out to commit certain suicide."

"With all due respect, sir, I don't recall anybody saying it was on you to send anybody anywhere," Castle told him. "By the same token, should certain folks take a notion to head Mexico way, I don't expect they'll be of a mind to need your say-so on that, either."

Scowling, Hardwick said, "Maybe I need to remind you—again—that what really has anybody stopped from actin' on such a recklessly foolish notion is the lack of horses."

"Maybe not horses," Mac spoke up. "But we ain't totally lacking for animals. Our chuckwagon is parked out behind the bunkhouse, and the mules to pull it are staked in that grassy patch back there, too. The rustlers never made it around that far."

Larabee frowned. "You ain't suggestin' somebody's gonna ride those jugheads, are you? And even if they'd hold still for it, how much good is only two—"

Mac waved him off in mid-sentence. "I'm not saying anybody rides 'em. I'm saying we hook up the team, and then we all pile on the wagon and head for . . . What's closest? A neighboring ranch? Town? Somewhere we can get hold of some mounts and hopefully round up some more men who'll join with us and ride out after those blasted long-loopers!"

This proposal seemed to stir a generally positive reaction among the others. Even Hardwick's despondent expression brightened some. "By God, it would at least be settin' something in motion. Beats just standin' here arguin' and moanin' about our sorry luck."

"Speakin' of luck," said Squint, "a piece of the good kind happens to be that us Double T men stowed our saddles and most of our gear in the bunkhouse, so it wasn't lost in the barn fire. All we need is to get to some cayuses we can tighten a cinch on and we'll be ready to ride."

"Let's quit jawing and get after it, then," declared Castle. "Mac, how about you take Otis and start hooking up those mules? The rest of us will commence gathering up our gear and getting it ready to load."

Chapter 35

A mix of anger and bafflement tugged at Stack Ketchum's expression. "Are you saying that what you saw . . . the ranch buildings shot to hell and partly burned, the horses run off . . . ? You saying somebody went to all that trouble just to steal a few cows?"

"More than just a few," Del Sol corrected. "More like a few hundred, based on the sign I tracked between here and the ranch. Appears like the rustlers made off with pretty much Hardwick's whole herd and drove 'em straight for Mexico, leaving the Box H bunch behind to put out fires, lick their wounds, and with no horses to give chase."

"Hell of a thorough job, if that's the way it went. You got to give the rustlers credit," said Ed Story from where he squatted beside the campfire, with a half-empty cup of coffee in his hand.

"Yeah. Credit for being thorough and credit for being quite a few in number," added Needham. "To drive off that many cattle and at the same time hit the ranch buildings so hard, you got to be talking a lot more than just a handful of rustlers, like what the Double T boys tangled with up on yonder hogback a few days ago."

"So what? What skin is it off our noses?" snarled Ketchum. "Whoever it was is in the cow-robbing business. We're about robbing money. The Box H's hard luck when it comes to holding on to their cattle don't affect us, other than it appears to have kept Otis from rejoining us."

"How about that, Jesus? When you went spyin' on the Box H, did you see Otis there with the others?" Story wanted to know.

"Yeah, he was there. Helping to get the fires under control and so forth," Del Sol reported. "The rustlers must have hit before he had a chance to slip away last night. After that, he was caught in the middle of everything and then stranded like everybody else on account of the horses being run off."

Ketchum shrugged. "Tough break for him. Good break for us, making it one less split of the bank money."

The other three eyed him. "We still gonna go ahead with the robbery?" Needham asked.

"Don't see any reason not to," came the answer. "Daylight has broke. Morning's coming on fast. About time for us to be heading into town, like we planned. The pile of sticks and adobe that Broken Spoke calls a bank is waiting as easy and inviting as one of those brothel gals back in Temecula."

"Yeah? And how did that work out for us?" Story reminded everybody.

"Knock off that complainin' talk, Ed. It's getting mighty tiresome," Ketchum growled. "Yeah, I know we're short Slater and Rico. And now Otis. But all he was ever gonna be on this job was a horse holder, anyway. If the four of us can't handle this on our own, then we got no right living up to the name we built for ourselves back in California."

"I agree with Stack," declared Del Sol, eyes gleaming dark and brittle. "This thing has dragged out long enough. We know the twenty thousand we came after—plus more—is waiting in that baked-mud bank. I say it's past time we claim it for our own!"

Needham and Story exchanged looks. Then Needham said, "What the hell. I'm plumb sick of just hangin' around here waitin'."

Story heaved a fatalistic sigh. "Okay. The Stack Ketchum gang shall ride again in all its tainted glory. But can we at least take time for a little more coffee? We don't want to ride in too early and draw attention to ourselves before the bank even opens."

Out behind the bunkhouse, Otis was glad to be busy helping Mac get the mule team hooked up. All during the night, once he'd become occupied fighting the raiders and the fires and the rest, he'd had little time to worry about Stack Ketchum and his bunch. That had put him in the cockeyed position of finding relief from concern over one bunch of outlaws by having to deal with the more immediate threat, which came with being attacked by an entirely different gang.

But now the fights with the raiders and the fires were done, and Otis was back to fretting over the situation with Stack. He was several hours overdue for rejoining his former cellmate, and with no mounts available, he couldn't make that up now even if he was moved to try.

What was more, if Stack went ahead with his plan to hit the Broken Spoke bank early this morning, the arrival of daybreak meant he and the others would already be primed to do that. Unless the absence of Otis gave them reason to hold off.

Otis suspected he wouldn't have been given a very important role, but couldn't be sure. He further suspected that by now, Stack had almost certainly sent Del Sol to find out why Otis hadn't shown up, like he was supposed to. Given the half-breed's skulking ability, aided by Stack's powerful spyglass, he could have positioned himself close enough anytime during the past couple of hours to get a reasonably accurate impression of what had taken place at the Box H.

That left the question of what Stack might decide to do based on the report Del Sol brought back. The way Otis saw it, as far as it related to him, it could go only one of three ways: either the gang would proceed with robbing the bank and leave him behind; they'd wait and somehow try to extract him from the Box H in order to include him in the robbery; or they'd complete the robbery and come for him later.

The most logical of those seemed that they'd go ahead with the robbery and leave him on his own. But maybe that was just wishful thinking on Otis's part. He'd love to be shed of Stack and the rest. Not only would it end the short-lived outlaw career, which he saw now he wasn't cut out for, but it would also leave him continuing his second chance with the Double T crew, which he was feeling more and more a kinship with.

That *seemed* the most logical way for it to go, but Otis had no way of being certain. All he could do until it finally played out was to keep a sharp eye on the skyline for any sign of Stack or Del Sol, hoping he never saw either of them.

God, let them want to be rid of me as bad as I do them,

was one of two recurring thoughts that kept running through Otis's mind. The other was the self-loathing question that demanded, *If you really want to solidify your second chance with the Double T crew, then why don't you tell them the truth about Stack and the double cross you've been working on his behalf?*

But Otis was now trapped in the middle, frozen from doing anything to effect an outcome one way or the other. Whatever Stack made up his mind to do, he would stubbornly attempt to follow through on. And as far as trying to level with Castle and the others at this late date—especially with no mounts for them to try to make it into town to possibly break up the bank robbery, which would include the deposit of Double T money—all that would accomplish would amount to Otis incriminating himself with the law and at the same time making himself a target for the Ketchum gang's revenge should they ever hear he'd squealed on them.

His plight made Otis want to groan out loud.

Instead, in an attempt to make conversation, which would give him something else to focus on, Otis said as he and Mac worked at buckling the mules into their harnesses, "I appreciate you speaking up for me the way you did a little while ago, saying how important the warning I managed to holler out was to everybody."

Mac shrugged. "Just telling the truth. If you hadn't been there like you were . . . man, I hate to think how bad it might have been."

"I'm glad about that. And I'm particularly glad I was able to do something good for the Double T crew. I know I did 'em wrong in the past, and I know they're sort of giving me a second chance. But they're still mighty edgy about me. Not that I can blame 'em. I only hope tonight will smooth off a bit more of that edginess."

There was genuine sincerity in Otis's words, even though hearing himself saying them brought on another sharp stab of guilt for what he *wasn't* revealing. For a crazy instant, he thought about blurting everything out to Mac and having it done with.

But the moment passed. Otis wasn't ready to face the consequences that telling the truth at this point would bring him. No, better to keep his mouth shut and cling to the hope that Stack and his bunch would pull off their robbery and make dust back to California, discarding him in their wake.

If it went that way, the loss of Box H cattle and Double T money stolen from the bank would be hard blows to those involved . . . but it would give Otis his best odds to remain in the clear and find a way to live with his regret and guilt.

"The Double T fellas are a pretty decent bunch from everything I've seen," responded Mac as he worked to jerk the knot out of some tangled reins. "You keep holding up your end of things like you been doing, they'll treat you right. And yeah, everybody's gratitude for what you did last night definitely ain't gonna hurt."

Otis smiled tentatively. "I sure hope so."

Yet even as he said it, his gaze drifted involuntarily off in the direction of the Ketchum gang's camp.

But it was Mac glancing in a different direction a moment later that yielded the sight of something much more welcome. "Hey, look yonder. Riders coming," he said. "Must be from a neighboring ranch. That could be a stroke of overdue good luck!"

Chapter 36

The five incoming riders were indeed from a neighboring ranch—the Barnstables' B-Bar-B. Frank Barnstable himself rode in the lead; his sons Leo and Brad came next, then two wranglers Mac had never seen before. They reined up in the open area between the main house and the bunkhouse just as inhabitants from each were emerging with armfuls of gear they meant to load onto the chuckwagon. Mac, his curiosity getting the better of him, left Otis to finish hitching the mules while he went out front to see what this visit might bring about.

From his saddle, a fiercely scowling Frank Barnstable raked his eyes over the scene—the fire damage, the sprawled dead bodies, the sooty, bedraggled condition of the Box H representatives gathering before him. His gaze came to rest on Hardwick.

"Some of my hands spotted the smoke over this way right after daybreak. When they alerted me and I got a look for myself, I could tell it was something serious. A grass fire maybe or a barn, I suspected. I gathered some boys, and we came to see if we could lend a hand. But good Lord, Hannibal! What happened here?"

"Rustlers," came Hardwick's initially terse reply. Then, his mouth pulling into a tight, straight line, he went on. "A whole pack of 'em, Frank, hittin' like nothing you ever saw. Like a guerrilla platoon from the war. Shootin', burnin', runnin' off our remuda—lookin' to do everything they could to kill or cripple so's we couldn't give chase when they ran off the herd."

"Your whole herd?"

"All but a handful of stragglers, which wouldn't yield enough meat for a good Fourth of July barbecue."

Jabbing a thumb at the dead bodies, Barnstable said, "Looks like you at least made the varmints pay plenty."

"Some. Not near enough."

"You lose any of your people?" Barnstable asked, his eyes turning anxious as they made another sweep of those who'd closed in around Hardwick.

"Thankfully, we only suffered a few cuts and bruises." The grim line of Hardwick's mouth pinched down lower at the corners. "If I don't get those cows back, Frank, the Box H will be finished."

"How much of a start do the rustlers have?" asked Leo, mounted to one side of his father.

Castle gave the answer. "Four hours, give or take. They hit shortly past midnight. The only thing we have left to head out with, now that the fires are under control, is a chuckwagon and a mule team to pull it with. We were just fixing to load up people and gear and try to make it somewhere we could get some mounts and maybe some men to ride with us."

"You can get all the mounts you need at the B-Bar-B," said Barnstable.

"And some men, too," spoke up his other son, Brad. "Including me. I'll ride with you after those thieving snakes!"

When several surprised and somewhat skeptical stares knifed into him, the younger Barnstable brother squared his shoulders defiantly and went on, "What? I can ride and shoot as good as most around here, can't I? And having recently got my head knocked more squarely into place"—here a meaningful glance directed Mac's way—"it seems plenty clear it's going to take some shooting and hard riding to have any chance at retrieving those cattle."

"Brad's right," agreed Leo. "And something else that's plenty clear is that a raid this ruthless ain't gonna end here. Not if they get away with it. The days of rustlers nibbling away a few head here and there will be over, and whoever is responsible for this will be back to wipe out the next rancher they set their sights on. If it don't get stomped out quick, it could be a matter of survival for every rancher in the territory."

"Your boys are not only makin' noises like men. They're also makin' a lot of sense," Hardwick said to Barnstable. "But there's something more to know for anybody thinkin' they want to throw in on this. The hombre behind it is Creo Davies. And even after we thinned his pack by the carcasses you see strewn about, he still has somewhere in the neighborhood of thirty men ridin' with him. Maybe more waitin' across the border."

"Creo Davies!" Barnstable spat the name like a bad taste from his mouth. "I thought that piece of trash conducted his bloody business down in Mexico."

"Appears he came north, lookin' for greener pastures. Or, to be exact, what he can find grazin' on 'em."

"All the more reason he finds out quick that what he'll

get instead ain't green . . . but ground stained red by his own stinking blood," insisted Brad.

"I like your sand and your sentiment, kid. I feel the same, as do all the Double T men riding with me," said Castle. "But how many others of a like mind are there around? And how soon could a dozen or twenty be rounded up?"

"All the men riding for my brand have sand. And I expect all of them would join in if I asked," responded Barnstable. "But I only have a half dozen besides my two sons. Since your chase is bound to take you into Mexico and last for an uncertain amount of time, I can hardly spare all of them."

"But there are other ranches around, Pa," pointed out Leo. "If we spread the word, surely all or most of them would pitch in. And you've got to figure there are also men in town who'd—"

The rest of what he was going to say was cut short by a shriek of pain and panic coming from behind the bunkhouse. As all faces snapped in that direction, another long, mournful wail sounded.

"It's Otis!" Mac exclaimed. "Something's wrong!"

He immediately broke into a run for the corner of the bunkhouse, with several of the others right behind him. As he rounded the corner of the building, Mac's eyes quickly locked on the form of Otis where he lay twisting and flailing on the ground at the rear of the wagon.

The cause for this became evident a second later when a writhing motion in the grass just beyond Otis revealed itself to be a fat rattlesnake in the process of slithering away after making its strike!

Mac's steps faltered momentarily, as he was torn between continuing directly to Otis or giving attention to the snake. His indecision was promptly settled by Boyd Lewis lunging past him, unleathering his .45 in a lightning draw and shouting, "Rattler!"

The big Colt roared a heartbeat later. The first slug drilled through scales and meat a couple of inches behind the viper's head. When the snake thrust up higher, hissing and baring its fangs even as the convulsing tail issued its telltale clatter, a second bullet blew its head into a pulpy, shapeless blob, and the rest of the body went limp.

Mac dropped to one knee beside Otis, and the fallen man clutched desperately at his shirt front. "Oh, damn it all. Damn my luck . . . That rattler nailed me good, Mac. It was coiled where I didn't see it behind the wheel, and . . . and when I leaned down to knock out the holding chuck, it shot straight up at me. Oh, damn."

Bodies crowded in close behind Mac. Squint said to the others, "Move back some. Give us room." Then, kneeling beside Mac, he pulled a bone-handled bowie from the sheath on his belt. "Get his shirt open, Mac. Find the bite. Larabee"—calling this over his shoulder— "work up a chaw of tobacco for a poultice."

Mac eased Otis onto the flat of his back and began tugging open his shirt, looking for puncture marks, which would indicate where the snake's fangs had sunk in.

"It's no use, fellas," Otis protested between choppy breaths. "He got me twice, both times near the base of my throat . . . too close to my heart . . . I'm a goner."

"Hush up that talk," Mac told him. "Just hold on. Keep fighting until Squint has the chance to—"

"No!" The word came out harsh, commanding. At the same time, Otis's right hand clamped with bone-crunching force around Mac's wrist. "Don't waste time on a lost cause . . . Listen to what I have to say . . . Where's Castle?"

The trail boss stepped close and leaned over. "Right here, Otis."

Otis looked up with a tormented gaze, which he swept slowly back and forth between Castle and Squint. Big beads of sweat were breaking out on his face, and his ruddy color was fading, taking on a faint bluish tint.

"I'm lower than the slimy belly of the rattler that just served me what I deserve . . . I been lying and double-crossing you fellas ever since I showed back up again. The only truth I told was that Stack Ketchum and his gang was out for that twenty thousand Castle used to carry in his money belt . . . But they weren't just *maybe* coming for it. They were here . . . close by . . . the whole time. And I never broke with Stack. I was still in it with him and the others . . . The only reason we didn't make our move as soon as we caught up was because Stack was suspicious about the Double T crew hanging around to help the Hardwicks. He wanted to be sure . . . you still had the twenty thousand. Stack sent me in with my phony story to be a lookout and find out for sure."

Otis was breathing with more and more difficulty, and his words were sounding steadily thicker, as if his throat were tightening around them.

Castle stared coldly down at him. "Did you get word to Ketchum that the Double T money is now in the Broken Spoke bank?"

Otis continued to stare up, barely blinking. His eyes seemed to be filming over, and it was hard to tell if he was seeing anything clearly. He rasped out, "That's why I'm telling you this . . . Yeah, I got word to Stack. He's planning to hit the bank right after it opens this morning . . . I—I was on my way to sneak out and rejoin him last night when I spotted the raiders moving in . . . You can believe it or not, but I'm g-glad it worked out that I was able to give everybody some w-warning . . ."

Otis squeezed his eyes tightly shut, and a spasm of pain shuddered through him.

"He's about done," Squint murmured. "Like he said, those bites were too close to his heart. The poison pumped through him mighty fast."

Castle said in a flinty tone, "There was poison in him long before the rattler added a new dose."

"Maybe so," Mac allowed. "But however it came about, he still saved our bacon last night. And if we act fast on what he just told us, maybe it'll be enough to save something more."

Castle gave him a sharp look. But before he could respond, Hardwick beat him to it, saying, "By God, Mac is right. There might be time to make it to town about when the bank opens. Maybe in time to warn the marshal and break up that robbery!"

Castle's eyes turned to Barnstable. "Will you lend us some of your horses?"

"You bet I will! Yours ain't the only money in that bank," came the answer.

"Everybody in our outfit can ride, but me, Boyd, and Mac are the best guns if it comes to trading lead with Ketchum's bunch."

"Take three mounts, then, starting with mine. Hank, Buster"—Barnstable gestured impatiently to the pair of wranglers who'd ridden in with him and his sons—"hand yours over, as well."

"How about me and Leo going with 'em?" said Brad. "We've raised enough hell in that town. It's about time we balanced it out some."

Barnstable's eyes pinched briefly with reluctance, but

then he replied, "Okay. You're spoiling for it so bad, go ahead. But not Leo." His eyes swinging to the older brother, he added, "You hightail it back to the B-Bar-B and fetch mounts for the rest of us. And while you're at it, send some riders out to other nearby ranches to spread the word about this raid. Tell 'em we need as many men and guns as they can spare. Once the damn bank robbers are dealt with, we've still got a crazy rustling pirate to chase down!"

Everybody scrambled into action. But Tara rushed forward and insisted on taking a moment to wrap Castle in an uninhibited embrace. At the same time, Mac found Sara pressing against him and also slipping her arms around his neck. Gazing up at him in that penetrating way she had, she whispered, "I don't know what lies ahead for the two of us . . . but don't you ride off and decide it by getting your fool self killed, you hear?"

Their lips touched briefly, and then Mac promised through a grin, "I'll do my darnedest not to."

A moment later he was up in the saddle of one of the wranglers' horses. Before wheeling away, he glanced down to where Squint continued to kneel beside a shivering, faintly writhing Otis.

"He'll be out of his misery soon," Squint reported.

Mac took a breath, let it out a bit unevenly. "I know he wasn't much, but I think a part of him was trying to do better. Give him some kind of decent burial, won't you?"

Squint showed no response right away. Then, grudgingly, his chin dipped a single time. "I'll see to it."

Chapter 37

Preston McCall felt restless, uncharacteristically anxious. He'd long demonstrated an ability to remain both inwardly and outwardly calm in even the most pressing of situations, including his military service during the recent war. It had always served him well. And on rare occasions when he was disconcerted to an unusual degree, he'd been able to put his thumb on the reason why and bring it quickly under control.

This morning was different. An uneasy feeling had started gnawing at him sometime in the middle of the night and remained after he woke and all through breakfast. He had a pretty good hunch what it was—waiting for news of how Creo's raid on the Box H had gone—but recognizing this still didn't put the feeling to rest.

The previous rustling done by Grimsby and his men had been widely scattered and smaller in scale, each raid far less ambitious in and of itself. But Creo's aim—to snatch away the entire Box H herd in one swoop, as envisioned by McCall—was something on a grand scale that would reverberate through the whole territory and be talked about for years to come. In a sense, it would be the grand battle McCall had never got the chance to command during the war. And though hopefully his name would never be attached to it, he would have the personal satisfaction of knowing the part he played.

But that satisfaction, along with the easing of his anxiety, would come only when he heard how the raid had gone. Surely, news of something that significant ought to reach town quickly. Anticipation of this, of word sweeping frantically up and down the street outside his door, made McCall eager to get to the bank that morning so he'd be in place when it happened.

He was always prompt, always the first one to arrive and begin making preparations for the day's business, but this morning he got there even a few minutes earlier than usual. Had he not been so occupied by wondering about the success of Creo's raid and when he'd hear news of it, he might have taken closer notice of the two individuals—a lean young man with darting eyes under oddly bent brows and a hard-faced half-breed with a drooping mustache and a cigarette hanging from one corner of his mouth—slouched against the wall of the feedstore across the street from the bank.

Once he'd let himself in at the rear, McCall went directly to the spacious desk located within a railed-off section on one side of the main room. After lighting a glass-domed coal oil lamp, he sat down and began shuffling through some papers in a file he'd left open atop his desk at quitting time the previous day.

Only a few minutes later, Oscar Hoyt, McCall's chief teller, arrived. He was a rumpled middle-aged man with bags under his eyes from being run ragged by the seven kids he and his wife had at home, but his desire to escape the household's commotion made him a devoted and dependable employee. He and McCall exchanged good mornings, and then Oscar proceeded to open the walk-in vault on the back wall and begin extracting the money drawers to bring over to the teller windows. A plump young woman named Rachel Goode, one of two part-time tellers McCall also employed, showed up to help him finish with this. It was unusual for a woman to work as a bank teller, but Rachel had a mathematically inclined mind and had proven to be quite good at the job.

"It's less than a minute before nine, Mr. McCall," Oscar announced. "Shall I unlock the front door and raise the shades partway before the sun gets too bright and hot?"

McCall looked up from his papers. "Yes. By all means." His eyes scanned the room. "Where's Karl?" Karl was an aging war veteran with a bullet-shattered leg who performed guard duty each day.

Oscar smiled tolerantly. "Appears he's running a little late. But I saw him starting down Brennan Street earlier. He moves a little slower some days than others."

McCall grunted. "It would help if he didn't lug that heavy old shotgun with him all the time. I've told him repeatedly he ought to leave it here at the end of each day and find himself a cane to help get around better. But you know how blasted stubborn he is."

Oscar's grin widened. "Yeah, Karl can be that."

Oscar had barely made it back behind his teller's window before the front door opened and two men entered. First through was a tall, trim man wearing pin-striped trousers, a bib-front shirt, and a yellow bandanna around his neck; all showed some age and trail wear, though they were of high initial quality and had recently been aggressively brushed.

Following behind him came a man of slighter build

with pale blond eyebrows, which stood out in sharp contrast to his ruddy complexion. The long duster coat he wore, which displayed much hard wear, including ragged fraying around its collar and cuffs, stood out in equally sharp contrast to the attire of his companion.

"Good morning," said a smiling Oscar as the man in the bib-fronted shirt stepped up before his window. "How may I help you?"

"We came here," Stack Ketchum told him, "prepared to make a deposit."

"Very good. We'd be delighted to accommodate you," Oscar responded.

Now it was Ketchum who showed a smile, a very thin one. "Don't be so sure about that."

"Begging your pardon, sir?" said Oscar, both his voice and smile faltering with uncertainty.

"You see, the deposit I am prepared to make," explained Ketchum, suddenly and smoothly drawing the Colt from the holster on his hip and thrusting it through the bars of the teller window until the muzzle was mere inches from Oscar's face, "is to plant a slug from this smoke pole right between your eyes if you don't do exactly what me and my partner tell you to do!"

As these words were issuing from Ketchum, Ed Story swept open his duster coat and swung from within its folds a long double-barreled shotgun. Leveling this in the direction of McCall, he added, "And if you think that gimpy old critter you used to call your lobby guard is gonna show up and save you, think again. He's permanently retired, and on his way out, he was obliging enough to leave me this handy gut-shredder."

Where he sat, McCall went rigid, except for the instant, visible rage that coursed through him. "You'll never get away with this!"

"That's where you're wrong, banker man. We already *are* getting away with it," Ketchum told him. "And if you want to live to cry about it later, you best haul your butt out of that fancy chair and drag it over here to help stuff some big, roomy bank bags full of all the paper money you got."

McCall didn't react at once, remaining seated behind his desk, still trembling from the rage inside, his face turning purple from it. Also, on the inside, a voice roared in protest: *This can't be happening.* Not now, not on the brink of succeeding at all he had so craftily been planning. He would *not* let this happen! He was a military commander, and he would stand his ground!

As he finally pushed to his feet, McCall's attempt to stand his ground was to try for the pistol in the shoulder holster under the lapel of his coat. The maneuver was bold and unexpected but had no chance against the shotgun already leveled on him. The pistol scarcely made it into sight before Story triggered one of his barrels and the double-aught blast hammered full force into the former colonel's chest. He was hurled backward against the high-backed chair on which he'd been seated, upending it and spilling him into a leaking, lifeless heap on the floor.

Near the opposite end of Broken Spoke's main street, Marshal Curly Strand had just stepped out the front door of his office with a fresh cup of coffee in hand. He intended to have a seat on one of the weathered wooden chairs positioned against the outside of the building, where he meant to enjoy the coffee before it got too cold, and the morning air before it got too hot.

He was in the process of lowering his bottom onto a dusty seat when the boom of a shotgun sounded from up at the bank. The sound was unmistakable and gave the marshal enough of a jolt that it caused him to slosh some of the coffee onto the back of his hand.

Straightening back up, Strand growled out a curse at the sting of the hot liquid. He tossed aside the cup and moved out into the street in long strides, automatically adjusting the gun belt around his waist and peering anxiously up toward the bank as he did so.

Across the way, Jep Stephens, who had been busily sweeping the boardwalk in front of his boot shop, stopped sweeping and craned his neck to also look up toward the bank. When he saw the marshal in motion, he called, "Was that a gunshot, Curly?"

Without breaking stride, Curly responded, "Afraid so. You got any customers in there, Jep, keep 'em inside until I see what's going on."

The marshal kept trudging steadily but cautiously forward, eyes and ears on sharp alert. Up ahead, he saw a man he didn't recognize run across the street and make for the front door of the bank. The fool. Curly tensed, fully expecting to hear more gunfire. But none came. The man entered the bank with no sign of a problem.

What the hell was going on? Had the shotgun report come from somewhere else?

Curly broke into a half trot, even though he was already starting to feel winded. As he drew abreast of Mike Grogan's barbershop, Grogan appeared in the doorway and called, "Hey, did I hear a shotgun go off?"

"I think there might be some trouble up at the bank, but ain't sure yet," Curly answered. "Do me a favor and send that boy of yours hightailin' out the back alley to fetch Virg Lamont at his hotel, will you? Have the kid tell him, in case Virg ain't already been rousted by the commotion, to come a-runnin'!"

"You got it." Grogan started to turn back in the doorway but then paused long enough to ask, "You want me to grab my hunting rifle and come up the boardwalk behind you in case you need more backup?"

"Ain't a notion I'd say no to, Mike," Curly allowed. "But if you come, stay close to the buildings and keep your head down until we know what's going on."

Curly continued in motion until he'd almost reached the intersection where Brennan Street fed in from the residential district that lay off to the left. From just around the corner, a ragged voice suddenly wailed, "Help! Somebody come quick. It's old Karl Vine, the bank guard. He's been hurt bad!"

The marshal immediately altered his course and veered over to where he could see down Brennan. Sure enough, only a short distance away, he could see the bulky body of a white-haired old man lying crumpled on the boardwalk. Dropped to one knee beside him was a young man named DeVrie, who worked at the telegraph office, apparently on his way to work. He was looking around every which way, near panic showing on his face, as he cried, "Somebody needs to get the doctor here in a hurry!"

Curly stepped up and laid a hand on one of the young man's shoulders. Looking down at the pool of blood Karl's head lay in and the deep slash that ran from under the hinge of one jaw nearly to the other, he said in a low, tight voice, "No need for hurry, son . . . Karl is past anything a doctor can do for him."

Jesus Del Sol burst into the bank lobby, agitation showing plainly on his face and in his tone.

"What the hell was that shotgun blast?" he demanded. "I thought we was gonna do this quick and quiet? Now half the town out there is stirred up. I can already see a lawman coming up the street."

From where he remained on the front side of the teller's counter, while Story had moved around behind it to help the pair of blubbering, sobbing bank employees stuff money into two large canvas bags, Ketchum said, "The shooting couldn't be helped. We had a would-be hero who had to be dealt with."

"How much longer?"

"As long as it takes!" Ketchum snapped. "You get back in the doorway. If any of those stirred-up townsfolk get too close, give 'em something to really worry about. When you step back out there, motion for Jack to bring the horses across to this side of the street. Looks like we're gonna have to spur outta here in a hurry!"

Del Sol frowned. "Those townies see getaway horses moving over, they're gonna know for sure what's going on, and it'll make 'em even more likely to try and take action."

"That'll be their tough luck, then," Ketchum responded. "Any of 'em get too close, see to it they pay hard for their nosiness."

Chapter 38

A hatless, tousle-haired Virg Lamont eased out the front entrance of the Ace Hotel just as Curly was drawing even with it. Virg's gun belt was cinched around his waist, the untucked tails of his shirt puckered by its grip; the six-shooter was drawn and gripped in the deputy's fist. As soon as he saw the marshal, Virg wanted to know, "Is it true there's a bank robbery going on?"

"Seems like. Something is playing out," Curly told him.

Strung out along the boardwalk behind Curly, Mike Grogan and two other men with rifles were edging forward. They were ducking in and out of doorways and pressing close to the storefronts as much as possible.

"I didn't hear it, but Grogan's kid told me there was a shotgun blast from the bank?" said Virg.

"Way it sounded." Then, jerking a thumb over his shoulder, Curly added, "Back yonder, just down Brennan Street, Karl Vine, the old bank guard, is laying dead, with his throat slit and his shotgun missing. I got a hunch it might have been his old boomer that somebody else used inside the bank."

"Damn!" Virg exclaimed.

A moment later there was movement in the recessed doorway of the bank. A sliver of a man holding a Winchester could be made out. He motioned at something, and just a couple of seconds after that, another man, this one on horseback, broke into sight from the opposite side of the street, just past the corner of the feedstore located there.

The rider was leading a string of other saddled horses, and he urged them along with a loud "Heeyahh!" as he spurred his mount to make the crossing fast, churning a cloud of dust, until they all disappeared into an alley on the west side of the bank.

At the same time, the man in the doorway leaned out long enough to trigger three rapid-fire rounds down the middle of the street, aimed at nothing in particular, just providing cover to hold Curly and the others in place.

"Everybody hold your fire! Don't expose yourself or shoot back unless I do!" ordered Curly.

"Getaway mounts!" declared Virg once the horses were across and the man in the doorway had ducked back out of sight again. "There's a robbery going on in there for damn certain, and the owlhoots are getting ready to make a run for it. How many horses did you count in all that dust? Was it four or five?"

"I made it only four. But that's four too many with us pinned down clear back here where we are," said Curly. "And we don't dare try to close in and pour lead in through the front windows, on account of the bank employees in there."

"The one piece of luck we got is that we're on the

same side of the street as the bank," Virg pointed out. "How about I go back through the hotel, pop out on the other side, and go up the rear alleys to get in a position where I can be waiting to make it hot for 'em when they try for their getaway? You hear me cut loose, the rest of you come guns a-blazing before they swarm me!"

Curly's brows pinched tight with concern. "That's a hell of a risk for you to take, Virg!"

"What's in that bank makes it worthwhile to me," blurted the deputy.

This sounded odd to Curly, under any circumstances. Before he could venture a question or comment, though, a shout from Mike Grogan demanded the attention of both lawmen.

"Look! Out there in the street!"

Halfway up toward the bank, coming from the other side, a man was walking slowly out into the middle of the dusty street. He was a short, plump individual with an oversized nose and a gray-flecked walrus mustache. He moved in shuffling steps, angling in the direction of the bank, with his hands held open and empty out before him.

"That's Homer Goode, the tailor. His daughter Rachel works part-time in the bank. What the hell's he doing?" Virg muttered.

The answer came a moment later, when Homer called toward the bank, "You men in there! Word is spreading what you are up to. I care not for the money or anything else save my beloved daughter Rachel, who is now trapped in your midst."

"Goode! For God's sake, get out of there!" Curly hollered.

But the man paid no heed, just kept shuffling forward and kept talking. "I beg you to spare her. She is so young and innocent. All I have left that matters in the world after the fever claimed her mother and sister. If you need to take a life or a hostage, take me. Me for her . . . I beg you. Just spare her."

The shadowy shape appeared in the bank doorway again. "Get away, old man! We don't aim to hurt nobody unless you force our hand. Now scat, before—"

He never got to finish. A shot fired from somewhere behind Curly sent a slug ripping up the street and smashing away a chunk of the bank doorway's adobe framing. The shape of the man who'd been standing there disappeared, but it was too much to hope that he'd been struck by anything more than some bits of adobe brick.

"Damn it! I told nobody to open fire until I said so!" bellowed Curly.

One of the men strung out behind Grogan stammered meekly, "I . . . I thought I had a clear shot."

Virg snapped, "You had a clear shot, all right . . . a clear shot to make sure the streets are gonna run red with blood!"

No sooner were the deputy's words spoken, like a prophecy of doom, than evidence of their truth busted wide open. Gunfire from the bank—from the shadowy man in the recessed doorway as well as from the rider who'd crossed with the getaway horses, now on foot just behind the building's far corner, also wielding a repeating rifle—began furiously raking the street and the building fronts along the south side.

Homer Goode, the plump little man in the middle of the street, was cut down instantly and mercilessly. Curly leaped into the hotel doorway with Virg. The rest of the men strung out behind him either flattened themselves on the boardwalk or found other doorways to duck into as a hail of lead hammered the row of storefronts, shattering windows and tearing long gouges in wood and adobe outer walls.

Squeezed tight in the hotel doorway, Curly rasped to Virg, "We'll keep 'em busy out here. You go ahead with that back alley plan. We got to try to stop 'em and make the buzzards pay. Keep your head down and make every bullet count. We'll work our way to you as quick as we can!"

A short distance out of town, with the silhouettes of the taller buildings starting to poke into sight, the men from the Box H were coming hard. Four abreast they rode, with Mac and Castle in the center spots and Boyd and Brad Barnstable on their respective flanks.

Above the rush of wind and the rhythmic thump of hoofbeats, Castle called, "I think I hear gunfire coming from up ahead. Damn, I hope we're not too late!"

"We ain't," a grim-faced Mac assured him. "If you hear gunfire, then that means the marshal and townsfolk are making their own attempt at stopping those robbers. With luck, we may be in time to help 'em turn the tide!"

Chapter 39

Having by now stomped around to the back side of the teller's counter, Stack Ketchum grabbed the money sack out of the hands of Oscar and shoved the man roughly out of the way.

"This will have to do," he barked to Story. "Lace up that sack of yours and let's get the hell out of here. The last thing I wanted was to have to try and shoot our way clear of this dust pile, but it looks like we got no choice."

"We can make it. At least we're getting a pretty good haul," Story told him as he gave the girl Rachel her own rough shove and then began tying the thongs that closed the mouth of the second money sack.

"What's going on out in the street?" Ketchum hollered over to Del Sol.

"Not much," answered the half-breed in the doorway. "The marshal and a handful of men are crabbing forward along this one side, but mighty slow and careful. I think the lead me and Jack poured their way might have put some heavy loads in their britches." Del Sol snickered. "I figure the only reason they ain't doing no more shooting back is on account of being afraid to hit the employees they know are in here with us."

"We can use the girl as a hostage, the way her old man said, to help us get in the clear," Story suggested.

Rachel, who had cowered away after Story's shove, suddenly straightened up defiantly. With tears running down her round face and her chin quivering, she said, "What became of my father? I heard him calling from the street. If you harmed him, I will not cooperate no matter what you do to me!"

"Shut her up," snarled Ketchum. "She's just as good to us knocked senseless as she is running her mouth."

Story reached out, grabbed Rachel by the hair, and yanked her closer to him. "You heard the man, girlie. One more peep, I'll coldcock you." Then, jerking his chin toward Oscar, he asked, "What about him?"

"Reckon he's served his purpose," Ketchum answered.

But as the gang leader was raising his Colt, thumbing back the hammer and starting to aim it at Oscar, Del Sol called from the doorway, "Better hold off on that! The marshal and his boys hear shots coming from in here and figure we're getting rid of these folks, won't give 'em no more reason to hold off cutting loose on us."

Ketchum paused, nodded, eased the Colt's hammer back down. The sigh of relief building in Oscar's chest never got released, however, before the barrel of the Colt instead slashed viciously across his temple and knocked him unconscious.

"Okay, we're heading for the back now, Jesus," Ketchum announced. "Give those brave city fathers out there another round in case they got any room left in their drawers. Then hotfoot it out to join us. Time to rattle our hocks the hell away from this scab on the desert!"

Mac, Castle, Boyd, and Brad Barnstable were within a hundred yards of the buildings on the north side of town now. They could all plainly hear the cracks of a fresh rifle volley shattering the morning air.

"The bank is toward the west end of the main street," Brad called out. "Sounds like that's where the shooting is coming from."

"Then that's where we want to be," Castle told him. "Take the lead on getting us there!"

Virg Lamont was right where he meant to be. At the back end of the alley running along the west side of the bank building, with good cover provided by a thick-walled old rain barrel and a discarded heavy wooden desk tipped over onto one edge. Further masking his presence was the cluster of four horses that had been driven into the alley a little while ago by the mounted robber who'd brought them from the other side of the street.

That individual was now on foot, stationed at the opposite end of the alley, using a repeating rifle to join with the man in the front doorway at pouring sporadic volleys of lead down toward Marshal Strand and the others.

If he'd wanted, Virg could have used his vantage point and the Henry repeater he'd grabbed before exiting the hotel to pick off this rifleman by now. That was tempting. Trouble was, it would warn the others inside of the deputy's presence.

No, what Virg wanted was to get *all* the thieving dogs

in the alley before he sprang his ambush. Having them before him in a bunch when he finally made his move might increase the risk to him, but it would also give him his best odds for disrupting their escape and significantly thinning their ranks before they could manage any response.

Putting his neck on the line this way had little to do with Virg's devotion to duty or the law or the town. Hell no. Anything and everything he could do to stop this robbery was for the sake of his own self-interest—namely, saving the money he and McCall were planning to haul off themselves. Virg had no way of knowing McCall's condition, though that initial shotgun blast loomed as a concern, but there was nothing he could do about it at the moment. He hoped the colonel was okay, but securing the money remained his main goal regardless.

The opportunity to do that was suddenly at hand when the bank's alley door burst open and people began hurriedly emerging. First came Ed Story, with a money sack in each fist, followed by Stack Ketchum—though Virg knew neither of them by name—who was jerking Rachel Goode by one arm.

Story called to Jack Needham at the mouth of the alley, "Come on! Time to saddle up and get out of here!"

At the same time, Ketchum was shoving Rachel toward one of the horses, snarling, "Climb up there and be quick about it!"

The girl was unexpected and caused Virg to hold off opening up on the alley full of robbers, the way he'd planned. *Damn!* The deputy had done some cold things in his day and had no qualms about snuffing out the life of another person . . . as long as that person was a man. So okay, he may have cuffed around his share of mouthy females, but that was a lot different than pulling the trigger on one. Yet if he cut loose on this crowded alley now, the way he'd been figuring to do, Rachel getting caught in the line of fire would be mighty hard to avoid.

Virg's hesitancy over this possibility suddenly gave way to a whole different development. Once Rachel was up in the saddle, as Ketchum was toeing a stirrup to climb up behind her, the girl twisted at the waist and swung one hand around and down at him with all the speed and force she could manage. Clutched in that hand was a pair of scissors, which she'd secreted within the folds of her dress, and now the point of these she plunged deep into the side of Ketchum's neck!

"You murderous pig! All of you! You killed Mr. Mc-Call and my father, and you all deserve to burn in hell!"

These were the words Rachel screeched as she followed her initial strike by hurling herself from the saddle, dropping her full weight onto Ketchum, and driving him to the ground as her arm rose and fell repeatedly, stabbing and gouging in a frenzy.

Virg was so surprised and stunned by what he was witnessing that he remained crouched in place, unmoving.

But Ed Story wasn't frozen to inaction. Exclaiming a curse, he dropped the money sacks, drew his pistol, and shot Rachel twice at point-blank range. The impact of the slugs lifted her off Ketchum and slammed her back to roll under the feet of the horses. In turn, these animals, reacting to the screeching and shooting and now the bloody body bumping underfoot, began wheeling and stamping in panic.

This was the scene that met Del Sol as he stepped out of the bank's alley door. His dark eyes flashed as he tried to take in the chaos. "What the hell?"

"It was the girl! She went crazy!" Story told him. "I think she might have killed Stack."

"That ain't the only problem we got," rasped the half-breed. "Just before I left the front doorway, I saw four riders coming down the street. Coming hard. I don't know who they are, but it's clear they're bent on throwing themselves into this."

"All the more reason we need to get out of here, then," wailed Needham, trying to catch the reins of one of the spooked horses. "Grab those money bags—and Stack, if you can get him up—and let's go!"

If he was going to stop the getaway and save the money, Virg had to act now. And so he did. Straightening up partway and extending the Henry so that it rested across the rim of the rain barrel, he called out, "You've gone as far as you're gonna go, boys!" while simultaneously stroking the trigger.

His target was Ed Story, and the slug hurled by the roaring Henry was dead on the mark—except for the fact that a fraction of a second before Virg fired, the agitated horse Ed was standing next to suddenly whipped its head to one side and effectively blocked the shot. The bullet smashed through the skull a thumbnail's width behind the animal's right eye and exploded its brain. The unfortunate beast was dead before its great body shuddered and collapsed heavily to the ground, emitting an agonized shriek on the way down.

That was enough to throw the remaining three horses the rest of the way into full panic. Sounding their own shrill protests, they wheeled and reared up, hooves kicking out and striking the sides of the alley, as they sought frantically to turn and bolt away. None of the unmounted robbers were quick enough or strong enough to hold them back. And, as one, the way they came rushing was toward Virg's end of the alley.

The deputy had no chance to take another shot. He was

suddenly too busy scrambling to get out of the way of a wall of boiling dust and the stampeding mass of straining, snorting, pounding horseflesh within it.

That didn't stop both Story and Del Sol from trying their luck, though. Pressing themselves against the bank's outside wall to avoid getting crushed by the uncontrollable horses, they still managed to raise their guns and snap off some wild rounds at the retreating shape of the meddler who'd fired on them and sent the animals into a final frenzy.

Running up behind the pair, pausing only to snatch the dropped money sacks from the ground, Needham shouted, "Save your ammunition until you've got a sure target. We can deal with that bushwhacker when we make it out of this alley. But right now we gotta catch those blasted horses!"

Chapter 40

"There's the bank, ahead on the left," Brad Barnstable shouted to the other riders barreling down the middle of Broken Spoke's main street with him.

Tossing barely a sidelong glance, they flashed past the marshal and the rest of the men working their way up the boardwalk. "The robbers are in the alley on the west side!" Curly called after them.

"Make for that alley! Swing out wide and come in on angles!" Castle called to the men riding with him.

The remaining distance to the bank was covered quickly. As ordered, the men from the Box H made a wide sweep, curving to the north side of the street and then curling back, so that they converged on the alley's mouth in a pincerlike fashion. As the pincer closed and they reined up their mounts with guns drawn and ready, however, they found the alley to be empty. All except for the trampled bodies of a young woman, a man, and a horse.

"The dust and gunsmoke is hanging too thick in there for 'em to have been gone very long," declared Boyd.

Seeing the accuracy of the statement, Castle promptly instructed, "Mac, you and Brad circle around this next building and meet us on the other side. Me and Boyd are going through the alley!"

South of the bank and the next building bordering the alley, a dry goods store, was a largely unclaimed section of the town. It was comprised of flat, barren ground, with a wood-frame warehouse off fifty or so yards to the west and a handful of broken-down adobe huts straight out.

Knowing practically every corner of the town from his numerous rounds while on duty, not even Virg had much familiarity with this part. When he ran from the alley to escape the stampeding horses, knowing the robbers would be right behind them, with guns already blazing, his eyes were searching desperately for some scrap of cover.

The answer was a broken-down, badly weathered old buckboard that somebody had left propped on adobe blocks, with all the wheels removed. It wasn't much, but it was close and would have to do. After making his decision, Virg veered slightly to his left, aiming for the buckboard, while the horses thundering out right behind him thankfully charged straight ahead.

Knowing what was bound to come next, Virg covered the final few feet to the buckboard by throwing himself into a diving roll, which carried him underneath the rig and brought him twisting around onto his belly partly behind one of the stacks of adobe bricks that served in lieu of a wheel. Even at that, he'd barely squirmed into place before bullets sent his way by two of the robbers came sizzling in. Some gouged low into the dirt, while others hammered against the already battered sides of the old buckboard.

Snarling a curse, Virg levered a fresh round into his Henry and began returning fire. Ironically, his targets were now finding effective cover behind the big rain barrel and overturned desk he had selected for himself only a short time ago. But the stack of adobe bricks he was flattened behind was serving him well enough for now.

But then, suddenly, that was no longer the case.

As the robbers in the alley tightened their shot placement, two or three rounds in quick succession came slamming directly into Virg's bricks. They didn't penetrate through; that wasn't the problem. But what they did accomplish was to finish what wind erosion had been nibbling at for all the years the stack had been holding up the rig. One of the bricks near the bottom cracked and broke apart, causing those piled above it to shift and slip and topple away. The front corner of the buckboard dropped directly down onto Virg, the hard, unyielding edge of the frame knifing high across his shoulders and crushing his spine at the base of his neck.

The deputy experienced an instant of piercing, unimaginable pain followed by a rush of numbing warmth . . . and then blackness.

Any satisfaction felt by Del Sol or Story at having dispatched their ambusher was mighty short-lived. No sooner had they ceased firing after seeing the buckboard collapse on Virg than they heard, filling the alley behind them, the clatter of hooves and a voice demanding sharply, "Drop the hardware! Try to turn around, you die!"

But, of course, they didn't take the advice. Cursing, leaping apart so as not to make a better target by staying jammed shoulder to shoulder, the two robbers attempted to spin and get off some defensive fire with their already smoking guns. The maneuver never came close to countering Boyd Lewis's lightning reflexes. From his saddle, the black man held his Colt .45 at waist level and fanned three rounds so close together it sounded almost like the roll of a single discharge. Castle got off a shot, too, though of little consequence. It was Boyd's .45 slugs that riddled Del Sol and Story and pounded them to the ground.

That left Jack Needham as the only member of Ketchum's gang still alive. While the other two were dealing with their would-be ambusher, Needham concentrated instead on going after the fleeing horses while also hanging on to the money sacks, which he gripped, one in each hand, as he ran. When all gunfire behind him suddenly stopped, he glanced back over his shoulder, expecting to see Del Sol and Story turning his way after successfully finishing their quarry. When he instead saw his partners sprawled in death just outside the end of the alley, his steps faltered, and he nearly stumbled and sprawled himself.

Once he'd regained his balance, the realization he was now on his own brought Needham to a momentary staggering halt. The words *Now what do I do?* screamed through his head.

For as long as he could remember, Jack Needham had been a follower, seldom on his own, sure as hell never a decision maker. But the instinct to survive beat within him, anyway, and the thousands of dollars now in his lone possession made it beat all the harder.

Seeing he had gained no ground on the horses, and knowing that at any minute the men who'd gunned Del Sol and Story would come boiling out of the alley, Needham changed course and veered toward the dry goods store in hope of perhaps finding a place to hide until he could somehow get his hands on a different mount with which to make his escape.

But the plan didn't take him very far. Needham had gone only a few steps on his altered course before two riders came pounding around the corner of the dry goods store directly ahead of him. They reined up sharply even as Needham once more ground to a halt. Each of the men held a handgun clenched in his fist.

One of them, aiming an old Smith & Wesson .44 Model 3, barked harshly, "Drop the bags and keep those hands empty . . . or die where you stand."

Needham's will held for a single ragged heartbeat. Then his fingers loosened, and the money sacks dropped to the ground. Ever so slowly, he raised his emptied hands.

Chapter 41

The blazing noon sun beat down on a far different scene at the Box H ranch than the one it had shone on at the break of day. Where once only a handful of soot-streaked, bedraggled survivors had stood alone facing loss and uncertainty, now twenty-odd riders sat their saddles, wearing expressions of grim determination for what they were about to undertake.

At the center of those gathered in a semicircle was Hannibal Hardwick, mounted square-shouldered and steady in spite of his wounded leg. He was bracketed by his two daughters, and fanned out close behind were Mac and the Double T men from Texas. Curved round on either side were Frank Barnstable and his two sons, three additional wranglers from their ranch, Marshal Curly Strand, Mike Grogan and two other townsmen, plus a half dozen wranglers from nearby ranches who'd heard about the rustling raid.

"I can't tell you how much I appreciate all of you

showin' up like this," Hardwick was saying. "Before we head out, though, I want to make double sure you're all clear that we're ridin' after some mighty dangerous hombres."

"Everybody understands that full well, Hannibal," Frank Barnstable said in response. "It's because of Creo Davies's reputation for being so ruthless and bloodthirsty that many of us are here. Sure, we want to help you get your cattle back. But we also know that if Creo gets away with something like this, it will only make him greedier for more. That means every other ranch and every decent person in the territory—maybe the town itself—will be at increased risk. We all need to pitch in and do everything we can to prevent that."

"For any of you who might be just catching up with the latest news," added Curly, "only a little while ago Broken Spoke *was* hit by a gang of ruthless criminals. Bank robbers. Luckily, their attempt got busted up. The bank's money was saved, but not without the terrible cost of innocent lives. I don't know what prompted the Devil to spew so much evil our way all at once, but Frank is right. We've got to beat it back and not let it take root, or we'll be even sorrier than we are now. That's why I'm joining in this chase, instead of staying and trying to comfort my suffering town. I figure that, in the long run, I can do more good by helping to eliminate Creo."

Castle shifted restlessly in his saddle. "Listen, I appreciate it's a good idea to make sure everybody understands what's going on. But we ought to be past that by now. And what's also past is more than ten hours since Creo and his pack of vermin rode out of here. I say we can't afford to waste a whole lot more time trying to hash things too fine before we get started after 'em."

"What we need to do," Mac said in a flat, hard voice, "is *settle* that varmint Creo's hash, once and for all."

"Hard to argue that," agreed Barnstable.

"What are we waiting for, then?" somebody asked.

"I'm all for making some dust. That's what we came for," spoke up Mike Grogan. "But it seems to me, considering the mixed bag of folks we got here and the dicey times sure to lay ahead, we ought to decide before we go much further who's leading this shindig. We got a couple ranch bosses who are used to calling the shots for their brands. And we got a marshal who—"

"Hold up on that one," Curly said, cutting him off. "I ain't shirking responsibility, but I also ain't here in no marshal capacity. First place, I'm plumb out of my jurisdiction. Second place, since we're bound to be going down into Mexico, I'll be even farther out. Hell, I'll be downright illegal . . . as will be all the rest of you. On top of that, other than a stint in the war, I've always functioned in a town setting. Out in broken country, I got even less experience than I got jurisdiction."

Hardwick chuffed sarcastically. "Don't set yourself up so high and mighty, Curly. Pretty soon you'll have us convinced you're so worthless, we might as well kick you back to your sufferin' town."

"Only convincing I see needs doing," replied the marshal, "is to state the obvious. It's your herd. You have the most immediate stake in this. You're clearly the one to do the ramrodding, Hannibal."

"I second that," said Barnstable.

Hardwick wagged his head. "Thanks for the vote of confidence, gents. I appreciate it. Ten years ago—hell, four years ago—nobody would have had to speak up for me. I'd've demanded taking charge, and made it stick. Only things are different now. For one thing, this bum leg of mine might not hold up for too much hard ridin'. You don't know how much I hate hearin' myself admit that, but fact is fact. I'm gonna give it a helluva try. We'll just have to see. Regardless, though, there's only one other man who's the right choice for leadin' this thing and seein' it through with the best chance to succeed. That man"—he jerked a thumb over his shoulder—"is Castle."

The old man paused, letting what he'd said sink in and giving time for some glances to be exchanged and a smidge of muttering to come from those who had had no exposure to Castle or hadn't even heard his name before. Then Hardwick went on. "Castle and his Texas boys have been nothing but willin' and useful ever since arrivin' in our area, startin' with savin' me and my gals from the rustlers a few days ago right through to helpin' bust up the bank robbery in town earlier this morning."

"I can vouch for that," said Curly.

Barnstable hesitated just a moment before giving a firm nod. "If Hannibal sees Castle as a man to ride the river with, then that's good enough for me. I say the matter is closed."

With all eyes suddenly focused on him, Castle swept a slow, level gaze in return and then signaled acceptance with a curt nod of his own. "All right, I guess that's the way it's gonna be. Right now the main thing is to get a move on and start closing the gap between us and that mangy pack. We can work out some of the finer details once we're rolling.

"But understand this. If I'm the one in charge, then that covers everything. From here on out, it's what I say that goes. Until this is over, nobody is riding for another brand or has any other allegiance except to this job. When we cross the Rio Grande, we're not only gonna have Creo's bunch to worry about, but there'll be Rurale patrols, other bandits, and maybe even some Apaches . . . all who'd be plenty anxious to relieve us of our lives and anything else that fancies 'em. The best chance to make it in and out of all that will be to think and act as one, to do what you're told when you're told to do it. That clear?"

Nobody spoke right away. Until a burly number named Mahoney, a wrangler from one of the outlying ranches, had something in his craw that needed spitting out.

"Now that we got a leader and you're laying down rules hard and fast," he said, "I got a thing been bothering me since I showed up a short time ago."

"Let's hear it and get it over with," Castle told him.

Mahoney made a gesture indicating the Hardwick sisters. "These two gals rigged up and ready to ride with us. You just rattled off all the dangers we might be running into. Don't the notion of taking a couple women along set wrong with nobody but me?"

"You raise a fair point," Castle allowed. "Time was I would have felt the same. But Tara and Sara have proven capable of riding and shooting as well or better than most men. Plus, considering the stolen beeves belong to them and their father, their stake in this is plenty solid." He paused long enough for one corner of his mouth to quirk slightly upward. "Besides . . . I'd hate to be the one to try and *stop* them from coming."

Mahoney didn't look wholly convinced, but then a shrug of his wide shoulders signaled acceptance. "Okay. I guess I got my answer."

They reached the river at dusk and made camp on the north side. Recognizing this might be their last chance for a while at a nighttime fire or hot food, Mac made a big batch of pan biscuits, which he passed out to everybody, while the rest cooked coffee and beans for themselves.

The Hardwicks and the Double T men were going on nearly twenty hard hours since they'd had any sleep, so it didn't take long after they'd eaten and darkness began settling in before they were more than ready for some. Before that, however, Sara motioned Mac to a shadowy spot on the edge of camp, where they could have a few minutes relatively alone.

"We've barely had a chance to speak, just the two of us, since those awful raiders showed up shooting and burning like hell itself," she started out.

Mac nodded wearily. "Yeah. Things have been mighty busy from then on."

Sara leaned close. "There's so much I want to say to you. So much I want you to know."

Mac placed his hands gently on her shoulders. The nearness and warmth of her, the *smell* of her . . . His exhaustion fell away, and a surge of passion like few he'd ever known coursed through him. There were things he wanted to say, too, feelings he wanted her to know. But what he felt and knew above all was that this wasn't the right time.

When he tried to explain, Sara pressed herself harder against him and said, "It's always the same with you. When *will* be the right time, Mac? What if you—or I, for that matter—don't come back from this trip? Think of the regret for not taking the time when it was available."

Perhaps due to his exhaustion, Mac became annoyed. "Available for what, Sara? Words? Promises? Sweet murmuring in your ear? I'm a man of deeds, not words, Sara. You've seen that. And you've also seen, must surely know, that I have feelings for you. But until I . . . I can *do*

something to back them up, it's just not in me to . . ."
Suddenly his hands were off her shoulders, and his arms
were wrapped around her, pulling her tighter still.

"It's okay, Mac," she whispered in his ear. "You're
right. Your actions do speak for you, and they've shown
your feelings. I saw you run through gunfire to try and
reach the house in order to save me from those savages.
How selfish would it be of me—of any woman—to ask
for more proof than that?"

Chapter 42

They crossed the river at first light the next morning. Before leaving, Castle shared with everybody some of the reasoning he and Squint had done the previous night, before turning in.

"Moving five or six hundred head of cattle, you can expect to cover an average of about fifteen miles a day," he said. "If everything goes real good, maybe eighteen or twenty. Now, we don't know how many good vaqueros Creo has in his gang. Since they've been rustling cattle south of the border for quite a spell, probably a fair number. So that means that's about what we should expect out of 'em."

"So how does that figure out to where they might be now compared to where we are?" asked Curly.

"If they pushed all night by moonlight and we know they left the Box H about one in the morning, that would have got 'em right about here at daybreak yesterday."

"With daylight, they would have kept on pushing all the harder, right?" said Grogan, the town barber.

"Not necessarily," responded Squint. "There's water here and halfway decent grass on this side of the river. By the looks of things, the land on the other side turns considerably harsher. Even though they'd want to eat up some miles ahead of the day's worst heat, I expect they more likely let the herd rest here for a spell to water and graze some."

"That fits the ground sign off to the west a ways," confirmed Boyd. "Big section of grass trampled and chewed down over there, and the riverbank along that same stretch is all dug up where the beeves crowded in to drink."

"The thing of it is, we got no way of knowing how long they stayed here," picked up Castle again. "I wouldn't expect no more than three, four hours. What it boils down to is that we got to figure they're still roughly a day ahead of us. The good news about that, though, is that a cattle herd moving fifteen or sixteen miles in a day is a lot slower than mounted horses being ridden in pursuit over that same period."

"You figure we'll catch up with 'em by the end of the day?" asked an eager-sounding Leo Barnstable.

Castle bared his teeth in a humorless smile. "I'm saying, depending what we run into in between, I think we got a good chance of getting *in sight* of them by the end of the day. That'll be far from the end of it, though. More like it will be where things turn even dicier."

Larabee emitted one of his dry cackles. "You can count on that, boys and girls. It sure as fire ain't like those skunks are gonna just hand the cows back on account of bein' good sports about us doin' such a dandy job of catchin' up and all."

"What it'll come down to at that point," said Castle,

his mouth straightening into a thin, tight line, "is the lay-out where we catch 'em, how big Creo's force actually is, and if there's anything that might give us an edge if we have to go gun to gun against them."

"Well, hell," drawled Hardwick, "here I thought this might turn into some rough piece of business."

As foreseen by Squint, the terrain south of the river quickly turned harsher, more barren. A wide, deep expanse of nothing but sand and dust speckled by cacti and clumps of scrub brush. The flatness of it made for easy going, though, and the trail of the cattle herd was plain, so they moved along steadily and at a good pace.

As the morning fell away, the land turned more broken. Long, crooked fissures, slashed into the dry ground like horizontal lightning bolts, became visible. Ragged-crested rock formations began thrusting up with greater frequency, some with shallow arroyos twisting through them. In the distance, an east-to-west line of saw-toothed mounds, not really big enough to be called mountains, rose up against the cloudless, sun-bleached sky. They were rusty brown in color, with little sign of any vegetation.

By noon, the baking, motionless air had grown brutal. Spotting a cluster of tall, sloping boulders with jagged peaks throwing intervals of shade along their base, Castle called a rest and motioned everybody to find shelter out of the sun. As soon as the horses were cooled off some, the men poured hatfuls of water for them to drink and only then sought what comfort there was for themselves.

After tending their own mounts, Mac and Sara sat together in a spot of shade, passing a canteen back and forth.

"This is worse than I imagined," said Sara. "I thought conditions got hot and dry up around Broken Spoke. How do people live in a place like this?"

"More like they endure," Mac told her.

"What about our cattle? No grass, no water for all this way . . . How long can they endure?"

"Cattle are pretty tough critters. Up to a point. The way Castle and Squint are reckoning, that ridge of low mountains we see ahead must not be very wide, and on the other side things likely open up to a valley or some such where there'll be graze and water for the beeves. The rustlers get 'em that far, they'll likely hold 'em there for a spell, give 'em a good rest before they start pushing 'em again."

Sara's eyes brightened in her pretty, sweat- and dust-streaked face. "Then there, if there is such a place, is where we can reclaim our herd. Right?"

Mac grinned. "Maybe. Though it may not be *quite* as easy as you make it sound."

"I know, I know. I heard all the things Castle said. But overcoming whatever we have to is exactly what we came to do, isn't it?"

"Indeed it is," Mac allowed. "And that's what we'll do. It's just a matter of seeing for sure what we're up against and then making the best plan to do the overcoming."

Sara regarded him in that way she had. "You have a lot of faith in Castle and Squint, don't you?"

"Sure do. They're good, solid men. A couple of the best I've ever run across."

"You realize they feel the same about you, don't you?"

"Well, I reckon I hope they do. But I got no way of being sure."

"Take it from me, it's true. I can see it plain, even if

you can't. And I'll tell you somebody else who thinks mighty highly of you Texans—and not just Castle, but all of you—and that's my father."

Mac grinned again. "I kinda got the impression, at least early on, that he wasn't overly keen on anything that came out of Texas."

"That might have been the case at one time. But it's possible for even ornery, stubborn old codgers to change their minds once in a while. Especially"—and here an impish twinkle suddenly formed in Sara's eyes—"when he's presented with the fact it's a Texan that his daughter is in love with."

"You mean your pa knows about Tara and Castle?"

"How could he not? He's got eyes, don't he? They've made it pretty doggone plain to everybody what's going on between them."

"Yeah, no getting around that."

"So earlier, while everybody was still assembling back at the ranch, they took Pa aside for a minute, and Castle stated his intentions to marry Tara as soon as this raider business is finished."

"Reckon the fact your pa bragged on Castle as the only man to lead this shindig we're on is a pretty clear sign he didn't have a problem with the notion of him as a son-in-law."

"So it would seem." Then, the twinkle not entirely gone from her eyes, Sara added, "Oh, by the way . . . after Pa got the straight of it about Tara and Castle, he wanted to know how things stood between me and you."

Any sign of a grin lingering on Mac's face was suddenly gone. "What made him ask that?" he wanted to know.

"Like I said before, he's got eyes, don't he?" Sara answered offhandedly. "We may have been keeping things more low key than my sister and Castle, but it hasn't exactly been a secret there are at least *some* sparks between us."

"Okay. So, uh, what did you tell your pa?"

Arching one eyebrow sharply, Sara snapped, "I told him that unlike Castle, who knows what he wants and is bold enough to go after it, you are . . . are just *a fence-sitter!*"

Mac wasn't sure what that meant and was even less sure how he should respond.

Luckily, he didn't have to. Because at that moment, Squint came slipping around the edge of a boulder, saying in a hushed voice, "Everybody pay attention! Boyd has spotted some riders comin' from the east. Likely a Rurale patrol. If they keep comin', they'll no doubt cut sign of the cattle herd trail. But our tracks will be hid in amongst them, so the Rurales shouldn't have no cause to look for us. Meanin' if we slip back deep in the rocks, keep the horses quiet, and stay still and low ourselves, we oughta be okay. Get on with it, then. Move back, slow and easy . . ."

Chapter 43

The approaching riders were indeed a Rurale patrol. Twenty heavily armed men riding two abreast. All were clad in sweaty, dust-caked khaki uniforms, with a single bandoleer over one shoulder, a pistol riding in a snap holster, and a repeating rifle snugged in a saddle scabbard. Steeple-crowned, wide-brimmed gray sombreros were on the heads of all but one. At their lead was a captain who somehow maintained a crisper, less sweat-stained uniform, splashed with a display of ribbons on the chest, and a black, stiff-billed cap.

Of additional note was a caisson wagon being pulled by the fifth pair of riders. It had a short bed and two tall wheels designed to travel over various sorts of rugged terrain. The bed was loaded with four wooden ammunition boxes and, in the center, an odd-shaped object draped in a canvas tarp.

"Is that what I think it is?" muttered Squint in a husky whisper from where he, Castle, Boyd, and Mac were wedged into a high crevice, out of which they were monitoring the oncoming column of men.

"If you're thinking it looks an awful lot like a Gatling gun with a tarp over it, then I'm afraid you're right," said Castle in response.

"A Gatlin' gun?" echoed Boyd in a low voice. "I thought Rurales was supposed to be rural policing outfits, not small armies all on their own. Those boys out there are geared up strong enough to fight a war, even without the Gatlin' piece."

"Like I told you, this country is full of killers," said Castle. "Injuns, bandits, owlhoots on the run from up North—"

"Like us, you mean?" Squint asked, cutting in.

"Plenty worse than us. But what they all got in common—including the local villagers and farmers—is that every one of 'em hates the corrupt Rurales more than practically anything else. The Rurales know this and keep themselves ready for trouble . . . the kind where all hell busts loose."

Mac took all of this in, just listening. He'd never seen a Rurale patrol before, and he sure as blazes had never had any encounters with a Gatling gun. He had heard about the terrible killing efficiency of such weapons and had even seen a picture of one in a newspaper once, but that was the extent of it. As far as he was concerned, he'd be satisfied getting no closer to one of the damn things than he was right now.

"They've reached the cattle trail," noted Boyd as he and the others continued to monitor the movement of the patrol.

"They're swingin' to follow it," added Squint a moment later. "And they didn't appear particularly surprised or bothered to run across it."

Castle said, "That Creo hombre may not have worked north of the river much before this, but by all reports, he's been active down this way, robbing and rustling and whatever, for quite a spell. If this patrol is any indication, you gotta kinda wonder why a bunch so well equipped as this one hasn't managed to pinch off Creo's fuse by now, don't you? If they really wanted to, that is."

"You sayin' you figure they're in cahoots with that pirate, that they're takin' a cut of his spoils to do some lookin' the other way when it comes to his shenanigans?" asked a frowning Squint.

Castle shrugged. "Like I said, the Rurales are notoriously corrupt. These outlying patrols especially have more of a reputation for skimming as much as they can get away with than they do for protecting the people."

"So," said Mac, finally adding to the conversation, "if this bunch we're looking at are on their way to meet up with the rustlers and end up spending any time with 'em . . . that all of a sudden makes what we might be facing a whole lot tougher."

"You said a mouthful there," grunted Squint.

"But *if* and *might*, those are the key words," declared Castle. "The presence of that patrol changes everything and means we need to hold off on bulling ahead like we were until we get a clearer picture on *if* and *might* and a few other things."

"What have you got in mind?" Boyd wanted to know.

"For starters, we're going to have to hold everybody right here for a while longer. Quite a while, I'm thinking. Nobody's going to like it, I know. It's hardly the lap of luxury, but at least it has a few splotches of shade, and it beats going back on the move through the hottest part of the day. Mainly, though, we can't afford to stir up a dust cloud like the one coming from the patrol that just passed.

You saw how far away we were able to spot them. If there are any lookouts in those high rocks ahead—or if that Rurale officer sends a man to check their back trail—we'll reveal ourselves a long time before we want to."

Boyd nodded. "Good point. We hold in place until late afternoon, near dusk. Goin' on the move then will be a lot easier on everybody and a lot less chance of bein' noticed. If there's a good moon again tonight, we can even travel some into dark."

"We'll lose time and distance on the herd again, though," Squint pointed out.

"Maybe. But not too much, I don't expect," countered Castle. "If there's a valley or graze of some kind beyond those high rocks, like we figure, the cattle will be there waiting. If not there, then somewhere damn close. Those rustlers *can't* run 'em beyond some time tomorrow without grass or water. Not unless they're aiming to run 'em to death, which makes no sense. But never mind so much guessing. With a little luck, I think there's a way we can get some facts."

The eyes of the other three quit following the fading patrol column and settled instead on Castle. Under their scrutiny, he said calmly, "Boyd . . . Mac . . . what would you say to a little scouting mission?"

Chapter 44

"There's the layout," Mac was saying from where he squatted beside some markings he'd scratched in the dirt. He was using the stick he had done the marking with as a pointer. "That about the way you recall it, Boyd?"

Boyd dropped to one knee beside Mac and, an intent expression on his dark face, studied the lines and shapes in question. "Appears you got it captured real accurate," he said.

Grouped around the two men, close but not so close as to blot out the wash of moon and starlight that illuminated the patch of ground under study, were the rest of those in pursuit of the stolen cattle. It was a handful of minutes past midnight, and by this point they had reached the ridge of high rocks and the mouth of a narrow, sandy-bottomed pass that appeared to cut a winding path through them. In the meantime, Mac and Boyd had completed their long, circuitous scouting assignment and had rejoined the eagerly awaiting main group only a short time earlier.

At this late hour, coming after a long, grueling day, having the scouts back with a more exact report on what lay ahead seemed to pump a wave of exhilaration through all present.

Getting on with the report, Mac said, "Through this pass, on the other side, the land pretty quickly changes, the way we were figuring it might. There's a wide stretch of grassland, with what appears to be a spring-fed pool off to one side, the west. That's where the cattle are now, settled in for the night, with a handful of nighthawks looking over 'em. Far as we could tell, it's the whole bunch still all together.

"If that was all of it, we'd be in pretty good shape to get done what we came for. But the kicker is here." With his stick, Mac tapped the series of lines and shapes he'd scratched along one side of the irregular circle representing the grassy area. "About a quarter of a mile in sits the sprawling hacienda of what has to be some rich Mex landowner. We reckon his name to be Delbacca, since that's the handle we kept hearing tossed around when we got in closer."

"Closer? How close did you get?" Hardwick wanted to know.

"Dang near within range to light a cigar for him," Boyd answered.

Castle frowned. "I sent you fellas to do some scouting, not stick your necks in so far you risked getting 'em slit."

"Tell that to him," Boyd said, jabbing a thumb at Mac. "Once it started getting dark, he took the notion we needed to gather all the details we could. I thought at one point he was gonna offer to help the cooks in the kitchen of the main house fix the big feed for the celebration the three he-bulls was enjoyin'."

"What celebration? What he-bulls?" Castle asked.

"The he-bulls," Mac explained, "were the Rurale captain we saw earlier in the day, some character in a bright red sash, who had to be the pirate Creo, and the overstuffed head honcho of the hacienda, who we reckoned to be Delbacca. Exactly what they were celebrating we can't say for positive, since they were yammering in Spanish, and neither me nor Boyd are much on that lingo. The way they were laughing it up while filling their faces with food and wine, though, it was sure something mighty pleasing to all of 'em."

"Probably deciding how much each would line their pockets from money made off the rustled cattle," said Castle.

Mac nodded. "That's about the way we figured it."

Frank Barnstable said, "If the he-bulls were gorging themselves in the main house and there was a handful of nighthawks out with the cattle, what about in between? What about the Rurale patrolmen and the rest of Creo's men? Was there any sign of them?"

Mac lifted his eyebrows. "Oh, yeah. Plenty." Pointing again with his stick, he proceeded to relate more. "This square is the hacienda's main house. These lines running off to the side and around front are meant to show a low adobe wall that makes what I guess you'd call a compound or courtyard. Along the inside of the west wall is a smokehouse, a chicken coop, a grain bin, and a few small sheds. In the middle is a well and a stone fountain. Along the east wall are some huts for the full-time vaqueros. For the time being, judging by the bedrolls spread on the ground through that same area, Creo's men are also camped there. Outside the front wall, the Rurale regulars are set up. They've got two rows of tents pitched, with the Gatling gun and rifle pyramids parked in the middle of 'em."

"The Rurale men, by the way," said Boyd, "were meanderin' pretty freely in and out of the compound to mingle with the vaqueros and Creo's bunch, passin' around jugs of tequila and joinin' in some singin' and guitar playin', all real friendly like."

"Another sign of the corrupt relationship between the Rurale captain and Creo . . . and how used the followers of each are to it," Castle spat disgustedly.

"Yeah, that's been established," Barnstable agreed. "So how many men, total, does that make at the hacienda?"

"Way we roughly added it up," answered Boyd, "it goes like this. Three nighthawks out with the cattle, another half dozen or so vaqueros in the compound huts, twenty Rurales, and twenty to twenty-five members of Creo's gang. I'd say about fifty-plus in all."

Somebody gave a low whistle.

"Yeah. Plenty to go around," Mac said solemnly.

"Dealing with the nighthawks and taking the cattle would be relatively easy," said Curly, as if thinking out loud. "But there'd be no chance of accomplishing that without rousting the hacienda. Would there?"

"None in hell," affirmed Boyd's voice in an ominous tone.

"So we roust 'em. That just means we have to be ready to deal with 'em," declared Brad Barnstable aggressively. "It was made clear from the get-go this wasn't gonna be no cakewalk. We figured all along Creo likely had thirty or more men."

"Thirty bandidos is one thing. But another twenty Rurales rigged out like full military," said the late-arriving wrangler named Mahoney, "is a bigger mess."

"The man speaks true," said Hardwick, a hint of dejection creeping into his tone. "I said all along I didn't want to see good men go out and commit what's shapin' up more and more to be dang near suicide for the sake of my cattle. They ain't nohow worth that."

"Now hold on a minute," insisted Castle. "We didn't push ourselves this far and bake our hides all day just to give up when things take an unexpected bad turn. Before we jump too quick to turning tail, we can at least stop for a minute to try and think of a way around or through what's been plunked in front of us."

"As a matter of fact," said Boyd, "me and Mac, havin' seen the situation ahead of y'all and therefore given a chance to already ponder it some, have hit on some ideas we think might work. You go ahead and tell 'em, Mac . . ."

Chapter 45

The ideas Mac and Boyd came up with were simply a matter of taking lessons from some of the tactics recently used against them by the outlaws/rustlers and turning them *back* on the varmints.

"We only need six or seven good wranglers—and we have plenty of those—to get rid of the nighthawks and set the herd in motion back out through this pass and headed for home," Mac laid it out. "That leaves the rest of us to take up positions at the hacienda and get ready to hammer everybody in and around the compound in ways that will make them being rousted not so much of a threat."

Castle was quick to catch on. "We do to them what they did to us at the Box H. We put 'em on the defensive and try to cripple 'em from any quick reaction to us driving off the cattle."

"Taking *back* the cattle—*my* cattle," Hardwick corrected, a sudden surge of enthusiasm overtaking the dejection he'd shown signs of earlier.

It wasn't long, as Mac presented his and Boyd's ideas and they got further discussed and refined, before Hardwick's enthusiasm spread through the rest of the group. With the goal of striking in mere hours, in the final murkiness of night, just ahead of dawn's first paleness appearing above the eastern horizon, final details and specific assignments began getting ironed out. It was a bold undertaking, requiring a degree of daring and close timing that would have tested even a trained military unit, but everyone involved was confident and stonily determined to make it work.

In the precious couple of hours available for rest and some final reflection before everyone had to start through the pass in order to get in position, Sara again sought out Mac and maneuvered him to a spot where they were somewhat apart from the others.

"You left on that scouting thing without even saying good-bye," she said in a soft yet scolding tone.

Gazing down at her face, once more so near to his and cast in an intriguing mix of faint shadow and silver-blue illumination from above, Mac felt she had never looked lovelier. With a touch of huskiness in his voice, he said, "There wasn't any time. Boyd and me didn't know what we were going to find, how far we'd have to go, or how long it would take. It was important to get started right away."

"And once you found what you did, was it so important to work your way right into the thick of those . . . those bloodthirsty dogs in order to put yourselves even more completely at risk?"

"It seemed like a good idea to eyeball as much as we

could as close as we could. In the long run, I think it paid off," Mac said.

Sara's eyes flashed. "What about the short run? Say, the length of a knife slash laying open your throat if you'd gotten caught? Would it still have been worth—"

She stopped suddenly. Her eyes closed and the furrows across her forehead slowly smoothed as she willed herself to regain composure. When her eyes opened again, she said in a softer voice, "Wasting time with petty anger is the wrong thing for me to do. Especially now. Let's face it, apart from the danger you and Boyd placed yourselves in, what we're all about to embark on comes with considerable risk and danger for everybody. Some of us likely won't make it."

"That's a heck of a thing to say," Mac responded. "We'll have the element of surprise. If we hit hard and fast and the timing is right, there's no reason to think we can't pull this off. We tangled with Creo the first time without losing anybody, didn't we?"

"Only the same couldn't be said for several of his men, could it? And they were the ones in the position we'll be in this time around . . . out in the open, attacking." Abruptly, Sara leaned into Mac and slipped her arms around his waist. "But never mind that. It will turn out the way it turns out. The real reason I wanted to have these few minutes with you was to talk about something else. Something that's been hinted at and danced around for days, so I'm just going to go ahead and say it. I'm in love with you, Dewey Mackenzie. If there was any doubt in my mind, the terror I felt at the possibility of you not returning from that scouting trip erased it."

As if by their own volition, Mac's arms were around her. Gazing down at her upturned face, he tried to find the right words, but all that came out was, "Aw, Sara . . ."

"That's all right. You don't have to say the word back to me. Not until you're sure. I know you feel affection for me, and I told you before I can be patient." She smiled. "Except, I guess, when it comes to myself. I just wanted to make it clear, in case . . . Well, I wanted to be sure you knew."

Finally finding his voice, Mac said, "Love is a wonderful thing, Sara. To feel and to hear expressed. I've known affection, and yes, I feel a great deal of it toward you. But I've only ever told one woman in my life that I loved her. She went on to viciously betray me after falling under the influence of someone she should have recognized for the evil cur he was." He sighed and shook his head. "I know none of that is your fault, and it shouldn't matter to the here and now. But it's a bitterness I carry deep in me, and until I somehow get it purged out . . ."

Sara put a finger to his lips. "It's okay. I could always tell there was some kind of sadness you were holding inside. When this is over, if you let me, I think I can be the one to help you purge it out."

They kissed then. Passionately, intently. And for the first time, Mac didn't give one damn if anybody was noticing or not.

Chapter 46

Mac, Castle, Boyd, and Mahoney would start everything off. They were positioned outside the compound wall, southeast of the hacienda's main house, where a large corral held the vaqueros' remuda. Also contained there, on this occasion, were the horses of Creo and his men.

Releasing these mounts and scattering them in a wild panic, thus making them unavailable to use for pursuit—exactly as had been done during the raid on the Box H—was one of the keys to successfully retrieving the cattle. Helping to propel the horses' flight, on top of shooting and hollering, would be to set ablaze two large haystacks piled close on either side of the corral.

This initial burst of chaos would be the signal for the wranglers now stationed with the cattle—the nighthawks previously in place having already been silently eliminated—to set the herd in motion toward the pass and then on north to where they belonged.

Handling this part of the operation were Hannibal Hardwick, his daughters, and the three men from the B-Bar-B. Putting this in the hands of the Hardwicks simply made sense. While Tara and Sara knew how to handle guns as well as cows, nobody in their right mind wanted to put them in the thick of the gunfire when there was an equally important option.

By the same token, though he'd held up amazingly well so far, it was no secret that their father's wounded leg was straining him and presenting some limitations that might prove disastrous if he tried to navigate in a lead storm. Driving the cattle would have its own challenges, but ones far more manageable.

Also ready to join in as soon as things broke at the remuda corral were Squint and Red, who were stationed along with two townsmen just outside the east compound wall, where the vaquero huts and the bedrolls of Creo's men were located. They would throw torches over onto the huts and then fan out along the wall to open fire on the men inside as they stirred into action. Across the courtyard, from behind the west wall, Curly and Grogan were ready to lay down an assisting cross fire.

Farther down from Squint's team, at the northeast corner of the wall, the Barnstables were poised to wreak havoc on the Rurale encampment—hopefully before the patrolmen completely knew what hit them—after first cutting loose and releasing the picketed horses, as had been done with those from the corral. Their father laid down a barrage of cover fire, aided by Larabee and one of the volunteers from an outlying ranch, who would shoot from the opposite corner of the wall. Leo and Brad meant to ride hell-for-leather straight through the rows of tents for the purpose of damaging or at least upending the

Gatling gun in order to render it temporarily useless against the raiders.

That was how everything and everybody was set.

The raid on the raiders was ready to be unleashed.

"Eeeyah!"

"Yip, yip!"

"Run for the hills, you nags!"

Castle and Mahoney yanked open the corral gate and began pulling down sections of the rail, all the while whooping and firing their six-shooters in the air to get the horses inside whipped into a frenzy that sent them trampling and leaping to get away. Mac and Boyd each raced toward one of the haystacks with a flaming torch in hand. In little more than a minute, the corral was in shambles and empty, the horses were thundering in wild profusion to the south, and the stacks of hay were crackling infernos, sending sparks and billowing smoke high into the fading night sky.

At the same time, the Hardwicks and the men helping them got the herd quickly and successfully in motion, pushing it toward the pass.

In between, hell was popping.

After leading with torches thrown over onto the thatched roofs of the vaquero huts, the four-man team led by Squint and Red followed up by beginning a heavy exchange of gunfire with the vaqueros and Creo gang members who had been flushed out as a result. As planned, Curly and Grogan also joined in from behind the compound wall across the courtyard. In no time, the air was filled with boiling black clouds from the burning huts as well as a thickening haze of gunsmoke.

Those within the courtyard, who were so startlingly aroused to all of this, scrambled either to flee or find cover for returning fire. Often as not, however, they were driven back by walls of licking flames or hammered down by a hail of bullets.

Outside the compound, at the northeast corner, the Barnstables quickly freed the picketed Rurale horses with a flurry of knife strokes to the picket line. That done, the father promptly shouldered his rifle and began pouring lead at the khaki-clad patrolmen as soon as they came clambering out of their tents. From the opposite corner of the wall, Larabee and one of the outlying wranglers cut loose on the same targets.

Veering in and out to avoid getting caught in the cross fire, Brad and Leo spurred their mounts through the line of tents until they reached the Rurale rifles precisely stacked in two pyramids on either side of the Gatling gun. A pair of expertly cast lassos closed around each of these, cinched tight, and then the bundles of weapons were dragged bouncing and clattering away, even as some of the men from the nearest tents staggered and lunged in vain to prevent their removal.

With the remuda horses in flight and the haystacks in flames and the rest of the raiders signaled into action, the plan now was for Mac, Castle, Boyd, and Mahoney to work their way down to join Squint and his team outside the east compound wall. However, as they began their turn in that direction, an unanticipated interruption popped up. Gunfire from some rear and side windows of the hacienda's main house suddenly crackled, sending a flurry of bullets aimed their way.

The shots seemed frantic and wildly off the mark. Castle called to the others, "We can't afford to waste time with a handful of house rats! Let's join up with Squint and Red!"

But a moment later, there was a new development that changed his mind. Out of the house's back door, a single man came running. He was barefoot and shirtless yet, incongruously, a bright scarlet sash was wrapped around his middle. He ran brandishing a long-barreled pistol in each hand while furiously screaming Spanish curses.

At the sight of him, Castle immediately jerked back on his reins and said, "Creo! On second thought, here's a pirate rat I *do* have time to sink the ship of!"

After wheeling his horse, Castle heeled it hard to meet the onrushing bandit leader. Creo fired two shots on the run. They sizzled high and wide, made even more so by Castle ducking low in his saddle and leaning over to one side of his horse's neck. Straightening up, the trail boss got off a shot of his own as Creo fired again simultaneously. Castle's shot missed, the slug gouging dirt to one side of the running man. Creo's shot missed its intended target but struck the horse instead.

With a shriek of pain, the wounded animal threw its head high as its front legs folded, and its forward momentum carried it into a toppling, tumbling fall. Castle was thrown from the saddle and sent into a rolling tumble of his own. Seeing this, Mac and Boyd immediately wheeled their own mounts and charged in the direction of their fallen comrade.

But not only did Castle keep a grip on his Colt, he also somehow managed to come out of the tumble clearheaded. Shoving up onto one knee, he promptly thrust the Colt out ahead at waist level and spun to again face Creo. The latter, continuing to advance on someone he expected would surely be stunned by the fall, was instead the one stunned by surprise.

In fact, it surprised him plumb to death when Castle

rapid-fired two rounds that blew apart the would-be pirate's black heart and knocked him flat onto his back.

As Castle rose to his feet, Mac reined up beside him and said, "If you're done hunting rats for a while, you want a lift?"

Castle glared at the hacienda's main house, from which no more shots were coming. "That Rurale captain might be in there, too."

"If he is, he can't be worth much," pointed out Boyd. "He didn't back Creo's play, and since the shootin's now stopped, it appears he might've found hisself a hidey-hole."

"Remember what you said about wasting too much time with rodents," Mac said.

Castle gave a grudging nod, and then, with him swinging up to ride double, they moved on down the outside of the east wall to join Squint and Red. Though the vaquero huts continued to crackle and burn, the shooting from all points around the compound had sputtered down to only a few sporadic reports.

"I think we got the cockroaches mostly stomped out," Squint said. "Don't see no reason to hang around no longer than we have to."

With no objection to that, Castle signaled Curly and Grogan on the other side of the west wall, and they all commenced moving to converge with Larabee and the Barnstables out in front of the compound.

There was good news waiting there. The Rurales had been routed successfully, another notch in the overall plan having worked as intended.

But there was some unfortunate news waiting, too . . . and it would turn out to be only the beginning.

Chapter 47

"His name was Nelson. Dev Nelson. He rode for the Lazy L, a spread not too far north of my place. Never knew much about him. But he came to join in as soon as he heard what we was setting out to do. Reckon that speaks well of him."

Those were Frank Barnstable's words as he described the young wrangler who had been siding Larabee at the northwest corner of the compound. He'd taken a fatal hit from a Rurale bullet.

But that wasn't all. The same volley of return fire that killed Nelson had also caught Larabee. Caught him bad. Two slugs drilling at an inward angle just under his ribs and lodging there.

"Don't that beat all." The old puncher grimaced as the others gathered around where he lay. "We finally get Mac aboard as the best dang grub cook I ever worked with, and now I go and eat a servin' of lead, which . . . which I fear I ain't gonna digest very good at all."

"Just lay still, you darned old slacker," Squint growled with a catch in his throat. "We get that bleedin' stopped, we'll rig you a drag litter so you can do the thing you do best—lay around on your backside—while we haul you back across half of Mexico so's Doc Washburn can finish healin' you up."

"Don't bother," Larabee protested. "I'll just slow you down, and it'll be a waste, anyhow. I been around long enough to know how it ends for a fella with a couple slugs in his gut."

He continued protesting, but nobody paid any attention as they worked on stanching the bleeding and making a hurriedly fashioned travois out of the canvas and poles from one of the Rurales' tents. They had just gotten Larabee loaded on, made him as comfortable as possible, and were ready to head out when Brad Barnstable came riding back from where he and his brother had dragged off the Rurale guns and pulled away the Gatling gun on its cart.

The young man's face was chalky white and his expression anguished even before his eyes fell on the dead and wounded. Taking only a moment to acknowledge this sight, he then said in a rush, "Y'all had better come quick. Old man . . . er, I mean Mr. Hardwick, is hurt bad . . . And so is one of his daughters."

"Which daughter?" Mac and Castle blurted in unison.

Brad's eyes turned sad as they settled on Mac. "I'm afraid it's Miss Sara."

They found them on the fringe of the grassy sprawl, just short of the entrance to the pass through the high rocks. It was light by now, the first edge of the sun getting ready to poke above the eastern horizon. The cattle were nowhere in sight, the B-Bar-B men evidently having taken them on through the pass.

Hardwick and Tara sat side by side on the ground. Even at a distance, both were clearly highly distraught, their faces flushed and tear streaked. Sara lay stretched out before them, her head in her father's lap. She lay very, very still.

As soon as he saw her, Mac's heart sank. He knew from bitter experience that kind of stillness came only with death.

Before anybody could ask or say anything, Hardwick lifted his tortured face and groaned, "It's like the most terrible nightmare . . . only it's real. The cruel hand of Satan . . . because no just God would do this to a man, a father." Then his head fell again, and he wept.

After a moment, in her own ragged voice, Tara explained it more completely. "It was one of the nighthawks we thought had been killed. He still had some life left in him . . . enough to lie waiting off in the grass until he saw a chance to try and get even. What he saw was Sara, riding drag after most of the herd was already in the pass . . . The nighthawk rose up, cursing and firing wildly. One of his shots managed to hit her . . . When Pa saw her go down, he turned and rode back before her killer was done shooting. Pa was too late to save Sara, but he got revenge for her . . . only not before he also took a bullet."

Frank Barnstable winced. "How bad?"

Tara shook her head. "Not good, I'm afraid."

"Damn right it ain't good!" growled Hardwick, lifting his head again. "I'm a goner, and I know it. You try to take me with you, all I'll do is slow you down and end up dyin' on you, anyway."

"That's the same thing I been tryin' to tell the hard-headed varmints," spoke up Larabee from his travois. "But they won't listen."

"Pa, there's no way in the world we're going to just leave you here," declared Tara.

"Nobody's leaving nobody," Castle seconded.

"Why not? Why not leave me where I can maybe do some good instead of bein' a bother guaranteed to turn out for naught?" Hardwick argued.

"How are you going to do any good if we leave you here?" Barnstable wanted to know.

"Between bouts of mournin', I been sittin' here studyin' on a couple of things." Hardwick pointed. "For one, there's that big pond of water over there. Makes me think how those horses that got scattered have been corralled and picketed all night and were likely countin' on havin' themselves a good drink this mornin'. We threw a wrench into that. But after they've run for a while, them nags are gonna start thinkin' again about gettin' that drink. Some of 'em, I expect, will remember this pond of water."

"And that matters how?" asked Curly Strand.

"It matters," answered Squint, "because there are bound to be a few pockets of survivors still in that compound back yonder. If they all of a sudden have access to mounts again, you think they won't take a notion to come after us? Especially if enough of 'em are Rurales—their captain havin' never been accounted for, remember—wantin' to get their Gatlin' gun back. Even though we didn't take the darn thing."

"But this time we'll be the ones with superior numbers. We cut down dozens of the scurvy dogs."

Squint shook his head. "Don't mean what's left can't still peck away and harass us, cost us more lives."

Hardwick spoke again. "If we had that Gatlin' gun is the other thing I was ponderin' . . . the rest of how I could stay behind and do the most good before checkin' out." He paused long enough to emit a short, wet-sounding cough before continuing. "Picture this. Plant me in a narrow spot in the pass, set me up with that bullet gobbler, and somebody show me how to use it . . . Then, for as long as I last, any mother's son tries to use the pass to come after the rest of you, I send 'em to hell lookin' like pieces of Swiss cheese!"

"Count me in on that, too," crowed Larabee. "For the love of God, people, let a couple of old rannies who know their time has come check out the way they want. With some dignity, maybe even some glory!"

"Pa, don't ask this of me. I . . . I can't do it," sobbed Tara.

Hardwick reached up with a blood-smeared hand and clutched one of hers. "Yes, you can. You've always been the strong one, Tara. That's what I need you to be now . . . Take your sister home. Put her to rest in that plot with Ma. Give her a nice monument . . . Where my old bones end up don't matter. You . . . you and Castle . . . get those cattle back and build the Box H into something bigger and grander than I ever could have. Have a passel of kids and see to it they carry on . . . *That* will be my monument."

Mac had been hearing all of this vaguely, listening as if from far away, never for a moment taking his eyes off Sara. So still. So lovely, even in death.

I'm in love with you, Dewey Mackenzie.

Those words echoed through his mind. And with each

refrain came the knifing pain of knowing how badly she had wanted him to respond in kind . . . yet he hadn't. Mac cursed himself. Why had he refused to give her that simple satisfaction? What was wrong with him?

At that moment the sun finally broke above the horizon. A line of golden brightness washed over Sara's face, and for just a second, it was as if life had been poured back into her . . . But it hadn't, of course. It was only an illusion. Her life was gone. Forever.

Mac rocked back from the moment, as if a man coming out of a stupor, and swept a sharpened gaze over all around him.

"The old-timers are correct," he declared abruptly, authoritatively. "They have the right to call their own shots and check out with what they see as dignity. They've earned it. If they view it as a final meaningful thing for themselves, then we owe them the chance."

Everything was stone silent for a long count. Until Castle met Mac's sharp gaze with one of his own. "Are you sure?"

"I am," Mac replied firmly.

And then Squint added, "Reckon I feel the same . . . They have a right to their dignity as they see it."

Tara choked back a sob but said nothing.

It was settled.

For the rest of the day and into evening, as they pushed the herd north across the barrens and nearer to the river, Mac would slow his horse periodically and twist around in the saddle. First, he would look down to check and make sure the blanket-wrapped form of Sara was still riding securely on the travois he was pulling. Then he would pause and wait for the right moment of silence to grip the vastness. When it did, if he listened hard enough . . . he could almost swear that, ever so faintly, he was able to hear the far-off chatter of a Gatling gun and the raucous whoops of two old cowboys going out in a blaze of glory.

Chapter 48

A week after the retrieved cattle were back on Box H grass, four Double T cowboys were ready to depart for the delayed return to Texas. Each wore a mixed expression of sorrow and determination.

Larabee was not among them, of course. Nor was Castle. Even before Hardwick's words back at that pass in Mexico, there had been a growing awareness among most that it seemed headed for this, Castle remaining with Tara. Now that the need, not to mention the feelings between them, was even greater, there was no getting around it.

In a stirring, widely attended funeral service, Sara's earthly remains had been put to rest in the family plot, alongside her late mother. Dev Nelson, the wrangler who'd died siding Larabee, with no known relatives, was given a much more sparsely attended service and then was buried on a crest of the Lazy L spread.

With these matters tended to and Castle and Tara having already signed on some reliable new hired hands, there were no more reasons for the remaining Double T men to stick around. On hand to see them off, in addition to Castle and Tara, were the Barnstables and Marshal Curly Strand.

"With you rowdy Texans gone back where you belong," Curly huffed with false sternness, "maybe things will settle down and turn peaceful around these parts again."

"Maybe so," Frank Barnstable allowed. "But if the wind ever blows any of you fellas off course and you drift back this way again, I reckon we could find a way to stand it."

"It ought to go without saying, but you know one place you'll always be welcome," Castle stated solemnly.

"I second that," said Tara from where she stood close beside him. "For one thing, there'll be a wedding shindig to come back to one of these days before too long."

Squint grunted. "Fat chance of Boss Tremaine turnin' us loose again anytime soon, especially if he thinks we'd head this way."

"That fat money belt you're taking back ought to calm him down some," Castle reminded him. "Either way, tell the old mossyhorn for me that I appreciate all the opportunities he gave me and was always proud to ride for the Double T brand. And tell the rest of those hombres in the bunkhouse that I ain't gonna miss the smell or sight of 'em hardly a lick . . . But I'll still hold on to some good memories of having worked with 'em."

That was about it.

Except for Tara stepping away from Castle and walking over to stand beside Mac where he was perched on the driver's box of the Double T chuckwagon. Pard was tied to the back of the vehicle. They had come across the horse during the return to the Box H, grazing along with some of the other horses stolen in Creo's savage raid on the ranch but freed during the assault on the hacienda compound. Recovering his trail partner was scant recompense for losing Sara, but Mac was glad to have Pard back.

Looking up, Tara said softly, "My sister was very fond of you, you know."

"I know," Mac affirmed somewhat huskily. "I was honored."

"She wouldn't have developed those feelings for just anybody. Way I see it, that must make you a special person."

Mac shook his head. "But not good enough for her."

Tara winced. "I'm sorry to hear you say that. I'm sorriest of all, naturally, that Sara is gone. But part of that is regretting the two of you didn't have more time together. Maybe then . . ."

"I regret it, too, Miss Tara. More than you'll ever know."

With that, Mac pinched his hat brim and nodded to her before slapping the reins against the backs of the mules and calling out to them. The vehicle lurched into motion and rolled away, leading the others on their way back to Texas.

You're never too old to fight for justice in a new trail-blazing series from legendary national bestselling Western authors William W. Johnstone and J.A. Johnstone.

OLD COWBOYS NEVER DIE
William W. Johnstone and J.A. Johnstone

From the bestselling masters of the classic western comes a blazing new series that proves that old cowboys only get wiser, bolder—and crazier—with age....

They say you can't teach an old dog new tricks. But old cowboys? That's a different story—especially when those cowboys are trail-hardened cattlemen like Casey Tubbs and Levi Doolin. When these longtime buddies learn that their bosses are getting out of the beef business, they figure it's probably time to retire anyway. Nothing left to do now but deliver the last two-thousand cows to Abilene and collect their pay. There's just one problem. Their bosses' lawyer is skipping town with all the workers' cash—which means Tubbs and Doolin have one last job to do....

Steal it back.

Sure, pulling off a robbery is a new challenge for these old boys. But they've learned a lot of tricks over the years—and they're one hell of a team. There's just one catch: once they pull off the perfect crime—and get away with it—Tubbs and Doolin start thinking they may have missed their calling in life. This could be the start of a whole new career . . . as outlaws.

So begins the wild, wild story of two old cowboys who are one step ahead of the law—and the young U.S. marshal who's determined to catch them....

Chapter 1

"Well, I reckon that about ties a knot in it," Casey Tubbs announced as he joined the little group of eight men sprawled on their bedrolls around the chuckwagon. "Any coffee left in that pot, Smiley?"

"Yeah," Smiley said, and poured a cup for him.

Like the rest of the crew, Smiley was anxious to hear what Casey had found out when he went to look for Ronald Dorsey. They had driven the last of the two thousand cows into the holding pens at the Abilene rail yards. Dorsey, a lawyer for Whitmore Brothers Cattle Company, was responsible for collecting the money when the cattle were sold. He was also the man who would pay the crew their wages.

"Did you find Dorsey?" Smiley asked.

"Yep, I found him," Casey said.

"Well, what did he say?" Eli Doolin asked impatiently. "When are we gonna get paid?"

"He said he figured it all up and we owe the company money for our horses and such," Casey said.

"Damn it, Casey," Eli said, "when's he gonna pay us?"

Eli, along with Casey, was one of the older cowhands for Whitmore Brothers. The two of them had been working cattle together for so long that each one knew when the other was joking. The rest of the crew, all but two were young men in their teens, anxiously waited to hear what Casey had found out.

"Dorsey said the payroll was deposited in the First Cattleman's Bank under each man's name. We have to go to the bank to draw our money out. And the damn bank's closed now, so we'll have to wait till tomorrow mornin' to get our money." His statement was met with a chorus of groans and complaints. Every man was eager to have money in his pocket tonight. It had not been a particularly long drive. But every drive was hard work, pushing ornery cows across a dusty prairie, driving them all day, watching them all night. The pay was forty dollars a month, so a drive this short wouldn't put much money in their pockets. It had only taken a couple of days longer than two months. But it was enough time for them to want to "see the elephant" and ride home broke but happy after a night in Abilene.

Eli got up from his blanket and walked over to talk to Casey. "Why the hell didn't he just hold the payroll and pay us tonight? They've always paid us before," he said to him. "All the years before this, when John Whitmore was running things, we got our money the same time he got his."

"Well, this year, thanks to the way Mr. Dorsey handles it, we'll rest up tonight so we can light up Abilene tomorrow, good and proper. You still got grub to cook on that wagon, don't you, Smiley?"

"I sure do," Smiley said, "and I'm supposed to get some money to feed us on the way back home."

"There you go, boys," Eli declared. "You'll have a good meal in your belly on top of a good night's rest when you attack Abilene tomorrow." He looked then at Davey Springer, youngest of the crew at the age of fifteen—and this, his first cattle drive. "This way, you'll be able to brag about it when you get back home. You can tell 'em you didn't spend all the little bit of money you made until the second night you were in Abilene." Still looking directly at Davey, he said, "You'd best be careful if you fancy one of those little gals that makes her livin' gazin' at the ceilin'. You reach in your pocket and her hand will already be in there, countin' your change."

"You talk like you ain't gonna go into town with the rest of us, Eli," Sam Dunn, an experienced drover at the age of eighteen, remarked.

"Oh, I'll be goin' in with you," Eli said. "Both me and Casey, I expect. But when you young bucks head for the saloons and the dancehalls, we'll most likely find us a good supper and a drink of likker afterward. Right, Casey?" Casey nodded in reply. "You see, I've left too many a little dancehall gal with a broken heart when I had to tell her I couldn't stay with her. I don't fancy breakin' any more hearts."

His remarks received the mocking he expected. "Maybe when you and Casey finish your supper, you can look for a dancehall where the old ladies are all rollin' around in their wheelchairs," Sam suggested.

"That's a right interestin' proposition," Casey commented. "I like the sound of that."

The jawing back and forth continued right through supper, and for a while afterward, because there was nothing else to do. Dorsey sold the remuda, as well as the cattle, so there were no horses to take care of except the one you kept to ride back home.

* * *

There was no reason to roll out of their blankets early the next morning. The bank didn't open until nine o'clock, which to a cowhand seemed more like noon. Smiley was up early as usual, however, to fix breakfast. They were all standing by the front door of the bank when one of the tellers came to open it. He hesitated when he saw the nine cowhands waiting there. Evidently surmising that they could break the door down, he proceeded to open it. They filed in and lined up at the teller's window.

"Good morning," the teller greeted Casey, who was the first in his line. "What can I help you with?"

"You can help me with my lack of spendin' money," Casey said cheerfully. He gestured with his hand at the men standing behind him. "The nine of us work for the Whitmore Brothers Cattle Company. We brought a herd of cows up here that were sold yesterday. And Mr. Ronald Dorsey deposited the payroll for us in your bank so each one of us could pick up our money this mornin'. My name's Casey Tubbs." He stood there waiting for the teller to do whatever he was going to do to give him his money.

The teller could only respond with an expression of complete puzzlement. He had no knowledge of any payroll the bank was holding. "I'm sorry, Mr. Tubbs, I'll have to get Mr. Skidmore to help you. I'm afraid I don't know anything about your payroll." When he saw Casey's immediate reaction, he said, "I'll be right back. Mr. Skidmore will know about it, I'm sure." He left the cage and hurried back to the bank president's office.

In a few minutes, the teller returned with the president following. Casey didn't like the expression on the president's face. It was one of concern, instead of confidence. "Mr. Tubbs," he said, "I'm Malcolm Skidmore. I'm the president of this bank. There seems to be some confusion about some payroll money?"

"This is the First Cattleman's Bank, ain't it?" Casey asked. When Skidmore acknowledged that, Casey asked, "You did have a Mr. Ronald Dorsey in here yesterday to cash a check for the sale of Whitmore Brothers Cattle Company's herd of two thousand cows, right?"

"Yes, we did," Skidmore said.

"Then there ain't no confusion," Casey declared confidently.

But Skidmore still showed plenty. "The check was honored and the cash was picked up by a special messenger before we opened this morning to be put on the train for Chicago. Those were Mr. Dorsey's instructions."

"But there was most likely a separate sum of money that was the *payroll only*," Casey stressed. "That was supposed to be left here in the bank for us to pick up this morning."

"I'm afraid there's been some misunderstanding," Skidmore said. "Mr. Dorsey said nothing about any payroll. He wanted the entire amount of the money from the sale put on the train to Chicago." Seeing the instant shock of all nine men, he quickly sought to explain his position. "Please understand, the bank is in no way involved with Mr. Dorsey's decision on how the money was to be paid. He had a legitimate check and we honored it. Then, as is often the case with a large sum of cash, the customer wishes to have it transported in the safety of the mail car on the train. In that case, we are happy to provide a guard to accompany the customer to the train station, as we did this morning with Mr. Dorsey before the bank opened."

"So you're tellin' us that the money we worked for went to Chicago this mornin' with Ronald Dorsey?" Eli asked.

Skidmore turned to answer him. "I'm afraid so," he said. "At least it will. That train isn't scheduled to leave here until nine forty-five."

Eli turned to look at Casey. They were both thinking the same thing. "We ain't got much time to find that double-crossin' lawyer," he said.

"No we ain't," Casey said, "let's get goin'!" They headed straight for the door, and Smiley and the six younger men followed.

Outside, they gathered around the three older men, looking for answers. "Whadda we gonna do, Casey?" Sam Dunn asked, plainly bewildered.

Casey looked at the lot of them, all as bewildered as Sam. He made an instant decision. "Me and Eli will take care of it. Smiley, you boys go on back by the creek where we camped and wait for us there. We'll meet you back there."

Too confused to offer any other suggestions, they dutifully climbed on their horses and went back to the place they had camped the night just passed. Casey and Eli headed for the train station at a gallop.

The train was still sitting in the station and still taking on passengers when they pulled their horses to a stop beside what appeared to be the mail car. The intention was to find Ronald Dorsey, so they climbed on the train and entered the passenger car behind the mail car. Since Casey was the only one who had actually talked to him, he led the way as they hurried down the aisle, looking left and right for Dorsey. Not seeing him in the first car, they went into the next car and looked for him with the same results. The same happened in the third car, where they bumped into the conductor.

"Can I help you gentlemen?"

"No," Eli said. "We're just lookin' for somebody. We'll look in the next car."

"That's the caboose," the conductor said.

"Oh, well, I reckon we'll look again in them other cars," Eli said.

"Can I see your tickets?" The conductor was now concerned with the two desperate-looking men.

"We left 'em with our suitcases up in the first car," Casey said, and started back up the aisle, Eli went right behind him. The conductor just stood there for a moment before deciding he'd better follow them and get a look at their tickets, if they actually had tickets.

They hurried back up the aisles with still no sign of Ronald Dorsey. When they got to the door they had first entered, they stopped to decide what to do. "I'm afraid I'm going to have to ask you gentlemen to get off the train, unless you can show me your tickets."

Ignoring his ultimatum, Casey asked, "What's in that next car?"

"That's the mail car," the conductor said. "You can't go in there." Casey ignored him and went to the door, but found it locked. "You can't go in the mail car," the conductor repeated, now past concern and approaching panic. Still, he tried to maintain his posture of authority. "Now, both of you, off the train, unless you show me a ticket."

"Here's my ticket," Eli said, and pulled his Colt .45 from his holster and jammed it in the conductor's back. "You'd best come up with a key to that door right quick. We ain't got time to argue with you."

"Yes, sir," the conductor said right away, abandoning all pretense of authority. "But it won't open if he's slid the bolt on the other side." He fumbled with his ring of keys until he found one for the mail car. With one hand on the back of the conductor's collar and the other holding the gun against his back, Eli pushed him through the door when it opened.

A startled mail guard looked up from a small desk and asked, "What's goin' on, John?" A second later, he realized what was happening and he started to bolt upright from his chair, only to flop back down when he saw Casey, also holding a gun. Regaining a portion of his valor, he had to exclaim, "Right here? In the station? You must be out of your mind."

"What's your name?" Casey demanded.

"Wesley Logan," he said, staring at the revolver aimed at him.

"Well, I'm gonna make this real easy for you, Wesley," Casey continued. "All you have to do is follow my orders and we'll soon be gone. First thing is to reach over with your left hand and pull that pistol outta your holster and lay it on the floor. Be real careful, Wesley, I druther not have to shoot you." When Wesley laid the revolver on the floor, Casey said, "Kick it over here." Wesley did so and Eli picked it up. "We're here for one sack of money that belongs to the Whitmore Brothers Cattle Company," Casey continued then. "The sooner you give us that sack, the sooner we'll be out of here."

Wesley looked confused. He glanced down at a ledger on his desk, then back up at Casey. "We don't have any bag for Whitmore Brothers," he said.

"How 'bout one for Ronald Dorsey?" Eli asked.

Wesley checked his ledger again and said, "We've got one for him." So Casey asked how much was in the bag. "Fifty thousand," Wesley said.

"Whaddaya think?" Casey asked Eli. "I ain't tried to figure it up."

"We could take two thousand and that oughta cover it," Eli suggested. They hadn't taken the time to figure out exactly what the total should be for the whole crew.

Casey nodded his agreement. To Wesley then, he said, "Open that bag and count out two thousand dollars."

"I can't open it," Wesley said. "It has a lock on it, and Ronald Dorsey has the key."

"Get the damn bag," Casey ordered, "we're wastin' time here." Wesley jumped to follow his demand. Casey followed him to a cabinet and held his gun on him while he opened it and pulled out a canvas bag. As Wesley had said, it had a lock on it.

Eli didn't wait. He stepped forward and stabbed the bag with his skinning knife, and left the knife sticking in the bag. He told Wesley to cut a hole big enough for him to pull the money out. "Reach in there and count out two thousand"—he paused and looked at Casey and shrugged—"three thousand dollars. Hurry up," he ordered when he felt the train jerk as if about to start. "Put it in one of them bags." He pointed to a stack of empty mail sacks on the floor. Wesley kept pulling money out of the hole in the bag until he had counted out three thousand dollars. He paused then and looked up at Eli to see if he was going to tell him to stop. "Three thousand," Eli said. "That's all we came for. Hand me my knife." Wesley dutifully extended the knife toward him. "Turn it around, handle first, you bloomin' idiot."

"Oops, sorry," Wesley uttered, and turned the knife around.

With their guns still trained on the two railroad men, Eli and Casey backed up to the door. "I wanna thank you fellers for not makin' us have to shoot one of ya." He looked at Eli and said, "Come on, partner, we gotta hit the north road outta here." They backed out the door and jumped off the train just as the wheels started to turn over. In the saddle, they dashed away from the station at a gallop, expecting to hear shouts of alarm at any second, but hearing none.

Back in the mail car, John and Wesley were both amazed to still be standing. It was the first train robbery for both and Wesley was still holding the ripped bag. "There's gonna be hell to pay for this," he said, staring at the bag and the ragged tear in its side.

"They were two desperate-lookin' men," John, the conductor, said. "With all the money in this car, I wonder why they didn't want it all. There's fifty thousand dollars in that one bag, and all they took was three thousand."

"Yeah, don't make sense, does it?" Wesley said, still staring at the bag. "They coulda took more and this fellow, Dorsey, wouldn't know the difference. Makes just as much sense if they had took an even five thousand."

"That's a fact," John said. "I'm glad there was two of us witnesses to the holdup, so we can tell 'im what happened. And I expect we'd better report it right away. That fellow, Dorsey, is riding in the caboose. I let him ride back there because he said he had a fear of riding in open passenger cars. He's gonna be fit to be tied when we tell him what happened."

"Right," Wesley agreed, "we'd best get goin'." He reached in the hole again and pulled out two thousand more and gave John half.

Approaching the south end of town, the two train robbers continued their escape at a fast lope. When it appeared there was no one chasing them, they reined their horses back to a walk and Eli pulled up beside Casey.

"What the hell were you talkin' about when we left back there and you said we gotta hit the north road? What's the north road?"

"There's gotta be some road outta here headin' north," Casey said. "So I said that in case they get up a posse to come after us. Wesley and John can tell 'em we were goin' out the north road."

Eli just looked at him and shook his head slowly. "We need to stop and figure our money out before we get back to the camp." Neither one was good at arithmetic, so they dismounted beside the road, and with the road as a blackboard and a stick as their chalk, they figured the split of the money. They finally resorted to moving off the road and into the trees, so they could divide the money in nine little piles. When they were finished, they returned to their camp and the seven anxious souls awaiting them. They all got up to crowd around the two, excited to see Eli holding a sack.

"Boys," Casey announced, "we're happy to tell you that you will all get your wages for two months' work, as the honorable Ronald Dorsey promised. Plus, you're each gettin' a one-hundred-dollar bonus for the delay in receivin' your wages." That brought forth a cheer from the young cowhands.

"What about the money for my supplies?" Smiley asked.

"You got that, too," Casey said to him, "more than they'll actually cost. We all got what was owed us, plus the bonus."

"You musta found ol' Dorsey," Smiley said. "Where'd you find him?"

"We maybe oughta chip in some of our money to you and Eli," Sam Dunn suggested. "We wouldn'ta got a nickel, if you hadn't gone after Dorsey to get it."

Casey and Eli looked at each other to see who was going to explain the special circumstances around the crew's payday. Finally Eli volunteered. "Boys, there are some special conditions that come along with your pay-off. It's best that you head straight back to Texas, and don't go into Abilene tonight to spend your money." He immediately captured everyone's attention. "You see, we never caught up with Ronald Dorsey. We caught up with the money he got for the sale of the cattle we drove up here. It was on a train that just left here for Chicago."

"You robbed a train?" Davey Springer asked.

"I guess you could call it that," Casey said to him. "But it seems only fair. We just took what was rightfully our money and left the rest in Dorsey's bag. If he had been honest with us, he wouldn't have had that money to take to Chicago in the first place. That was ours, and me and Eli just went to get it back."

"That does seem fair," Smiley remarked, "but the Union Pacific Railroad ain't likely to see it that way. You had to break into the mail car to get the money, didn't you?"

"We had to persuade the conductor to unlock the door, so we could get in the car," Casey said. "But we didn't break down no doors, or destroy no railroad property, did we, Eli?" He paused, then said, "Except for that money sack you had to cut open with your knife."

"That weren't railroad property," Eli reasoned. "That belonged to Ronald Dorsey."

"That don't make no difference," Smiley insisted. He was genuinely worried about the two old cowhands. "How'd you persuade the conductor to let you in the mail car?"

Casey looked toward Eli again, but saw no tendency to answer the question, so he said, "We told him they had something that belonged to us in there."

"And he just unlocked the door for you?" Smiley asked.

"That was pretty much what happened," Casey said. After a pause, he added, "'Course, when Eli stuck his .44 into the conductor's back, he knew we weren't just wastin' his time."

Smiley shook his head, scarcely able to believe what the two of them were telling him. "I swear, Casey, you're talkin' about armed robbery of the Union Pacific Railroad. It don't matter if it was for that little bit of money. You're gonna have Union Pacific detectives lookin' for you, for sure."

"I hope they take the north road to start lookin'," Eli mumbled to himself. Then he announced, "If any of you don't want your share of the money, we'll be glad to take it back." No one opted to return the tainted money, including Smiley, which was of no surprise to Casey or Eli.

Given the special circumstances that insured their pay, plus bonuses, the rest of the crew were in agreement with Casey and Eli's recommendation to leave Kansas at once and return to Texas. All the younger hands were planning to ride the grub line in hopes of finding permanent employment with some of the bigger ranches. The coming winter would be a little easier on their efforts with the extra money Casey and Eli had procured for them. Each man thanked the two for their sacrifice on their behalf and promised to never tell where they got the money.

Smiley was the only one of them who had a place to go. He had already agreed to go to work for another rancher in North Texas he had worked for before. He was replacing an old cook who was making his last trip to market that year. That left the two train robbers to decide what to do.

Visit our website at
KensingtonBooks.com
to sign up for our newsletters, read
more from your favorite authors, see
books by series, view reading group
guides, and more!

BOOK **CLUB**

BETWEEN THE CHAPTERS

Become a Part of Our
Between the Chapters Book Club
Community and Join the Conversation

Betweenthechapters.net